DEVIL'S RETRIBUTION

BOOK 2 OF THE DEVEREAUX CHRONICLES

Debbie Boek

Publisher's Cataloging-In-Publication Data
(Prepared by The Donohue Group, Inc.)

Names: Boek, Debbie, author.
Title: Devil's retribution / Debbie Boek.
Description: [Lafayette, New York] : Wolf Rider Publishing, [2018] |
    Series: Devereaux chronicles ; book 2
Identifiers: ISBN 9780692128329 (paperback) | ISBN 0692128328
    (paperback) | ISBN 9780960077571 (ebook) | ISBN
    096007757X (ebook)
Subjects: LCSH: Blizzards--Fiction. | Brothers--Fiction. | Alcohol
    trafficking--Fiction. | Sasquatch--Fiction. | Retribution--Fiction. |
    LCGFT: Paranormal fiction. | Thrillers (Fiction)
Classification: LCC PS3602.O42255 D482 2018 (print) | LCC
    PS3602.O42255 (ebook) | DDC 813/.6--dc23

ALSO BY DEBBIE BOEK

If Not For The Knight

Sommers' Folly

Devil's Bait
Book 1 of the Devereaux Chronicles

Devil's Gathering
Book 3 of the Devereaux Chronicles

5 STAR REVIEW FOR DEVIL'S BAIT

Devil's Bait was a great book! I could not put it down. I am not an avid reader so a book really has to catch my attention in order for me to get through it. I finished this book in two days. Absolutely LOVED it! You will too! I am waiting for the sequel!
    --K. DeGroot

5 STAR REVIEW FOR DEVIL'S RETRIBUTION

All my reviews are spoiler free, but it's really difficult to write a review of these first two books, Devil's Bait and Devil's Retribution, in what will hopefully be a really long series, without giving spoilers because all I want to do is recount moments from both books! Which in itself is probably the best recommendation I can give because these are a lot of fun.
    -A. Emin

5 STAR REVIEW FOR DEVIL'S GATHERING

Debbie Boek has done it again! Devil's Gathering: Book 3 of the Devereaux Chronicles is the best yet!
-R. Mason

Visit the author at:
debbieboek.com
debbieboek.blog

CHAPTER 1

"Where the hell are you, Tim?" Joey Montclave mumbled, as he stared intently into the evergreen trees that surrounded the cabin. "You don't get here pretty quick, there won't be no reason for you to show up at all."

Joey was a large man, and the heavy winter parka and wool hunting cap made him look even bulkier than usual. The snow hadn't arrived yet, but it would be coming soon, and the temperature was dropping fast.

Joey kept to the safety of the porch that wrapped around the front and sides of the rustic, old cabin.

He wasn't nervous, didn't even know what that felt like, but he was concerned. The creature was nearby, Joey was sure of it because he could hear it moving around, snapping branches and crunching the frozen ground.

He was constantly on watch, twisting his body from side to side as he trained his rifle on the spots where he thought the sounds were coming from. But, even with a high-powered scope, he still couldn't catch a glimpse of it, just its fleeting shadow as it ran from cover to cover in the thick copse of trees.

And, in less time than he could raise his rifle again, he would begin to hear the noises in a completely different area. Joey felt relatively safe where he was, there was a small clearing surrounding the cabin and he was confident that he would be able to fatally wound the creature before it could cross that space and get to him.

But, it would be dark soon and that advantage would be lost. The creature was too fast to hunt alone, which was why he was so impatient for Tim to arrive. Once the darkness arrived, any chance they had of killing the creature before it killed them would be severely diminished.

Joey's head jerked around to the left as he heard the sharp snap of a branch. He moved down a few steps, his rifle steady in his hands as he stared through the scope, trying to catch even a brief look at it through the dense pine trees.

A sudden rancid smell assailed his nostrils and Joey realized, seconds too late, that the beast was smarter than he was, after all. No one could hear his screams as he was lifted up onto the roof of the cabin, where the creature tore open his chest with one strong swipe. The pain was excruciating, but brief, and the life faded from his body quickly and mercifully.

*   *   *

"Where the hell are you, Tim?" Scott was so angry that he had to restrain himself from yelling into the phone when his brother finally answered.

"None of your business, I'm heading out to help a friend."

"None of my business? Since when? I thought we worked together."

"Scott, let's be real, okay? I didn't want to have to have this conversation on the phone, but I'm sick of dancing around it with you. I don't think you have your head in the game anymore. You're not focused, you're not concentrating, and you're too dangerous to work with right now."

"What the hell are you talking about?"

"You got drunk again last night, didn't you?"

"I did not get drunk," Scott replied, unable to keep his bloodshot eyes from wandering around the cheap motel room, trying to ignore the dozen or so empty beer bottles strewn across it from one end to the other.

"Close enough though, or else you would have heard the phone ring, and you would have heard me packing and leaving, but you were passed out cold."

"Alright, so I had a bad night, that's suddenly enough for you to sneak off and not want to work with me anymore?"

"Those bad nights are happening more and more often and I can't keep dragging your hung-over ass around with me. You need to figure out what you're doing. It's been what, almost two years, right? Emma's not leaving her husband for you. She's gone, and you need to get that through your thick skull and move on, or its going to kill you, one way or the other."

"Go to hell, she's got nothing to do with this."

"See, that's the problem, Scott. Emma has everything to do with this and you just refuse to see it. I warned you back when we were helping get the demon out of her house that this would happen, but you went ahead and hooked up with her anyway. You're still paying for it, which is fine, but now I am too, and I'm done with it. I'm not even sure if I can keep working with you. She's not worth it, Scott. Not worth the risk to both of our lives."

Scott went deadly quiet on the other end. Tim knew that this was a very touchy subject for his brother, which is the reason he avoided bringing it up for so long, but it had been eating at him way too long and he couldn't keep silent about it anymore.

"I'd rather be on my own than have to continue to worry about you every day. Maybe you need to think about getting out of this business altogether, or at least go to her, confront her, find out for yourself, one way or the other, so you can move on with your life. This is destroying you, man, and I can't keep watching it happen."

Scott's voice was low and cold when he finally responded. "No worries, brother, there's nothing more for you to worry about. I won't be getting in your way anymore, ever. Guess we're done here."

He threw the phone across the room, ran his fingers through his thick, brown hair and took several deep breaths, trying to calm down a little. He couldn't remember ever being this angry at his brother.

They got on each other's nerves and squabbled frequently, but this was different, Tim had crossed a line that he shouldn't have, and Scott wasn't sure if they would ever be able to mend this rift.

Scott felt a familiar stabbing pain in his chest, almost as sharp and debilitating as the ones that attacked him every time that he thought about Emma Draper and what they almost had together.

He grabbed a half-empty bottle of beer from the end table by the bed and swallowed down most of the warm, amber liquid, grimacing at the taste, his stomach revolting in disagreement and almost getting the best of him.

"Breakfast of champions," Scott muttered, as he laid back down on the bed, hoping the pounding in his head might let up a little if he just chilled out for a while.

But that wasn't to be. His thoughts drifted back over the past, to the time when he and his brother had first started hunting with their father. The game they hunted was paranormal, sometimes classified as cryptids, creatures of folklore that science had not yet been able to prove existed. But, he and Tim had learned at a very young age that the beasts that owned the night were very real, and that they were worse than any child's nightmare could conceive.

After their dad passed away, Scott and Tim carried on his legacy and continued the good fight. They were members of a small but elite group, a group that very few people even knew existed. They hunted monsters and kept their tales to themselves. To share them would lead to chaos and panic, so they continued on with their deadly work, neither expecting, nor receiving, any thanks for risking their lives daily to save others.

Tim was the rational one, the one that could keep a cool head no matter what the circumstances were, which helped Scott stay focused on the matter at hand. He had always been more of a hot-head, more passionate and direct and, sometimes, he had to be reined in for his own good. And only Tim was capable of doing that.

They'd always been there for each other, they were able to be braver and do more good, having the confidence of knowing that the other had their back and would always be looking out for them.

The two of them travelled across the country to wherever they were needed and spent pretty much every hour of every day together. They knew each other like no one else ever could, but now it seemed that they would be parting ways and would have to learn to get along in this world without the other at their side.

"Probably for the best, anyway," Scott muttered, knowing he wasn't likely to be able to forgive Tim for a long, long time. They were like two halves of a whole and Scott knew this wasn't going to be an easy transition, but he chose not to dwell on it any further right now.

He decided to just ignore the pounding in his head and the butterflies in his stomach and swallowed a handful of aspirin, showered, shaved, and threw his meager belongings into his duffle bag.

Feeling a little more human at that point and having nothing else to do at the moment, he headed home to see his mother.

*   *   *

"What a surprise, Scott, it's so good to see you." Doris Devereaux was a handsome woman, with short silver hair and dark, probing eyes, very much like her son's.

She stepped out onto the porch of her tidy little home to give him a hug. Standing on her tiptoes to look over his shoulder, Doris asked, "Where's, Tim?"

"He went off to help one of the other guys."

"And you didn't go with him?"

"Leave it alone, Mom." Scott bent down and kissed her cheek, ignoring the questioning look on her face. "You look good, how's everything here?"

"It's fine," she replied. "I just finished my latest book and sent it off."

"Which one is this?"

"The Shapeshifter, out in Ohio."

Scott nodded, that hunt was still fresh in his mind, and it had been a doozy. It was only through their ability to work so well together that he and Tim were able to kill that evil freak of nature before it killed them. It was touch and go for a little while, but they were eventually able to do what had to be done.

Scott and Tim also continued their father's tradition of sharing the details, as much as they felt was needed anyway, with Doris. She was able to rewrite them in such a way that she had become a successful author, with a fictional series of supernatural books for teenagers. The royalties from those books financed Tim and Scott's hunts.

"Tell me the truth, Scott, why aren't you with Tim?" Doris asked, once they were settled down on the comfortable sofa, sipping a glass of iced tea. She couldn't help but notice that the two of them seemed to be drifting further and further apart lately.

She thought she knew the reason but couldn't be sure. Doris had a very close relationship with both of her boys but there were things they would never share with anyone, including her. She knew their safety, their lives, depended on each other, and she was worried, very worried, about what was happening between them.

"He's an ass. He took off in the middle of the night on me."

"That's not like him, didn't he have an explanation for it?"

"Sure, he did, same crap as always, he just blamed Emma again. He even had the gall to tell me he no longer wants to work with me. Apparently, I'm not up to his standards anymore."

"That's pretty extreme, even for Tim. Is he right, Scott? Is this all because of Emma?"

"Hell, no, I should have known you'd jump right on the bandwagon and blame it all on her, too. You never liked her to begin with." Scott stood up and began to pace restlessly around the room.

Doris' heart ached for him, he had really loved that woman and it didn't appear, no matter how much time went by, that he would ever give up hope that they'd eventually be together. She was torn, trying to decide whether or not she should tell him about the call that she'd received.

She couldn't fathom how a married woman, with children, could play so fast and loose with so many other people's emotions because of her own selfishness. It was inconceivable to Doris, and she didn't even bother to try to understand how or why it had happened.

Scott was right, she despised Emma from the very beginning and watching her son suffer these last couple of years had only cemented those feelings. Which was why she was struggling with such indecision about that damned phone message now.

"Do you still think there is a chance that she'll leave her husband and family to be with you? It's been a long time, Scott."

"I know that, and, yes, I do. We had something special, Mom, something I've never experienced before or since. I'm not giving up hope. I know that it's been a long time and maybe I'm just kidding myself, but I can't give up on her. Emma unlocked something inside of me that no one else has ever been able to."

Doris was silent as she watched him struggle with his emotions.

"Oh, hell, sometimes I don't even know anymore. Maybe I'm just being stupid and stubborn." Scott ran his hand roughly through his hair and his dark brown eyes were blazing with all of the frustration and anger that were roiling around inside of him.

"Regardless of that, just because I think about her once in a while, doesn't mean that I can't do my job anymore."

"I know, son." Doris responded, her own dark eyes were clouded with indecision as she debated what was best for Scott, and what she should do.

"You remind me so much of your father. You have his tenacity and his passion, and sometimes the two just don't go together. Maybe you just need to take a little time for yourself, to think things through."

"So, you don't think I'm up to snuff anymore, either?"

"Don't put words in my mouth, Scott, you know that's not what I said."

"You didn't have to. I'm going to head into town for a little while. Don't wait up for me," he added, roughly running his fingers once again through his hair.

Scott knew his mother had no alcohol in the house and, right now, he definitely required something stronger than iced tea.

Doris watched him walk out, her brow wrinkled in concern, but she didn't argue any further with him, knowing how futile that would be on this particular subject. Besides, now she had time alone to think about what she was going to do about that damned message.

*   *   *

"Joey, where are you?" Tim arrived at the cabin shortly before nightfall, but the cabin was dark, and Joey wasn't answering him.

Tim wasn't at all sure about what to expect, Joey had been pretty cryptic on the phone and he felt like he was walking into the situation blind, which left him more than a little uncomfortable.

He'd spent the remainder of the trip thinking about his brother and wondering if he had severed his entire relationship with Scott by finally being honest about Emma. Tim truly hoped not, he couldn't imagine not having Scott as a part of his life. They were a team, always had been, and it would leave an enormous hole in his world if Scott wasn't a part of it.

But, somehow, he had to get through to him and get Scott to stop moping around about Emma and start living his life again. Tim wouldn't have been able to live with himself if he wasn't honest with Scott about the situation, he'd kept his thoughts on the subject to himself long enough. Now, he would just have to wait and see how it would play out between the two of them.

In the meantime, Tim knew he had to clear his head and figure out what the devil was going on at this cabin. Joey was a tough guy and rarely asked for help, so Tim realized that he needed to focus all of his attention on what was happening right now, he'd have to worry about Scott another time.

The temperature here in the wilderness had dropped below zero, and Tim could see his breath as he slowly circled the cabin, looking for anything that might be out of place. He was glad that he'd taken the time to grab his warm suede coat, and pulled the Sherpa lined collar up around his neck to keep the biting wind at bay.

Heading back up onto the porch, he spotted a few drops of dried blood on the steps, at least that is what he assumed the rusty colored stains were, but there was no telling how long they had been there.

Tim's uneasiness grew when he stepped up onto the porch and spied a wool hunter's cap in the bushes, off to the side of the steps. It had a suspicious red stain on it also, and when he plucked it from the bush, he was able to feel the dampness and knew the blood was fresh.

He quietly drew his pistol and moved towards the front door. Just as he swung it open, Tim was assailed by a rancid, horrible stench that made him want to gag.

*   *   *

"Now, Candy, that's not very ladylike."

"I know." The voluptuous brunette had snuggled in between Scott's legs, which were hiked up onto the barstool, and now she was leaning her pouty red lips toward him with determination.

The bar was hopping tonight, and Scott realized, a little too late, that it was probably a mistake to come here. The music was too loud, people were elbow to elbow and, if one more person drunkenly bumped into him, he'd probably end up spending the night in jail. His head was still throbbing from the night before and he tried a little hair of the dog that bit him, but even that wasn't touching it. And, to top it off, Candy had moved in and was doing her best to seduce him. But, he hadn't had nearly enough alcohol for that just yet.

Scott leaned back to avoid her incoming lips, but didn't have much further to go, the edge of the bar was already digging viciously into his back. He glanced over at his mug of beer, grabbed it and raised it to his mouth just before she was able to make contact.

Candy leaned back and frowned at him, although she still didn't remove herself from between his legs. "You never did play nice."

"And you were always too much to handle, even back when we were kids."

With a coy smile, she tilted her head to the side, and said, "Oh, you always managed just fine. You gonna be in town for long?"

"No, I'll be leaving first thing in the morning. In fact, I should be heading back to the house now."

He gently backed her out from between his legs, collected his money from the bar and stood up.

"Scott, we used to have fun together, didn't we? What have you got to lose by spending a little time with me tonight? Maybe I could even get you to put a smile on that frowny face of yours."

He looked at her intently, trying to make up his mind about something. Candy was an attractive woman, although her clothes fit a little too tightly, and the thick makeup couldn't hide the signs of the rough life that she'd been living.

She was right, though, they had shared some fun times when they were younger. Candy didn't worry about anything other than the here and now, she let tomorrow's problems take care of themselves, the exact opposite way that Emma lived her life. Scott realized that maybe it was time for him to forget about Emma once and for all, and Candy would make just as good a first stepping stone as anyone else.

Scott ran his hands roughly through his thick hair as he stared intently at Candy, trying to make up his mind. Deep down, he stilled believed that Emma would come back to him, but he could hear his brother's words echoing in his head and finally came to a decision.

He reached for Candy's hand, ready to lead her outside, take her up on her offer and try to eliminate any more thoughts of Emma Draper. But, before they could even begin to make their way through the crowd, his phone rang. Scott hesitated when he saw that Tim was the caller. After their last conversation, he knew Tim wouldn't ring him unless it was serious, life and death serious. He had to take the call.

"Tim, what's going on?"

For a moment, there was only static and then a few words, 'Joey', 'dead', 'hurry', then the call was cut off completely. Scott couldn't be sure of what he heard because there was so much background noise in the bar. He tried to call Tim back several times, but it always went straight to voicemail.

"Candy, sorry, I've got to go." Scott hurried out of the bar, pushing people impatiently out of his way as he left the building and headed for his car.

Candy watched him go and sighed in frustration. He still looked great, even after all these years, and she had come so close to getting her hands on him again. She was very disappointed and, this time, the pouty look on her face was actually expressing a real emotion, something she rarely put on display.

"Pour me another, Ed," she called to the bartender, as she looked around at the crowd, checking to see if there was anyone else there that might be worth her while.

CHAPTER 2

Scott hurried back to his mother's house to grab his gear. He was hoping she'd already be in bed so that he could just leave a note for her. He hated lying to her, particularly straight to her face, but he didn't want her worrying unnecessarily.

Luck was not with him and she was wide awake when he arrived, still worrying about how to fix the mess she may have made with her own deception.

"Hi, Mom, hey, I thought you might be in bed by now. I'm sorry to do this, but I have to leave."

"Why, what's wrong? Is it Tim?"

"Of course not. There's nothing wrong, I just had a friend call and ask me for a favor and I promised I'd get to him as soon as possible."

Doris frowned, she could tell that he was not being completely honest with her, but she always trusted him to do what was right. If he didn't think she needed to know what he was up to, then she would give him the benefit of the doubt.

He grabbed his duffle bag and leaned down to kiss her cheek. "No worries, Mom. I'll stop back as soon as I can, okay?"

"Alright, you stay safe."

"I will." He headed out to his car, checked the GPS for his brother's phone location and hit the road.

*　　*　　*

Scott drove through most of the night and was able to locate the remote cabin just after daylight. His throbbing head had subsided hours ago and a couple of large black coffees had gone a long way to help him stay awake during the trip, but the caffeine also had adrenaline pulsating through his veins in overdrive.

He parked the car, grabbed his pistol and cautiously made his way over to the front porch. The door was ajar and had obviously been forced open, there were shards of wood sticking out of the frame, indicating that great force had been used to kick it in.

Scott frowned at the rusty spots sprinkled over the steps and his heart started to race when he realized that might very well be his brother's blood.

"Timmy," he yelled, "Timmy, are you here?" Scott thought he heard a muffled noise coming from inside the house but couldn't be sure. Stepping into the gloomy interior, he slowly made his way through the downstairs, or what was left of it, someone, or something, had virtually torn it apart. The furniture had been thrown into the walls and there were pieces of wood and cushions strewn all over the room.

A loud thump upstairs caught Scott's attention and he made his way to the bottom step, peering intently up into the dark hallway. He was unable to make out anything of consequence and took the stairs one at a time, trying to keep his step light and not make any noise.

The pistol was gripped tightly in his hand as he cautiously continued up the stairs. But, after hearing another loud thump, followed by a drawn-out groan, he had no choice but to hurry up the last few steps, regardless of the amount of noise he made.

The sounds were coming from the first door at the top of the stairs and, even in the murky, early morning light, Scott could see the deep gouge marks on it and the smeared blood along the walls.

"Tim, you in there?"

"Yeah, is it gone?"

"Is what gone?" Scott asked, as he quietly turned the knob on the door and pushed it inward. It stopped abruptly when it hit a bureau laying sideways on the floor, blocking it from moving any further.

Tim was breathing heavily and groaning as he tried to move the bureau out of the way. Scott placed his shoulder against the door and shoved with all his might. Together they were able to get the heavy piece of furniture to move enough so that they could get the door at least partially open.

"Is what gone?" Scott repeated. "How bad are you?"

"I'll be okay, a little light-headed, I think I lost a bit of blood."

"You think?" Scott asked, looking at his brother in concern. His coat was open and the entire front of his shirt was soaked in blood. "Where did it get you? And what is it?"

Tim peeled the front of his shirt away from his skin and gingerly unbuttoned it, baring his chest, which had four long, deep lacerations across it.

"It's not all my blood, so you don't have to look quite so concerned," he said, smiling slightly. "I'm not sure exactly what it was but, if I had to guess, I'd say, and don't you laugh, it was some sort of Bigfoot creature. Real tall, real hairy and with real long claws. And it stunk to high heaven."

"Did you shoot it?"

"No, it came up from behind me when I was about to go into the cabin, I turned and it swiped me with its claws. I was able to stab it a few times before I got away, ran in the cabin and blocked myself off in this room before it broke in. I heard it slamming around until just a short while ago. When I heard you, I thought it might be coming back."

"From the looks of the place, you only hurt it bad enough to piss it off royally."

"Man, I hit it at least three or four times, but I don't think my bowie could penetrate all the way through its hide, so the stab wounds probably aren't deep enough to do any real damage."

"It must be bleeding pretty good so we should be able to track it, but it would be a lot easier if there was snow on the ground. You stay here, I'll take care of it."

"No, Scott, it moves faster than anything I've ever seen. We'll both go, it's our best chance to kill the thing once and for all."

Scott hesitated. "Alright, let's go before it gets too far ahead of us."

Before they left, Scott turned to him one more time. "What about Joey, have you seen him?"

"No, but his truck is here, and I found blood on the steps and on a cap off the side of the porch. I don't think he made it, but I don't know where his body is."

"Damn," Scott said quietly, "he was a good man."

"I know, and a good hunter, too. Since his wife died, that's all he seemed to do, all day, every day, just to keep himself busy. We'll have to get the word out about him once we get this situation squared away."

"Definitely, he deserves an appropriate send off."

They made their way through the woods quietly and slowly, able to find droplets of blood periodically, leading them deeper and deeper into the forest. Rubbing their hands together and blowing warm breath on them, they tried to prevent them from going numb in the freezing cold.

"You are such a freakin' twatwaffle," Scott said in disgust at one point, watching his brother trudge slowly along beside him, obviously in a great deal of pain. "Why the hell didn't you wake me up, so I could come with you to begin with. Then you wouldn't be so banged up and we'd have already bagged this thing."

"Okay, first, I've told you before, there is no such word as twatwaffle. Second, you already know that answer. I didn't have the time, or the energy, to deal with you on one more job where you were so hungover that I couldn't trust you to do what had to be done."

"Google the word, my friend, it means contemptible person. And, as far as the hangover, uh, oh," Scott said quietly, coming to a complete stop and unbuttoning his wool peacoat so that he could grab his pistol from its shoulder holster. He looked around, peering through the dense growth of trees and brush.

"What?"

"Kind of thinking we may have been led into a trap," he said, his voice quiet and even, as he continued to turn in a circle and stare into the foliage.

Tim had his gun out by now and was also scanning the area. "Why?"

"The blood trail goes off into two different directions ahead of us, I think the bastard doubled back and…"

Scott was cut off by a horrid, ear-piercing roar that almost brought them both to their knees. They had no time to think before the creature was upon them. It appeared out of nowhere and knocked Scott aside with a brief swat of its long apish arm, then headed straight for Tim.

Tim had his pistol raised and was able to get off one round before the creature put him in a bone-crushing bearhug. Tim couldn't breathe and was being held so tightly that he couldn't maneuver his gun into position and get off another shot.

The pain was excruciating, and Tim thought he might have felt at least one of his ribs cracking when the pop, pop, pop of Scott's gun broke the silence and the creature released its death grip.

Tim slid to ground as the creature fell backward, its lifeblood soaking into the dirt and pine needles beneath it.

Scott cautiously leaned over it, his nose wrinkled in disgust at its ungodly stench. Its chest was still and there was no movement from it at all. He gingerly poked it with the toe of his scuffed work boot, ready to jump out of the way if necessary, but there was no reaction from the creature. It definitely appeared to be dead.

He fired one more round, pointblank into its forehead. Scott was usually confident in his Blackhawk .44 Magnum but, in this case, he needed to be absolutely sure the creature was dead. Once that was done, he walked over to check on his brother.

"Can you make it back to the cabin?" Scott asked.

"Might need a little help," Tim said breathlessly. "I think he cracked a rib or two."

They both stared curiously at the grotesque hairy beast laying lifeless on the ground in front of them. Neither of them had ever seen anything like it and couldn't tear their eyes away. But, when Scott noticed that Tim's breathing seemed to be a little labored and he was making an odd wheezing noise, he realized that he needed to get Tim some help as soon as possible. They turned and began to make their way slowly back to the cabin.

"Houston, we have another problem," Scott said, a couple of hours later, as he stomped back into the cabin.

"What now?" Tim asked.

After killing the creature, Scott managed to get Tim back to the cabin and started a warm, cozy fire for him. They warmed up in front of it while they argued over whether or not Scott should go back and retrieve the creature's body.

"Scott, I'm fine, really. This might be our only opportunity to figure out what this thing is. And we have no idea if there could be more of them out there. We can't fight them if we don't learn more about them first."

"I can hear you wheezing and struggling to take a breath. That's nothing to fool around with, we need to get you medical attention, stat," he said, unable to keep from grinning. "I always wanted to say that, but, seriously, that thing can wait."

"No, it can't. You go get it and I'll rest up and be ready when you get back."

They went back and forth a few more times until Scott finally acquiesced and headed out to drag the creature back to the cabin.

"It's gone."

"What do you mean, it's gone?" Tim said, sitting up, throwing the blanket off his lap and reaching for his pistol, which was on one of the nearby end tables.

"Was I speaking in tongues? What don't you understand?"

"But, how can it be gone? It was dead, wasn't it?"

"Of course, it was. I have no doubt that it was dead."

"So, what happened, wolves? Bear?"

"No clue, it wasn't torn apart, there were no drag marks, it was just gone."

"Damn," Tim said, grabbing his coat, and whistling through his teeth at the pain as he shrugged into it. "We should go try to find the body. We still don't even know what it was."

"No, not now. We don't have the right equipment for a long trip into the woods. And you are in no condition right now, anyway. Let's get to Mom's and get you stitched up, then we can figure out our next move."

"We'll never find it if we leave now."

"Them's the breaks, it can't hurt anyone any more, and I'm not concerned about getting my picture in Nat Geo with a new unidentified species, so let's get the hell out here."

Tim was about to argue some more, but his whole body ached, and it was getting more and more difficult to draw a deep breath, so he reluctantly gave in. "Alright, let's go now, before the sun gets any lower. I don't relish the idea of another night in this place and, as it is, I don't think that I'll ever get this stench out of my nose."

"Agreed, and you smell almost as bad as it did, good thing we came in different cars. Can you drive?"

"Yeah, I'll be fine. We may have to stop once in awhile along the way, but I can do it."

Neither of them realized how timely their exit was as they drove away from the cabin, unable to see the gigantic, hairy creature staring at them through the dense woods, his eyes glowing almost red as he filled his nostrils with their scent.

*   *   *

"My goodness, what happened?" Doris asked, as Tim stumbled in through her front door.

"It's not as bad as it looks." Tim said weakly, trying to reassure her.

But, Doris could see how pale his face was and how shallowly he was breathing and was not fooled in the slightest by his attempt to discount the extent of his injuries.

"Go up to your room, I'll get my supplies and be with you in a minute. Scott, get the water boiling and grab some rags out of the pantry."

They'd all been through this drill before and knew what was required of them. It took awhile, but Scott and Doris eventually got Tim cleaned up and stitched back together.

"Nothing personal, Tim, honey, but you stink to high heavens. Hit the shower and when you're done, I'll wrap your ribs for you."

"Okay," he replied, popping a couple of Ibuprofen.

"Oh," Doris stopped and turned back to him. "I hope you don't mind, but I think it would be best to just burn that shirt that you were wearing, and maybe the coat, too. That smell will never come out of them."

"That's fine," he replied. "You can burn everything that I had on, I don't ever want to catch a whiff of that stench again."

Once Tim was showered and his bruised ribs were wrapped tightly, they made their way downstairs to get something to eat. Doris put some soup on the stove as Tim explained what had happened.

While they talked, Scott walked back and forth in front of the bookcase with all of his mother's novels, which were also a kind of diary of the cases they had worked on, and their father before them.

"Mom, did Dad ever talk about seeing or hunting Bigfoot, or any similar kind of creature?"

"He actually used to laugh at the stories about them, never felt they were for real. The closest thing I can remember was a Wendigo, back before you boys started hunting. I think he hunted it in Oregon or Washington, up that way. But, it wasn't a hairy creature like the one Tim was describing."

She carried the pot over to the table and started ladling up bowls of hot tomato soup for her boys.

"What the hell is this?" Scott asked, his voice was frigid as he picked up a small piece of paper from the desk in front of the bookcase.

Doris' heart dropped when she realized that it was the note she had written from Emma's answering machine message.

"Mom, what is this? Did Emma call you?"

"Scott, don't get mad, I was just looking out for you. But, yes, I did get a message from her a couple of weeks ago."

"And you didn't tell me?" His dark eyes were snapping in anger.

"I figured that if you wanted her to be able to reach you, she would have your number."

"You know we had to trash all our cell phones after that nasty little incident in Yuma. She wouldn't have my new number."

"Oh." Doris frowned. "I'm sorry, I forgot about that."

"What did she say? Did she leave you a number?"

Doris hesitated, she knew he was already very angry, but she wouldn't lie to him. "If it was on the message, I didn't think to write it down and I deleted the message. She called on the landline, so I can't go back and find the number."

"Damn," Scott said, running his fingers through his hair.

"I'm sorry, son. I should have told you, but I just didn't want her to be able to hurt you anymore, and I was hoping that you might finally be starting to get over her."

"Mom," Scott shook his head in frustration, "I won't ever get over her, please try to understand that. It's not your decision to make, it's mine. And I made her promise never to contact me until she was ready to be with me."

"Holy shit," he said, as a huge grin lit his face. "She's ready to be with me. Now, I just have to find her."

Doris hesitated, but she couldn't deny the happiness that lit his face, and knew she had to step out of this and let Scott find his own way, no matter how difficult that might be. She could only hope that Emma's intentions were honorable and that she would not hurt her son any more than she already had.

"Emma said she would be at the Algonquin Ski Resort in New Hampshire for the next few weeks, and that you could find her there."

Scott ran up and kissed his mother's cheek. "Thanks, Mom, I know you worry about this situation, but you shouldn't. It's all good, trust me."

Dark eyes met dark eyes and Doris cupped his cheeks with her hands, trying to hold back the tears that were threatening to fall. "I can't abide anyone hurting you, son. I just want you to be happy."

"I know, and I will be, as soon as I find Emma. Tim, you ready for a road trip or still too banged up? Think hot toddies, hot tubs and hot little ski bunnies......"

"I thought you two were in the middle of a big fight?"

Scott looked straight at Tim as he replied to his mother. "We aren't done with our problems, there's obviously more we need to straighten out between us. But, with any luck, I think this road trip might put an end to this one particular issue."

"Besides, it's hard to stay mad at him when he keeps stepping up and saving my life." Tim shrugged and winced in pain. "Let's go, a good soak in a hot tub sounds like just what I need, but you're driving."

"You are not leaving tonight, and don't argue with me, Scott." Doris' stern matronly tone stopped him flat. "You can leave first thing in the morning. Both of you need a good night's rest, especially Tim."

Scott was anxious and frustrated, but knew she was right. Tim was hurt, and he couldn't even remember how long it had been since he slept, so it was the smart move.

"Fine, Tim, get some rest, we're leaving at first light and you'd better be ready."

CHAPTER 3

"When you realize that you belong with me, I'll be waiting for you. No matter how long it takes."

"When, not if?"

"When, not if."

Emma had replayed that scene with Scott hundreds of times in her mind over the last couple of years. With every fiber of her being she had believed him. But, now she was realizing that they were obviously just empty, meaningless words to him, something he thought she wanted to hear.

He wasn't waiting for her after all, and it made her sick to her stomach to think that it hadn't been real for him. Maybe those were just the platitudes that he used to placate all of the women that he hooked up with, lulling them into believing that he actually cared when, in reality, it was only a temporary situation and just a matter of time before Scott was able to move on to his next conquest.

In her heart, she just couldn't believe that was who Scott was, or that there wasn't something special, something real between them. But he wasn't here and that told her pretty much all that she needed to know.

She sighed heavily and grabbed her suitcase, ready to head out the door of the Lodge and on to points unknown.

Emma had been so excited and nervous to see Scott again that it never occurred to her that he might not feel the same anymore. She left the message for him almost two weeks ago. He hadn't shown up, or even called for that matter, so it was time to face the inevitable.

"I guess it took me too long to get back to him and he just couldn't wait any longer."

It left Emma feeling completely numb inside and she had no idea where she would go next, but with a blizzard heading their way, this was not the place she wanted to be. If she got stuck here for an extended period of time due to the storm, it would just be a constant reminder of the path that her life was not going to take. Her heart hurt almost as much as it had when they first split up to live their own lives over two years ago.

"Come, Callie," she called, brushing away an errant tear and heading towards the exit doors.

Emma stopped short when she reached the end of the length of the leash and Callie hadn't moved. Turning back to the dog in surprise, she repeated the command. "Come, Callie."

But the big, black German Shepherd ignored her and continued to look towards the check-in desk, whining softly and rhythmically wagging her tail back and forth.

Emma lifted her gaze to find what had captured Callie's attention and her heart stopped beating in her chest as she met Scott's gaze across the room.

Neither of them moved, neither blinked, they just stared in stunned silence at each other, not really believing what they were seeing.

Callie barked suddenly, breaking their spell and startling everyone in the vicinity. The young, red-haired bellboy closest to Emma jumped so violently that he narrowly avoided falling backward into a large potted plant.

Scott slowly started walking towards Emma, stopping only to pat Callie's head, which made her tail move even more spastically back and forth.

Raising his dark eyes back up to meet Emma's, he took the last few steps, covering the distance between them.

Still no words were exchanged as he raised his hand to her face and softly caressed her cheek. She leaned into his hand and caught her breath as his thumb slowly rubbed against her lips.

Sliding his hand around the back of her neck, he drew her towards him and bent down to capture her lips with his own. They were as sweet as he remembered, and he had to force himself to step back and release her.

"Hi," he whispered hoarsely.

"Hi, yourself," Emma answered, tears sparkling in her eyes. She couldn't look away from him, afraid that if she did, he would disappear, and she would have to accept that this was all just a figment of her imagination.

"You are real, aren't you?" she asked, placing her hand on his broad chest, feeling his erratic heartbeat.

"Yes, I am, and I am so damned happy to see you again. You look amazing, even more beautiful than I remember."

"And you're still full of it, aren't you?"

"Technically, yes, I am, but not about this. I mean it. Come here."

Scott pulled her into his arms and she wrapped hers around his waist, laying her head against his broad chest.

"I didn't think you were coming. I didn't think you wanted me anymore."

Scott could feel her tears soaking through his shirt and ran his fingers through her thick, blonde hair. "Never that, it was just a miscommunication. Once I got your message, I came as fast I could. Dragged Tim along too, hope you don't mind."

"Of course not, it'll be good to see him."

"Were you leaving?"

"Yes, there's a blizzard coming soon, and I thought I'd get out ahead of it. This place is close to being shut down, most of the guests left already."

"I think we can still get you another room, might be nice to get snowed in and have some time together. I think we have a lot of catching up to do."

Emma was in a daze as she followed Scott back over to the check-in desk, still not quite believing that this was really and truly happening.

"We're all on the first floor, hope you don't mind. I think they are trying to keep what's left of us together."

"That's no problem for me. Did you want to get your stuff and put it in my room?"

His dark brown eyes burned into her. "I thought about that, but I don't want to put any pressure on you, not yet anyway," he added with a devilish smile.

"I thought we could ease back into this reunion kind of slowly, savor it so to speak."

"Savor it?" Emma couldn't keep the amusement out of her voice.

"Yeah, we'll take baby steps until we get used to each other again. I've waited so long, Emma, I don't want to mess this up now."

"That is genuinely so sweet," she replied, wiping a tear from the corner of her eye. "Trust me, there is no chance of you messing this up. You are all that I've thought about for a long time, too, but I'll try to be patient and do it your way, okay?"

He didn't reply, just moved so close to her that she could feel the heat coming off his body. Scott cupped her face in his hand and slowly lowered his lips to hers.

He wouldn't have minded staying that way indefinitely but forced himself to step away from her.

"Drinks in the cocktail lounge in thirty minutes."

He walked towards the door but stopped and gave her a dazzling smile. "God, it is so good to see you again, Emma. You make my heart smile."

The lobby was a hub of bustling activity as people tried to check out and get on the road before the blizzard started. But, Emma might just as well have been standing there completely alone.

She neither heard, nor saw, any of it, as her brilliant green eyes filled with tears of happiness while she watched Scott walk away. Her heart felt lighter than it had in years and she vowed that, this time, she would make sure that nothing would ever be able to separate them again.

*   *   *

Emma kept checking her reflection in the mirror, but it didn't change and there was nothing more she could do to hide those extra lines around her emerald eyes. But, they sparkled with excitement and the cashmere pullover fit her curves snugly, its soft peach color complimenting her blonde hair and white alabaster complexion, so she felt some of her self-assurance returning.

"You can do this," she said quietly to her image. "You've waited way too long for this moment, you cannot chicken out now."

Taking a deep breath, Emma released it slowly and headed for the door, feeling slightly overwhelmed now that her dreams had become reality.

She hesitated at the entrance to the cocktail lounge, Scott and Tim were already bellied up to the bar and seeing them together took Emma back to when the three of them were trying to rid her home of demons, to the time when she and Scott first fell in love.

Emma reached out and placed her hand against the wall to steady herself. She felt dizzy for a moment as the past rushed in at her and the intensity of her emotions swelled. It was so unreal to finally be here with him after all this time, after all those nights of longing for him, dreaming about him, wondering where he was and how he was. And now he was here, right in front of her and she was afraid to go to him.

His broad back was to her and the long corduroy shirt he was wearing hid the trim body beneath it. There were some grays dispersed casually throughout his dark brown hair which looked as tousled and unkempt as it always had, due, no doubt to his constantly running his fingers through it while he worked something out or when he was agitated.

Her heart caught in her throat when he suddenly turned towards her, almost as if he felt her burning gaze upon him. Their eyes met and held.

He was incredibly handsome, with pronounced cheekbones, full lips, a chiseled jaw and deep, dark brown eyes that looked as if they could see right into her very soul. Emma couldn't help smiling, it felt so good to just be able to look at him, and her body stirred of its own accord at the thought of being held in those strong, muscular arms again.

Scott waved her over and Emma had to mentally shake herself in order to get a grip and be able to move. She walked to the bar and Scott made room for her between him and his brother. Tim got up off his stool to give her a hug.

"I am so happy to see you," he said.

"I'm really happy to see you, too." Tim was a handsome man also, not as attractive as his brother, to Emma anyway, but they did have very similar features. Tim was a little tidier and buttoned down, his hair, a shade or two lighter than Scott's, was neatly trimmed and his eyes were softer, not as probing. He was just as muscular and broad but was a bit taller than Scott. And where Scott could be playful and devilish, Tim was more serious and focused, or at least he was when she'd first met them.

"Sounds like a but in there somewhere," Tim said with a smile.

Emma shrugged. "We didn't always agree on what was going on between your brother and me. I just wasn't sure what kind of reception to expect from you."

"Trust me, I have had plenty of thoughts about you that weren't exactly nice, but right now, you are a sight for sore eyes. I'm hoping you can help Scott turn back into a human being again, he hasn't been doing all too well in that department lately."

"Shut up, Tim, I've been fine," Scott replied irritably, as Emma turned to give him a quizzical look. "Here, have a seat, I ordered you a glass of wine. You still drink wine, right?"

"Yes, I do, thank you." Emma couldn't wipe the smile from her face as she watched Scott. He seemed as nervous as a teenager on his first date, his hand even shook a little when he handed her the glass of wine.

"Damn," he said, downing whatever fiery liquid had been in the shot glass in front of him. "So, catch us up, what has been going with you? Where are your kids?"

Emma noticed that he didn't mention her husband, Jeremy, but he was looking directly at her ring finger and must have noticed that she no longer wore a wedding band.

They were both staring at her intently and Emma found it more than a little unnerving. She took a long sip of wine to help herself calm down and began to update them, as best she could anyway.

"Where do I start? I guess with the house, you guys did a great job with it. We never had another ghost or demon problem, ever. Shelly finished high school and has just started her second year of college in Boston."

Emma had forgotten how close these two brothers were and how much of their lives were shared. When she envisioned how this reunion would go, it was always just her and Scott. But, the reality was that these two spent most of their lives together, there were no secrets between them.

So, as uncomfortable as it was, there would be no quiet, private conversation between her and Scott as she tried to explain what had happened between her and her ex-husband, so Emma continued on.

Scott hid a smile as he watched Emma reach for her ring finger. When they first met, she would endlessly twist her wedding ring whenever she was stressing over her relationship, with him, or with Jeremy.

But, she was no longer wearing the ring and stared blankly at her finger for a moment. Unable to alleviate her tension in that way, she reached up and gently started twisting her earlobe.

Scott had always been able to read people, mainly from learning how their physical actions reflected their emotions. Seeing how Emma had replaced her self-pacifying behavior enabled him to gauge the full extent of her emotional discomfort.

A slow rage began to burn inside of Scott as he watched her and realized how uncomfortable she was becoming, just at the thought of her ex-husband. It was the same rage that he'd felt when he'd first met Jeremy, not because he was jealous, but because he could see the emotional toll that Jeremy's treachery and dominating personality had taken on Emma, and it infuriated him.

Emma was unaware of the thoughts swirling through Scott's mind and braced herself to talk about her ex-husband. There were times that she wondered if she would ever be able to understand or accept what had happened to her marriage. She had been with Jeremy most of her adult life and his betrayal had wounded her so deeply that wasn't sure if she would ever completely heal from it.

As much as she tried to empower herself and not take the blame for what Jeremy did, she knew she must bear some of the responsibility. A marriage didn't end solely based on the actions of one spouse and they both had to answer for what they'd done, both before and after cheating on one another.

With one last tug on her earlobe and big swig of wine, Emma stared into mirror behind the bar. Most of it was hidden behind the stacked liquor bottles, but she could see enough of Scott's face to know that his jaw was set and he looked very tense, so she talked fast and tried to keep it brief.

"Jeremy and I did try to make our marriage work, but there had been too much deception, on both our parts, and neither of us were ever able to really trust the other again."

Scott waved the bartender over and indicated a refill was needed for all three of them.

"Jeremy eventually moved back to the city and got his own apartment. James and Collin stayed with me and we remodeled the old mansion and turned it into a Bed and Breakfast. We did quite well for ourselves, if I do say so myself. Although it was a lot of work, I really enjoyed it."

"So, you still live there?" Scott asked quietly, sipping his drink.

"No, the boys were old enough this year to go to prep school. We found them a good one in the city, it's a great foundation for them as far furthering their education and getting them into good colleges. They were both really excited about it, particularly because they could go together. I swear the two of them are almost like twins, they are inseparable."

There was no way to miss the bittersweet sadness that crept into Emma's voice when she talked about her children. They were the most important thing in Emma's life when Scott and Tim first met her, in fact they were the reason that Emma wouldn't be with Scott at that time. And they obviously still were, even though she could no longer be with them every day.

"Anyway," she said, "they are happy and it's a great opportunity for them, so we all agreed that's what we would do. They stay at the prep school and Jeremy has a room for them at his apartment when they are on vacation, or if they want to visit him for the weekend."

She was quiet for a moment as she sipped the wine.

"And you?"

"Jeremy and I officially got divorced. I had to sell the house because I couldn't afford to buy it from him. So, I am currently homeless."

"How long ago?"

"A few months."

Scott was quiet for a several moments, swirling the liquid around and around in his glass, the muscle in his jaw twitching. When he finally spoke, there was an edge to his voice that hadn't been there before.

"Why didn't you try to contact me before this?"

"I'm not sure, as soon as Jeremy moved out I almost called you, but I still had the kids to think about and I needed time. I wanted to be sure that I wasn't jumping from the frying pan into the fire, so to speak."

"I see," he replied gruffly, but Emma could tell that he did not understand at all.

"Scott, I had to make sure that I was making the right decisions, for myself and for my children. I'm sorry if you can't understand that."

"All I can see is that you took your sweet time, and apparently didn't give a shit about how that would affect me."

"That's not true, I thought about you all the time, I just wanted to be sure I did things right, for everyone's sake, yours included."

"Right." He drained his glass again and stared straight ahead, his eyes blazing with anger.

"Alright then, I still have to grab my stuff out of the car and take it to our room, so I'll leave you two alone for a little while. Scott, if the room doesn't have a jacuzzi, then I will be getting a different one, so you better check at the desk before trying to get into the one they already gave us."

"Sure, whatever," Scott replied, waving the bartender over for another round.

Emma placed her hand over his and shook her head. "No more, Scott, not right now. Can we go somewhere quiet, where we can talk? I'm sorry that I hurt you, but we do need to talk about this."

He threw some cash on the bar, grabbed her hand and turned towards the door, smashing into another couple in the process.

"Sorry, buddy," Scott said, grabbing hold of the guy to catch him before he fell on his ass. "Didn't see you there."

"It's okay," the tipsy young man replied. "I haven't been able to see anything but my beautiful bride since we got married last weekend."

They were both in their early twenties, very tanned and very attractive. He was tall and thin, she was a lovely young woman, petite with large blue eyes and striking red hair.

"Lauren and Craig Jeffries," he said, extending his hand to Scott.

"I'm Scott Devereaux and this is Emma Draper, congratulations to you both."

"Thank you," Craig said, barely glancing at them, as his gaze wandered back to his new wife. "Nice to meet you."

"You too, well, I'm sure we'll see you around."

"We don't get out of our room much," Lauren said with a giggle, "but, maybe we'll run into each other around mealtimes."

32

They grabbed hold of each other and headed over to a table in the corner of the bar, giggling and touching each other the whole way.

Scott had a strange look on his face as he watched them walk away and surprised Emma by turning towards her and slowly lowering his lips to hers until they were barely touching. His hand snaked around her waist and pulled her up tightly against him and she surrendered herself completely. The feel of his lips and his hard, muscular body against Emma's had her own body aching for more. She wrapped her hands around his neck and clung to him for dear life.

The bartender cleared his throat loudly and Scott and Emma stepped apart, realizing that their little display of passion had not gone unnoticed by the other patrons of the bar. Some were looking at them curiously, others enviously. Emma was blushing in embarrassment and Scott gave a slight bow to the crowd, grabbed her hand and walked out the door.

Scott stopped abruptly once they were in the hallway and turned towards Emma again. He ran his hand through her hair and cupped the back of her head, staring so deeply into her eyes that Emma couldn't have broken free from his gaze if she'd wanted to.

"You don't have to explain anything to me." Scott's voice was low and tender and gave Emma goosebumps. "I'm sorry that I over-reacted. I'm just a puddle of nerves and I don't know what I'm doing right now. I still can't believe I'm really with you and I think I'm a little scared. I don't like that feeling and I'm not sure what to do about it."

"I feel the exact same way," Emma murmured, her eyes still trapped in his gaze. "I only have one idea of how we might get over our silly teenage nervousness and accept that this is real, and that we aren't suddenly going to lose one another again."

"To hell with the baby steps?"

"Definitely, I need you to hold me and to kiss me and to make me yours again, completely. I need that desperately."

He continued to stare into her eyes for a few more seconds and she could see the glint of excitement in them. Grabbing Emma's hand, he turned and led the way to her room.

Callie greeted them enthusiastically and, feeling guilty for leaving her alone, Emma and Scott decided to take her for a long walk before consummating their own plans.

CHAPTER 4

Emma managed to calm down a bit and her heart slowed to an almost regular beat as she pulled on her coat and gloves and searched the room for Callie's leash.

Scott, although a little disappointed at the delay, realized that they both might need a few more minutes to get used to the idea and decided that the walk would be good for all of them.

Besides, when they'd been working together on the haunting of her home, it was their long walks with Callie that gave Emma and Scott the opportunity to get to know each other, and to eventually realize the depth of the feelings developing between them.

Once outside, they headed down one of the pathways off to the left of the building. They walked close beside each other, their arms touching as they slowly meandered down the trail. Callie was stopping periodically to check out the scents along the way and Scott and Emma followed along in a comfortable silence.

"Yoohoo, Emma." Emma didn't want her time with Scott interrupted by anyone and had to bite back her disappointment when she saw John and Rosemary Hubbard approaching them with their chocolate lab, Sally.

"Hello, Rosemary, hi, John." Callie went up and greeted Sally, they had walked these trails together quite a few times over the last week and were very familiar with each other. Emma noticed Rosemary and John looking at Scott curiously.

"This is my friend, Scott Devereaux. He and his brother just arrived today."

"Nice to meet you," John said, reaching out to shake Scott's hand. "Your timing's a little off, isn't it?"

"I don't think so," he replied, smiling over at Emma.

"John means because of the storm," Rosemary added. She was all bundled up with coat, scarf, hat and boots but, from what Scott could see of her, she was a good-looking woman, with large sparkly brown eyes and a trim figure.

"I know, and I have no problem being stuck here for a few days."

Once again, his eyes moved involuntarily to Emma, anticipating the afternoon they would be spending together today and, hopefully, many more just like it while the storm raged outside.

Rosemary raised her eyebrows at Emma, who blushed and looked down at the dogs.

"John and Rosemary and I got to know each other while walking the dogs along these trails. Sally is a little older than my Callie, but they get along great and I think they enjoy the company as much as we do."

"I think so, too," Rosemary added, her eyes losing a little of their sparkle as she looked down at the dogs. "My poor old girl is having more and more trouble getting around. I can't even think about losing her though. So, for now, we just spoil her like crazy and appreciate that she is still here with us."

"Amen," Emma replied, patting the lab on the head. "Well, we're going to head down the trail for a bit. The sky is starting to look pretty angry and I imagine the storm will be starting anytime now. We'll see you later."

"Nice to meet you," Scott added, as he grabbed Emma's arm and headed in the opposite direction that the Hubbard's were going.

As they slowly wandered down the trail, Scott found himself becoming very introspective. It was still difficult for him to believe this was happening, that he was finally here with Emma.

He reached out to grab her hand, not wanting to be any further away from her than he had to be. He needed Emma's touch to anchor him to reality. Scott was a brave man, but she was his Achilles heel, and in the dark recesses of his mind, he was afraid that she would somehow vanish from sight and he would, once again, wake up in a sweat, realizing that it was just another nightmare and Emma wasn't really with him after all.

Scott had been tormented by too many of them over the last couple of years and never wanted to experience another. The dreams were always pretty much the same, he and Emma walking side by side, holding hands, her brilliant green eyes shining up at him with unconditional love.

Even in the depths of his unconscious, Scott could feel pure joy flowing through his veins as they walked together into the sunshine, and he was filled with a sense of completeness that had eluded him his entire life.

But suddenly teardrops began spilling from Emma's eyes and she let out a desperate scream as something unseen tore her out of his grip. He wasn't able to move and couldn't go after her, as she faded further and further away from him.

Scott always woke then, his heart pounding heavily in his chest, his body covered in a cold, clammy sweat and Emma's screams echoing in his head as the pain of her loss hit him yet again.

Those dreams were one of the reasons that he had started drinking so heavily, hoping he might be able to sleep through the night, at least once in awhile. Not even Tim was aware of the Emma nightmares that had plagued Scott since the two of them went their separate ways.

Tim already blamed Emma for everything that had happened between them, which was ridiculous because he knew his brother and, knowing him, Tim had to also know that Emma couldn't have been the catalyst in their situation.

Regardless, Scott was not prepared to give Tim any more fuel for that particular fire, so he kept quiet about his nightmares.

Emma noticed that Scott seemed to be lost in his own thoughts and, after a few minutes of silence, she decided to try some small talk to bring him back to her.

"Sorry about this place, it isn't exactly five star, but it is pet friendly, and that's pretty much my biggest priority right now. There were quite a few other dogs staying here, but I'm not sure how many left because of the storm. Thank goodness Callie is such a good girl, she gets along with all of them, even some snarky little Morkie Poo that keeps trying to hump her leg."

"It's not so bad," Scott replied absently.

"Are you okay?" Emma asked, moving even closer against him. "You're awfully quiet."

"I'm fine, just fine now. And, maybe later, I'll even let you explain to me what the hell a Morkie Poo is." He wrapped his arm around her and they leaned against each other as they made their way back to the Lodge

Once they were back in her room, the two of them sat awkwardly on the bed, side by side.

"I feel like this is my first time, ever," Emma said, her voice was shaking, and her heart was beating so fast in her chest that she was afraid she might have an actual heart attack.

Emma wasn't just pulling on her earlobe now, she was twisting it painfully between her thumb and forefinger.

Scott grabbed her hands and held them in his own, staring intently into her eyes, searching for answers to questions that only he knew.

"I love you, Emma. I never stopped, and I never stopped believing that we would be together." His lips trembled as he spoke, his emotions pouring out with his words.

"To be honest, so much time had passed, I was starting to think I might be wrong, but I never gave up on us. I know we were only together a short time and maybe I'm just crazy, but I've missed everything about you and I am so happy to be with you right now. I can't bear the thought of ever losing you again, so you need to be straight with me, about everything."

Emma eyes glittered with unshed tears. "Oh, Scott, I'm sorry that I did this to you. I missed you so much and from the moment that I met you, all I ever wanted was to be with you. But, after the mess that I made of my marriage, I didn't want to screw things up with you, too, so I had to be sure of myself first. Can you forgive for making you wait so long?"

"You're here now and there is nothing to forgive. The past is behind us and we can't change it. All we have is this moment right now and I intend to make the most of each and every one that I have with you."

Scott slowly ran his finger along her chin and then her lips with a featherlight touch, moving his hand through her hair to the back of her head, he drew her in, capturing her lips, kissing her long and passionately, drawing a soft moan from her as she moved up against him.

They fell back onto the bed, their hands and lips reacquainting themselves with the other's body, with no more thoughts, no more worries or nervousness, just the passion of two people that had been separated for far too long. Their bodies eventually moving in perfect sync as they brought each other to fulfillment. Neither were able, or willing, to let go, so they continued to hold each other close for quite some time afterwards.

No words were necessary, it was enough to just feel the warmth of the other's body against them, and to know that, this time, it was real.

And at last, they were both able to take comfort in the fact that they had all the time in the world to get reacquainted, and whatever else had to be hashed out and discussed could be done at their leisure.

For now, they just enjoyed the peacefulness of their new beginning, blissfully unaware of how quickly their tranquility was going to shatter and turn into complete chaos.

*   *   *

Scott brought his bag in through the side door, the floors were hardwoods and the walls were light brown and littered with pictures of winter scenery, mostly snow-covered mountains with athletes showing off their agility, slaloming, weaving their way through obstacles, twisting and leaping through jumps, or just showing absolutely perfect form as they conquered the slopes.

Scott appreciated the athleticism required but had no interest in trying it out himself. He passed by the pictures without paying them much attention and made a quick left turn at the end of the hallway, stopping short in front of Room 107. He tried his keycard, unsuccessfully, several times and finally gave up and started banging repeatedly on the door.

He heard footsteps approaching and then it finally started to crack open.

"Thanks, assho...oh, I'm sorry, I thought this was my room."

On the other side of the door stood the perpetually smiling newlywed. This time, his hair was dripping wet and he was wearing nothing but a towel.

"No problem, I thought maybe you were room service, finally, but I guess not."

"Craig, right? I do think this is my room, see I have the key card for 107."

"They must have moved you to a different one, man. We got sent over here a little while ago. We were out in one of the Yurts and they made us come inside. They only have a few people on staff, ergo the very long wait for room service, and I think they want us all in the same vicinity to make it easier for them."

"Okay, thanks. I guess that I'll have to check at the front desk." Scott started to walk away but stopped suddenly. "You were out in one of the whats?"

"Yurts."

"Come again?"

"Yurts, there are a few of them outside, separate from the building. They are kind of like an octagonal hut, with all the amenities and a great skylight. We thought it would be more private for us than a regular room, you know, 'cause we make kind of a lot of noise."

This last he added with a proud smile. Scott couldn't help but nod and silently give him kudos for at least having his priorities straight.

"Well, sorry I bothered you, Craig, maybe we'll catch you later."

"Maybe, but if that room service ever gets here, it's more likely you won't see us until sometime tomorrow."

"Have fun, then," Scott replied, with a smile of his own as he headed down the hallway towards the reception desk.

Scott had no way of knowing that this couple would be the catalyst into the nightmare that would begin all too soon.

*   *   *

The main lounge was a large room with oversized windows along the wall that faced the mountains, so that those who were so inclined could relax with a hot toddy and watch the others do the hard work out on the slopes.

There were hardwood floors with throw rugs scattered around the room, and comfortable furniture positioned to accommodate the guests for whatever they chose to use the room for. The walls were made of cedar planking and there were open rafters above, giving the illusion of being in a comfortable handmade cabin. There were guests sitting at some of the tables playing cards or board games, and others were relaxing in front of the roaring fire, just soaking up the warmth.

The back side of the lounge held the bar, separated only by a short half wall about three or four feet high and live plants hanging from the rafters above the wall.

The set up worked well for the guests, they could warm up in front of the fire after a busy day of skiing, then grab a drink in the bar to relax before heading into the dining room for a gourmet meal.

Scott, Emma and Tim met up for dinner later that evening. Tim noticed the flushed cheeks on the other two, couldn't miss the way they kept glancing each other and smiling secretively. And they were constantly finding a reason to touch one another, Emma would tenderly adjust the collar on Scott's chambray shirt or he would move a piece of her hair back off her face.

There was no doubt in Tim's mind that the two of them had found a way to rekindle the passion they'd walked away from two years ago.

Back when they'd all first met, he had warned Scott about getting involved with Emma, not because of who she was, but because she was a married woman and had children that were and, obviously, would always be, her first priority. Tim knew that it would end bad and it did. He was angry at both of them about it for a long time, because he saw how torn up Scott was every single day after they separated.

Surprisingly enough, right now, Tim was willing to admit that he was truly happy that they had finally found their way back to each other. But, he hadn't quite forgiven Emma for all that she had put Scott through and he was a skeptic. He'd seen a lot in his almost forty years and, if there was one lesson that he had learned, it was that life didn't give happiness willingly, not without making sure there was sufficient suffering along the way.

"These two had better have already paid their dues then, because there is no way I will go through that with Scott again."

He kept his thoughts to himself and tried to make an effort to see the glass half full and hope the future had only good things in store. He decided to let go of the past and give Emma this chance to prove her sincerity where his brother was concerned. Tim had never been able to tolerate deceit or dishonesty and he would know before long if she was playing them and, if that was the case, he would address it as he saw fit, because Scott would never be able to.

"So, Emma, you look like life has been treating you well. You're dressed all chic and, you cut your hair, didn't you? It looks nice."

Emma ran her fingers through her blonde locks self-conscientiously. "Thank you, Tim, it's all the rage with the Hollywood starlets, it's called a Lob."

They both just stared at her blankly.

"It's a long bob, a Lob, get it?" She couldn't help giggling at their vacant looks, and added, "Never mind, it's not important. If I remember correctly, you two prefer burger joints and greasy spoons. Isn't this a little upscale for you?"

"When in Rome," Scott replied, before shoveling in another mouthful of steak.

"And how is that salmon, Tim, it looks delicious?"

"It's fantastic, melts in your mouth, but you haven't touched your food, is there something wrong with it?"

"It's fine." Emma's meal did look tasty as she moved the scallops aimlessly around on her plate, but she had no appetite for it. Her body throbbed with excited tension just to be near Scott again, and only he could fulfill her hunger. She couldn't seem to concentrate on anything other than the fact that he was really right here beside her.

They sat close to each other and just the heat from his body was enough to get her heart tripping in her chest. Emma felt the heat blossom in her cheeks as she remembered the feel of his hands and lips caressing every inch of her body just a short while ago. And all she could think about was being alone with him again.

"So, what kind of cases have you been handling? Anything interesting?" Emma asked, trying to direct her thoughts elsewhere as she shifted in her seat.

The two brothers looked at each other for a moment and then Scott gave a slight nod.

"Actually, our most recent case was very interesting and very dangerous. We lost a close friend to the creature."

"I'm so sorry, I didn't mean to bring up something that would upset you."

"It's alright, we all know the risks. But, he was a good man and it's still hard to accept that he's really gone. By the way, Scott, I did get ahold of his son, Bobby, to let him know what happened. He's going to spread the word and plans on having a send-off for Joey in a few weeks. He's going to grab some of the guys and they are going to the cabin to see if they can find him."

"I feel bad, Bobby's a good kid, too. Not as good a hunter as his dad, but damn close. I hope they can find Joey, that's the worst of it."

"I know, he was pretty broken up. I did notice that the cell service is pretty spotty here, it took quite awhile before I could even get through to him and then we disconnected before we were finished talking."

"It's been like that since I got here," Emma added. "What exactly happened to your friend? And do I understand correctly that he died, but you can't find his body?"

"I forgot what an inquisitive little thing you are," Tim replied with a patient smile. "Scott and I weren't there all that long and we didn't really have a chance to look for him. His truck was there, so was his bloody hat, but he was nowhere around."

"What kind of creature was it?"

"We aren't exactly sure," Scott said. "All we do know is that it was very big, very hairy and very smelly."

"Like Bigfoot?" Emma asked, the tone of her voice indicating how absurd his remark sounded.

"Maybe, we didn't think Bigfoot was real ourselves, but I don't know what else it could have been."

"I'm six feet four and that thing towered over me," Tim added. "We've never come across anything like it before."

"How close did you get to it?" Emma wasn't smiling any more as she tried to grasp the fact that Bigfoot, or at least a bigfoot type creature, did actually exist.

"Oh, real up close and personal," Tim said, subconsciously rubbing the lacerations across his chest that were still healing. "Close enough to kill it."

"Isn't there some government facility, or somewhere that you could take it and have them identify what it is?"

Scott nodded. "That's exactly what we would have done but something absconded with the damn critter before we could drag it out of the woods."

"What took it?"

"No clue, it had to weigh around five or six hundred pounds, easy."

A loud crash and a shrill scream abruptly stopped their conversation and they all quickly turned around to see what was going on.

One of the bus boys stood in the middle of the room, his prominent cheekbones blooming almost red enough to match the color of his hair. He looked down at the floor, now littered with shattered glass and china, and tried to hide his embarrassment from the entire room of people that were staring at him.

The portly manager hurried over, his face almost as red, but not in embarrassment.

"If you weren't one of the last employees I have left here, you'd be out on your ass, you know that don't you, Gabriel?" His words carried through the room, in spite of the fact that he was trying to keep his voice low.

"Yes, sir, Mr. Noffsinger, I'm sorry, sir."

"Get it cleaned up, now, and get out of the dining room, leave this to the girls, who aren't quite so clumsy and accident prone, you dipstick." He stalked out of the room, a fake smile plastered to his face as he nodded to the guests on his way out.

The poor boy was even more flustered now and was having a hard time picking up the debris from the floor. Emma couldn't bear seeing how uncomfortable he was and went over to help.

"Is there a broom closet nearby? I'll grab one so that you don't cut yourself."

The young man smiled gratefully at her. "Just through the swinging doors over there," he said, gesturing towards the kitchen. "Thank you, Ma'am."

"No problem," she responded, heading over to look for the broom and dustpan.

Once they had most of it cleaned up from the floor, he took a deep breath and released it slowly. He was tall and thin, and Emma thought he probably looked younger than he really was. He seemed to be trying to cover up the thin layer of freckles on his fair-skinned face with a scraggly beard, which, unfortunately, didn't quite accomplish its goal.

"Thank you, Ma'am, that was very kind of you."

Emma appreciated how polite the young man was and knew his mother must be very proud of how he turned out. She could only hope that her own children would be so respectful under similar circumstances.

"It was my pleasure. I waited tables myself, many years ago, and I know that it's not as easy as it looks. My name is Emma Draper, what's yours?"

"Gabriel Freve, my uncle got me the job, but if it wasn't for the storm, I would have been fired days ago. I seem to be nothing but a stumble-bum, and I've broken so much stuff already that I don't know if I'm going to get paid, or if I'll have to pay them."

"Don't worry, Gabriel, I'm sure they'll take care of you, after all, they need you right now."

"I only agreed to take this stupid job so that I could spend some time snowboarding, but holy crap balls, between Mr. Noffsinger hating me already and the storm making all the trails off limits, this is not turning out the way I planned."

His natural exuberance was starting to return as he picked up the garbage bag along with the broom and dustpan. Emma did have to lunge forward to give him another hand when he immediately started to drop everything, and the broom handle just about poked one of the other patron's in the eye.

Gabriel regrouped and got a better grip on them all, and with his brown eyes twinkling and red hair askew, he gave her a broad grin and walked back towards the kitchen.

Scott and Tim stood when Emma walked back over to their table. She couldn't help noticing that Tim was wincing in pain.

"Are you okay, what happened to you?"

"It was nothing," he replied. "I'm just a little sore is all."

"They have a masseuse here, bet she could make you feel a lot better. I had a couple of massages with her last week and she is good, and very nice looking."

"Thanks, but, no thanks, I'm good."

"Give it a go, Tim," Scott interjected. "You wanted a whirlpool, get the massage and then do the whirlpool, you'll be good as new, hell, you'll be better than new."

"I don't know, what are you guys up to now?"

Emma and Scott looked into each other's eyes, and Tim didn't have to be a mind-reader to understand the silent messages they were sending each other.

"Yeah, well, maybe I will try to find that masseuse after all. See you two in the morning."

CHAPTER 5

The massage parlor was already closed when Tim finally found it. He was restless and not sure what to do with himself, his body still ached but he needed some sort of physical release, so he threw on some sweats and a tee shirt and headed to the gym.

His ribs were still tightly wrapped and pretty sore, but he anticipated that there would be some piece of equipment that he would be able to use without causing himself any additional harm.

He was completely underwhelmed when he finally located it. They called it a gym in the Lodge brochure, but that was quite an overstatement considering that there was only a weight bench, a few barbells and two treadmills.

Just to make him even more cranky, there was already someone in there. The man was almost as tall as Tim and was sitting on the weight bench doing curls when he walked in. The man's biceps positively bulged when he lifted the weights and Tim was duly impressed.

They nodded to each other and Tim walked over to the treadmill to get started. Having nothing else to do as he ran, Tim checked out the mirrors that ran floor to ceiling around that side of the room, able to watch the man without being overly conspicuous.

The guy was not young, although he did have a great physique. His dark hair was just beginning to recede, and his nose was slightly bent, making Tim wonder if he might be a boxer, or, at least had been at some point in his life. He had small, dark eyes and glanced furtively at Tim every once in awhile, obviously not comfortable with someone else in the room.

Finally, after one last inquisitive look at Tim, he set down the weights, grabbed his towel and walked out of the room.

There was something off about the man and Tim decided that he might be someone to keep an eye on if they ran into him again.

*   *   *

"Did you want to come with us, Tim?" Emma asked, setting her empty coffee cup down on the saucer. "It finally started snowing, but it isn't that bad yet. We should be able to get one last long walk in before the storm really hits."

"No, thanks," he replied, stretching out his sore shoulders and wincing again. "The masseuse had closed up shop by the time I got there last night. I think I might try her again this morning and then find that whirlpool. I just want to sit and relax for the day. I can't remember the last time that Scott and I had time to just do nothing. I may even read a book, a novel, one that has nothing to do with creatures or folklore or anything monster–related."

"Bet you can't actually go through with that, but good luck trying. We'll catch up with you later."

As Tim was leaving, Emma's new friend, Gabriel, approached their table to collect their dishes.

"Good morning," he said enthusiastically.

"I see they let you back in the diningroom, after all. Does that mean things are going a little better for you today?" Emma asked.

"So far, so good, and they didn't have enough staff, so they kind of had to let me work in here again. Hey, I remembered where I saw you before, you had the big black dog in the lobby yesterday, right?"

"Yes, I did. That's right, you were the bellboy, weren't you?"

"Yeah, I tried that too, but kept dropping everyone's luggage and making them mad, so they switched me into the dining room. Up until a couple of days ago, I worked in the kitchen, but I didn't do so good there either."

"I'm sure you'll find your niche eventually. By the way, are you alright? I seem to recall that you almost fell into a plant when Callie started barking. Were you hurt?"

He flushed and looked down at the table. "I'm fine. I just get a little nervous around dogs, especially big ones. We had a cat once though, she was okay, until I had to get rid of her."

"What happened?" Emma asked curiously.

"She had a litter of kittens and started acting funny. I took her to the vet and he gave her a Valium prescription, said the cat had, I think it was called post-partum depression. My mom had a fit, the script cost over three hundred dollars. She made me give the cat away, along with all the kittens, of course."

"Your vet actually diagnosed your cat with post-partum depression?" Scott asked.

"Yup, he did."

"Where the hell do you live?"

Gabriel looked up from the dirty dishes on the table and was about to provide them with all the details about his hometown, but Scott cut him off before he could get started.

"Never mind, kid. Take it easy." He pushed his chair away from the table and stood up, extending his hand to Emma.

"Bye, Gabriel, we'll talk to you later," she said breathlessly, as she hurried along beside Scott. They headed to Emma's room where Callie stood impatiently wagging her tail as she watched them get bundled up for their little trek through the winter wonderland.

Callie was super-excited by the time they got outside, she'd been cooped up in that room way too much lately, so Emma unhooked the leash and let her run free. Even though Callie was getting up in years, she played like a puppy in the falling snow and Scott and Emma just followed along, enjoying her antics.

"She's getting a little gray, isn't she?"

"Yes," Emma replied, "she sleeps a little more and moves a little slower than she used to, but she's still the best dog ever. She's been my one constant in all this craziness the last couple of years, the kids are growing up and becoming their own people. They don't need me much anymore, but Callie still does, almost as much as I need her."

Scott tried to wrap his arm around Emma, but between his heavy wool coat and her bulky down jacket, he wasn't able to get much of a grip on her.

"For good or for bad, you also have me now, to help you through everything, okay?"

"I like the thought of that," she replied, as he leaned down to capture her cold lips with his own.

"Come on. We better get moving before we freeze in place out here. The wind seems to be picking up and the temperature is dropping fast."

He was right, the snow was suddenly coming down much harder and was mixing in with icy pellets that were stinging their cheeks.

"Where did Callie go?" Emma asked, she looked around but couldn't see the dog anywhere.

"This way," Scott replied, pointing to her prints in the snow. "Call her, these tracks are going to get covered up fast."

Emma called frantically for the dog, but her voice was getting drowned out by the wind that was beginning to whip even more furiously around them.

They continued along the trail, Callie's tracks getting fainter as the snow quickly filled them in. Emma's voice was becoming hoarse as she tried to scream above the wind.

"Hold up," Scott said, putting his arm out to keep Emma from going any further. He couldn't believe his eyes and hoped the incoming storm was playing tricks on him, but right in front of him were humanlike footprints in the snow, huge prints, at least eighteen to twenty inches long, and they were still very noticeable as they went much deeper into the snow than the dog's prints did. Whatever left them had to weigh at least eight or nine hundred pounds.

It looked like the prints had been coming towards them, but turned and went away, back into the woods, and the dog tracks followed.

"What is it?" Emma asked anxiously.

"It looks like Callie headed into the woods here. We can't keep going after her. With the snow and wind, we'll be lost in no time. We can't do it, Emma. We have to go back."

"No, I will not leave her out here alone."

"Emma, don't go getting stubborn on me now. She'll find her way back. We won't. Trust her, she'll come back to the Lodge on her own."

"No, I can't, Scott. I just can't do that."

"Please, Emma, we have to go back now. It's not safe." The wind was whipping even more furiously, and it was difficult to talk. The icy flakes pelted them in the face and they had to squint to protect their eyes.

Scott's stomach churned, he didn't want to lie to Emma, but he was afraid Callie may have run into the creature and, if so, most likely, they would never see her again.

He wasn't armed well enough to go into the woods after them right now, and he was frustrated at himself for coming outside so unprepared, even though there was no way that he could have known what might be out here waiting for them.

Scott couldn't bring himself to tell Emma about the creature's tracks. Not yet, anyway, let her keep her hopes up for the dog, for a little while at least, until he figured out what to do about this situation.

"Come on, Emma, we have to go."

The trail was filling in, but they were able to slowly make their way to the Lodge. Emma had tears frozen along her cheeks, she hadn't been able to hold them back and couldn't stand the thought that she'd left Callie out in this storm all alone.

Fortunately, for Emma, she had no idea of the extent of the danger that could be waiting for Callie out in those woods.

*   *   *

The bell overhead jingled quietly as Tim stepped through the frosted glass door marked Massage Therapy. There was no one behind the desk in the small room, but there were several doorways off of this main room, none with doors, just curtains and hanging beads separating them.

He heard a soft voice call out that she would be with him in just a minute.

Tim made himself comfortable on the soft, overfilled settee along the wall and stared around the room. He assumed the color scheme must have been intentional because, unlike the rest of the Lodge, these floors had a rich, thick, dark blue carpet. The walls were painted a pale grayish blue and Tim recalled reading that blue is one of the most soothing colors, that it reduces tension and calms your mind.

There was a white wrought-iron bookcase and filing cabinet behind the desk, other than those and the settee, there were no other pieces of furniture, just large plants placed around the room and pictures of sunsets and flowers sprinkled over the walls. It felt very peaceful.

A beautiful, young woman, probably in her late twenties or early thirties, pushed aside one of the curtains and walked into the room, gracing him with an angelic smile.

"Are you the masseuse?" Tim asked, not quite believing his luck. Her dark hair flowed down around her shoulders and she was wore a long black skirt and a soft, purple sweater.

She had a calmness and serenity about her that gave Tim the impression that she was a bit of a hippie throwback, someone that probably would have fit in very well back in the seventies.

"Yes, are you in need of a massage?"

"I believe that I am," he replied, immediately captivated by her dark blue eyes and soft, melodic voice.

"I'm Skylar, what type of service can I provide you with?"

Tim blinked, not exactly sure what she was offering. Skylar chewed on her lip, trying to bite back a smile while she handed him a laminated piece of paper which listed all of the various services that were available.

"What's your pleasure?"

Nothing on the list came even close to what had popped into his mind when she made the offer, and Tim decided that some of those pheromones running rampant around Scott and Emma must have rubbed off on him, focusing his thoughts in a direction that he hadn't even been aware of. Or maybe it was just the pretty blue eyes and curvy body standing a couple of feet in front of him that was doing it.

She continued to watch him with a curious look on her face, so he shook his head and tried to collect himself, looking away from her and back to the list of available items.

Clearing his throat, he said, "I've never had a massage before in my life, so maybe you can make a recommendation for me?"

"Oh, this is going to be so much fun," she replied, her voice low and sultry. "First of all, do you have a name?"

"Of course," he replied irritably, "Tim Devereaux."

He stood up and extended his hand to her out of force of habit, surprising himself yet again when little shards of excitement ran through his palm and up his arm as she delicately grabbed hold and shook it.

"Well, Tim Devereaux, we have a couple of options." She placed her finger on her lips and furrowed her thick, dark eyebrows as she walked in a circle around Tim, sizing him up.

"Maybe the Myo tuneup, no, not that."

"Why not?" Tim asked curiously.

"It involves acupressure and I generally use it for people who can use a tune up, or who need to restore weak muscles. That doesn't seem to be an issue for you," she said, gently squeezing his muscular triceps. He wore a long, untucked flannel shirt over his jeans, but they were tight enough to show the muscular thighs beneath them.

Tim smiled, starting to relax and enjoy himself.

"A Reiki Addon?" Skylar asked, continuing her slow circle around him. "No, you seem centered and well-grounded. I think the most beneficial service that I could offer you would be a deep tissue massage."

"What does that involve?"

She moved closer to him, looking up into his light brown eyes, her body just inches from his.

"I use firm pressure and slow strokes to reach deep layers of muscle, it relieves aches and pains and releases muscle tightness. Does that sound like something that might interest you?"

"Sure," he croaked, then cleared his throat. "Sorry, I think I'm getting a cold. That would be fine."

They moved over to the desk and finalized the financial arrangements, then Skylar said, "Go into the changing room and grab a towel, it's the small room over behind that paisley curtain. There is a second doorway in there for you to use to enter directly into the massage room. That way you don't have to worry about coming through the lobby, in case another client is here waiting. Come through the drapes and I'll get you situated on my table."

"I'll be wearing just a towel?"

"Is that going to be a problem?" she asked, with a wicked little grin.

"Of course not," he responded gruffly, heading over to the room she had indicated, trying not to show how silly and uncomfortable he felt.

Tim took his time removing his clothing and letting them fall into a pile at his feet. Taking a couple of deep breaths, he wrapped a towel tightly around his waist and bravely walked through the long gray drapes.

The main piece of furniture was a large massage table in the center of the room covered with a blanket. This room was done in various shades of green, another calming color, the walls were a pastel, the rug a richer, deeper green and the blanket a tint somewhere in between the two. The lighting was muted and there was a rustic, copper wall fountain to add to the ambiance.

Once he got himself situated on the table and the massage began, it didn't take long until Tim was feeling completely content and more relaxed than he could remember. Even though she hit more than one sore spot and made Tim's face screw up in pain as tried to keep from moaning out loud, he could have laid there under her skilled hands for the rest of the day, but that was not to be. Unfortunately, he'd only paid for a thirty-minute session and that had been up for more than ten minutes already.

"Do you mind if I ask how you got these cuts on your chest?" Skylar asked, after she helped him slowly sit up on the table. She traced one of them with her finger and Tim felt his skin break out in goosebumps. "They look fresh and from the color of those bruises, you banged up your ribs pretty badly, too."

"Long story," he said, hoping she didn't run her fingers over any more of his skin while he was face forward with just a towel on.

"I see," she said, narrowing her eyes at him, debating whether or not to try and get a little more information. From the set look on his face, she didn't think she'd be very successful and decided not to pursue it any further, although she very curious about what could have possibly caused those lacerations.

"You were tight as a drum, do you feel better now?"

"Yes, I do," he drawled, even his voice was feeling lazy and relaxed. "Thank you, that was really terrific."

"I'm glad, come back tomorrow and I'll give you a follow up, free of charge."

"Nice, why would you do that?"

"I like the feel of you under my hands."

At that moment, Tim decided that the towel was not enough protection at all and rested his hands over his lap.

"That would be great. I'd love to buy you a drink, what time do you get off?" he asked, as he slid off the table and made his way around her towards the dressing room.

"I can get off anytime that I want."

Again, the towel was not providing the protection he needed, and Tim just hoped he'd made it all the way past her before she was able to see the effect her words were having on him.

"Okay then, I'll give you my cell number before I leave, maybe we can meet up tonight."

"Definitely," she replied with a giggle. Tim looked back over his shoulder at her and from the amused look on her face, he knew that he hadn't been able to hide anything at all from her.

*   *   *

"Tim, we have to talk."

"What's up?" From the tone of Scott's voice, it sounded like his little mini-vacation was about to come to an abrupt end.

"Scotch, neat," Scott told the bartender, as he planted himself on the barstool next to Tim.

"I was wondering why you wanted to meet here. Little early, isn't it?" Tim asked.

"Callie took off into the woods today and she's still gone "

"Damn, and the storm is hitting hard already. Emma must be a mess."

"She is, but she doesn't even know how bad it really is, not yet, anyway." Scott stopped talking and ran his fingers through his hair while the bartender dropped his drink in front of him.

"What do you mean?" Tim asked, as soon as the man walked to the other end of the bar.

"It happened just before the snow started coming down real heavy, we followed the dog's tracks right up until they headed into the woods. They seemed to be following another set of tracks, made from some kind of monstrous size creature, it had to weigh at least eight or nine hundred pounds based on how deep those tracks were, oh, and did I mention it was upright, on two feet?"

Tim and Scott's eyes met in mutual concern. "Like our creature at the cabin?"

"I'd say so, but the size of this one would have to be even more massive than that one was. I think Callie took off after it. And I don't think there's a chance in hell that we'll be seeing her again."

Scott sighed heavily, he hated to admit that, didn't even want to think it because he really liked the dog, and he knew that Emma was going to be crushed, but that was the most likely scenario.

"And Emma saw the prints, too?"

"No, I kept her away from them and then we came back to the Lodge. She doesn't know about them, yet."

"Better keep it that way for now. What do you want to do? We can't go after it in this storm. We'll have to wait until it lets up a little, which could be days."

"Let's keep it between us for now and we'll figure out what to do once the weather clears up."

"What to do about what, Callie?" Emma asked, as she approached, sidling up close to Scott when she reached them.

She was wearing an oversize beige sweater, black leggings and a pair of leather Uggs with a slight heel. Scott wrapped his arm around her and felt his heart slam against his chest as he looked at her and, forgetting for a few moments about Callie and the creature, he was filled with immense gratitude that she was his, for so many different reasons.

There were bags under her eyes today because she'd been crying about Callie, but even that couldn't detract from her natural beauty. Scott wanted to hold her and protect her and not let anything bad happen to her ever again, but he knew as much as he wanted that, it couldn't ever be that way. That wasn't how life worked.

Instead, he just pulled her even tighter up against his side. "Yes, Tim wants to help look for her, but we need to wait until the snow lets up a little, okay? She'll be alright, Emma."

Tears glittered in her brilliant green eyes, and Scott felt a little squeeze around his own heart, wishing he could somehow make this easier for her, but knowing it was only going to get more difficult.

"Come on, let's go get something to eat and figure out what we are going to do with ourselves for the rest of the day."

He downed his drink and they made their way into the dining room. Only about half the tables were made up since there were so few guests and there didn't seem to be any currently available. As they were trying to decide what they were going to do, they noticed a couple in their sixties smiling and waving frantically at them.

"Do you know those people?" Tim asked. Both Scott and Emma shook their heads.

"Well, there are no other empty tables, so let's go make nice," Scott said, leading the way.

"George and Katherine Carmichael," the gentleman said, standing to shake hands with the three of them. He wasn't heavy but was solidly built and just about as tall as Scott. "Please join us."

"Thank you, I'm Scott Devereaux and this is my brother, Tim, and my, and Emma Draper."

"So nice to meet you," George said, pumping Tim's hand vigorously and smiling up at him. His eyeglasses were fairly thick, and he had to keep pushing them back up into place when they slid down his nose. "We haven't had a chance to meet anyone yet and it looks like we'll all be locked away together here for a bit."

"Well, hey," Tim said, "I hate to be rude, but I have to hit the gym before I get anything to eat, so I'll catch up with you later."

He was barely able to contain his laughter when he saw the trapped look on Scott's face. "Come find me when you're done, and we can talk more."

Scott shot daggers at him for leaving them at the mercy of the Carmichael's, but had to give Tim kudos for coming up with an excuse to leave before he could. Without having any other choice, he and Emma sat down to join them.

Emma almost forgot her worries about Callie as she watched Scott squirm uncomfortably during lunch. He was sitting close beside Katherine, and she just stared at him and giggled every time he talked or looked in her direction.

She had a cherubic face with a pert little nose and bright pink lipstick. She wore no makeup other than that and had the perfect Sixties flip hairstyle, bringing Marlo Thomas to mind for Emma.

Katherine's clothing looked very chic and expensive, but slightly out of place. She was wearing a wool poncho with a lovely multi-colored pattern on it, but the tassel fringe hanging from the edges kept dragging through her plate and collecting various condiments on it. Between her fawning on Scott and dragging her tassles across her plate, it was a little uncomfortable to watch.

"I love that necklace," Emma said, at one point, trying to break Katherine's death stare at Scott.

"Oh, thank you," she said, her voice was high-pitched and always seemed to be followed by a loud giggle and rapid blinking of her eyes. "George, here, gave it to me as my first gift after we won."

"After you won what?"

"Why the lottery, of course." She giggled loudly again and turned coy eyes back to Scott.

"Congratulations," he said, "I've never met an actual winner before."

"Six mill," George replied, leaning back with his chest puffed out in pride. "Course we lost almost half of it to taxes, but it left us enough to get by."

This was followed by a loud guffaw and Katherine giggled in sync with him.

"Of course, he's still the same man that he was before," she said. "Still so country that he thinks a seven-course meal is a possum and a six pack."

The two of them laughed loud and hard, and Scott and Emma just smiled and hoped that lunch would go by just a little quicker than it currently was. With so little staff on duty, service was very slow and the wait for their meals seemed to go on forever.

Eventually their food did arrive and, as lunch dragged on, Scott and Emma nodded and pretended to be interested in what their hosts were saying, but both found it more and more difficult to pay any attention to them.

Scott was preoccupied, trying to figure out how the same type of creature that they just killed hundreds of miles away had somehow turned up here. It was a little too coincidental for his peace of mind.

Emma had completely zoned out and stopped even trying to ignore the sadness and worry that she was feeling. Callie was out in the storm and, unless she found some place safe to ride it out, Emma might never see her again. She couldn't seem to keep that from dominating her thoughts anymore.

"So that's why the license plate on our new BMW Z4 reads COWTIPN," George finished loudly, with Katherine's accompanying giggle, which brought both of their attention back to the couple.

"That's something," Emma responded lamely, having no clue what he'd said before making that unusual comment.

The couple looked stricken, as if her lukewarm response had really hurt their feelings.

"Please forgive me, I'm not very good company today. My dog got lost outside this morning and I'm really worried about her. Excuse me for being rude, but I'm going to have to leave. I think I'll take a quick walk, just to see if she came back and is trying to get inside."

"I'm so sorry to hear that," Katherine responded sincerely, and, for the first time, she did not giggle when she spoke. "But, you haven't eaten hardly anything, that's not good for you."

"I'll be fine, it was nice meeting you. Hopefully, we'll run into you again soon."

"You are not going anywhere alone, I'm coming with you." He turned towards the Carmichael's and nodded to them. "Good to meet both of you. We'll see you again, I'm sure."

They stood and made their way out of the dining room, stopping once so that Emma could say hello to her new friend, Gabriel, who was once again trying to balance dishes on a tray, and barely managing it.

"Emma," Scott said, once they reached the hall leading to their room, "please, promise me that you won't go outside by yourself."

"I just plan on going right outside the front, I won't go far enough to lose my way."

He grabbed her arm, not hard, but firmly. "Emma, promise me, that you will not go outside alone, not at all. I'm right here, I'll go with you anytime you want. Just don't go by yourself."

"Why not, what's going on?"

"Nothing, I just can't worry about losing you, too. Promise me."

"Okay, I promise." Emma looked at him curiously, there was something he was not telling her, but she couldn't imagine what that could be.

CHAPTER 6

"I didn't see your name on the sign-up sheet."

Tim opened one eye to see who owned the haughty, deep voice, that was apparently speaking to him. He'd been relaxing in the hot tub after working out and had almost fallen asleep, until this guy showed up and started talking at him.

"Excuse me?" Tim asked, resting both of his muscular arms along the edge of the tub as he looked up.

"There is only one hot tub, and you must sign up for it. Samantha and I have this time booked every day for the next week, so you must leave, now."

The man was in his thirties, with perfectly coifed hair and well-manicured nails, but the speedos and flip flops made him look just plain silly. Tim still didn't move, and he could see the man's face getting red with indignation.

There was a woman standing behind him and off to one side. She was slim and filled out her hot pink swim suit nicely. She might even have been pretty, if her lips weren't pinched together so tightly in anger.

As if those two weren't annoying enough, they had a little yapping dog with them, it also looked ridiculous, wearing its own pink bathing suit with a matching bow. Tim could actually understand the dog's frustration, he'd be pretty pissed if he was dressed up like that, too. But, he was beginning to find the incessant barking close to intolerable.

"Yeah, I don't think so," Tim replied casually, turning his attention back to the man who had ordered him out of the hot tub. "I'll be done in a few minutes. It's big enough for all of us, so hop in, or else you can come back later."

"We will not be getting in there with you," the woman, Samantha, stated firmly, her voice almost as tight as her lips. "Travis, let's take this up with the manager."

They stalked out the room and Tim couldn't help but smile as he closed his eyes and slid back down into the warm, pulsating water, able to enjoy the peace and quiet once again.

*   *   *

"Callie's not here," Emma stated sadly, looking around the front parking lot of the Lodge. "I didn't really think she would be, but, I can't accept the alternative."

She turned to Scott, her eyes glittering tearfully, and he pulled her into his arms as best he could, their bulky winter clothing keeping them from getting too close. The snow was coming down fast and furious, and you couldn't see much beyond an arm's length away.

He didn't feel comfortable with Emma outside. The creature could be right beside them and they wouldn't be able to see it until it was too late.

"Come on, Emma, let's get back inside. I'll come out and check for her again later."

Once they got to their room, Emma couldn't stop the tears from falling unbidden.

"Scott, you must think I'm an awful baby. I always seem to be crying when we're together."

It wrenched Scott's heart to see the tears flowing down her cheeks and the pain clouding her eyes. He wished he could do something to help her, but knew he couldn't, and that just left him angry and frustrated.

He was a man of action, when there was a problem, he fixed it. With every fiber of his being he believed that Callie had met up with the creature and, if he was right, there was absolutely nothing that he could do for her at this point, and Scott hated the impotent way that made him feel.

"No worries, sweetheart, I know how much Callie means to you." Her pushed her hair back out of her face and kissed her forehead. Pulling her tightly against him, he stood silently as her tears burned through his shirt and sobs wracked her body.

"Why don't we lay down for a bit, maybe take a nap and forget about things for a little while."

"That's probably a good idea, I feel pretty wiped out right now."

Once she got undressed, Scott laid down and gently cradled her in his arms until she cried herself to sleep.

When he was sure that Emma was truly asleep, he quietly extricated himself and wrote her a quick note before leaving to track down Tim.

"Seriously dude, what are you, a girl now?"

"Don't knock it till you try it," Tim said, stepping out of the hot tub, releasing a long sigh of contentment and stretching every muscle.

"It feels great, between this and the massages, I have never been so relaxed."

"Just don't go getting soft on me, you're not finding your inner female, are you?"

Tim laughed as he wrapped a beach towel around his waist. "I'm pretty sure that ain't happening."

He walked over and opened the door, surprising Travis, who almost fell head first into the room. Samantha was right behind him, her face still twisted up in frustration, followed by the manager, Jerry Noffsinger, according to the name tag that he wore, with the little yapper still going at in between nips at Noffsinger's ankles.

Tim just nodded at them and strode through the door with Scott right behind him.

*   *   *

"So, what do we do? Do you think there is any risk for the people here at the Lodge?" Tim asked, once they got back to his room.

"I have no clue. I wouldn't think so, what with the weather being what it is. But, once it clears up, who knows what we'll be dealing with. I just can't believe it's a coincidence that the same type of creature showed up here."

"What's the alternative? That it followed us?" Tim walked into the bathroom to finish drying off and get dressed, raising his voice as they continued their discussion. "How could it possibly do that, across all those miles, and when we were in a car? And why would it?"

"Because we killed one of them, obviously. This one is bigger than the one we offed, maybe they're related, maybe they run in packs, like wolves, or something. I don't know. Are you sure there was only one back at the cabin?"

"I can't be positive, but I only saw the one that attacked me when I first got there."

"And that's the one we followed into the woods and killed, so if there were two of them, why wouldn't the other have attacked us then, to protect the first one?"

"I have no idea."

"Oh, hell," Scott said, running his hand roughly through his hair, "as crazy as all this sounds, maybe that's why the body disappeared. It wasn't dragged and only something really big could have carried it away."

"Well, the only thing that I do know is that I'll be carrying my pistol at all times, and I'd suggest you do the same. I didn't think we'd need one here, but I guess I was wrong."

"I left mine locked up in the car, I was actually happy that we could take a little vacation and not need the damn thing. But, that obviously isn't in the cards for us. I'm going run out and get mine, along with some extra ammunition. Need anything else while I'm out there? That weather is brutal already, you can barely see in front of your face."

"More ammo is all I need," Tim replied.

"I'm going to check on Emma first and then I'll be back. Send me a quick text if you plan on trying out any more girly stuff while I'm gone."

Tim threw a pillow at him as he scooted through the door.

Emma was still sleeping, so Scott grabbed his coat and gloves and headed back to the main entrance. It was difficult to even open the front door with the wind blowing so savagely, but he managed and made his way around the side of the building to the guests parking lot.

There were a couple of Lodge employees out trying to keep the sidewalks clear, but the wind was vicious and just blew the snow back in to the areas they had just cleared. They didn't even bother with the parking lot and all of the vehicles were covered in snow by now. It took Scott a few minutes to find his car, and few more to clear the snow off so that he could get to the trunk.

He felt naked outside without his weapon, and hurriedly removed his gloves so that he that could unlock the trunk and grab the guns and some extra ammunition.

Stuffing them into his pockets, Scott had to close his eyes to a squint, protecting them from the little ice shards in the snow that were cutting his face. He got into the vehicle through the front passenger door and rifled around in the glove box until he found a pair of sunglasses, they would cut down on the glare and protect his eyes a little from the sleet.

Then he ran back to the front of the building, but paused before opening the door, the hair on the back of his neck stood on end as he sensed something out in the blinding snow, something that was watching him.

Ignoring the icy bits stinging his face, Scott turned slowly and stared out into the white abyss, he couldn't see anything but the wind-driven snow, but it was there, he was sure of it.

*   *   *

"Who's the chick?" Scott asked Tim a couple of hours later. Tim had been standing in the lobby speaking with a very attractive young woman who walked away just as Scott reached him.

"My masseuse," Tim answered with a grin.

"No shit, you really are turning into such a girl, is this a regular thing now?"

"I think it might be," Tim replied absently, as the two of them watched the gentle sway of her hips while she walked away. Skylar had changed into a gray knit maxi dress that hugged her body, right down to her little leather ankle boots with the death defyingly high heels.

"She is not bad looking at all, at least from behind."

"And you wouldn't believe her magic fingers," Tim added, looking over at his brother now that she had turned the corner and was out of his view.

"A little too much information, Tim. There's Emma, want to get a drink before we go in for dinner?"

"Sure. Skylar's going to join us at the bar in a few minutes."

"Who's Skylar?" Scott asked.

"Hello, my masseuse, the woman that just walked away, who do you think?"

"How the hell would I know that? Feeling a little edgy about her, are you? After all, she is young enough to be your daughter."

"She is not and don't be such an asshole."

Scott just raised an eyebrow at his brother, putting his arm around Emma's waist and hugging her close to him when she arrived.

"What's going on?" she asked, sensing something odd in the air between them.

"He's just being girlie, come on, let's get a drink. We get to meet his new little friend in a few minutes."

"Don't start, Scott, I mean it. So help me, I'll kick your ass if you embarrass me."

"Now, seriously, would I do that?"

"Not if you know what's good for you."

Scott chuckled and the look in his eye was positively devilish as he helped Emma up onto a stool at the bar.

"What is going on?" she asked, feeling more light-hearted than she had all day, finally able to forget about Callie for a few minutes.

"Tim found himself a new friend."

"Here she comes, I mean it, Scott," he warned ominously.

Emma swung her stool around and instantly understood as she saw the masseuse, Skylar Carrico, walking towards them.

"Emma," she said in a soft, whispy voice, "it's good to see you. I thought you left before the storm hit."

"I almost did, but my friends showed up just in time, so here I am. You've met Scott and Tim, have you?"

"Tim, yes, this handsome fellow, I think not."

"Scott Devereaux, nice to meet you." He extended his hand towards her. She gave a him a Madonna-like smile and shook it briefly before directing her attention to Tim.

"I thought you'd at least have my drink ordered already."

"Oh, yes, um, sorry, um, what would you like?"

Emma and Scott struggled not to laugh at his nervousness, which was completely out of character for him. Although, it was apparent that it was nothing out of the ordinary for Skylar to deal with.

"Pinot Grigio."

Tim called the bartender over and they all gave their drink orders. Scott leaned back on his stool, prepared to relax and enjoy the show that Tim was putting on. He'd obviously been without a woman way too long.

Unfortunately, Scott didn't get the entertainment that he expected because Tim had pretty much regained his composure by the time he polished off his first beer.

The cocktail lounge was fairly small and was filling up with the remnants of the guests. Scott could see the Carmichael's wandering around the main lounge, stopping to speak to everyone that they happened upon. He could hear Katherine's manic giggling no matter what part of the lounge they happened to be in, and it grated on him like fingernails on a blackboard. When he saw that they were heading towards the bar, he quickly suggested that the four of them go into the dining room where they could sit and relax. There was just something about the Carmichael's that didn't sit right with him.

"So, what it is that you all do?" Skylar asked, once they found a table and got comfortable.

Tim and Scott looked at each other, not answering immediately. They had an unusual job and people did not always understand, so they found that they had to be cryptic about the details.

"Is it a secret?" she asked curiously, as she watched the silent communication taking place between the two brothers.

"Of course not," Tim replied. "We are consultants."

"What kind of consultants?"

"We fix problems, problems people can't find a solution to."

"Well, isn't that vague?" she asked, staring hard at him and then looking around at Scott and Emma, trying to read their faces.

"You, Scott, I can't tell what you are thinking, any more than I can your brother, which is unusual for me. I'm generally pretty good at that. But, Emma, you're an open book. You know that Tim is being less than truthful, you don't like it, and you are trying to avoid any eye contact with me so that you don't give anything away."

"What are you, some sort of psychic?" Scott asked.

"No, just a student of human nature."

"Well, I think you're heading in the wrong direction with this. Tim is not being deceitful, there's just some information that the general public doesn't necessarily have to know about. Why don't we just leave it at that?"

Skylar gave him another curious look and turned to Tim. "My mistake, Tim, I didn't realize that I was just 'the general public'. I thought maybe we had a connection."

"We do," he replied, no longer nervous, but still trying to figure out how much he could, or should, share with her. "Look, what we do is help people. That is the absolute truth and it's really all you need to know."

She opened her mouth to respond but was interrupted by Gabriel, his hands were full and all of them held their breath when it looked like he might dump the entire tray that he was carrying.

"Hey guys, Skylar, I didn't know you were friends with Heather Locklear and her crew."

"Who?"

"Emma, don't you think she looks just like Heather Locklear, you know, from TJ Hooker?"

"Only prettier, right?" Scott asked.

"Of course," Gabriel said, smiling shyly at Emma.

"Isn't that show a little before your time?"

"I'm into retro," he replied, completely serious. "Shit balls, there's Mr. Noffsinger, see you guys later."

Gabriel headed off with the items on the tray wobbling unsteadily, but he made it safely into the kitchen without any incident.

Their meal arrived a few minutes later and conversation was reduced to small talk about the food. By the time they finished, Scott could see that Emma was getting a little too introspective and assumed she was worrying about Callie again.

"Do you want to take a quick walk outside?" he asked quietly, knowing she'd understand what he was really asking.

Emma gave him a grateful smile. "Yes, I would."

"Goodnight, you two, behave yourself." Ignoring Tim's warning look, he winked at Skylar, grabbed Emma's hand and walked away.

*   *   *

They bundled up and headed for one of the side doors but couldn't get far once they were outside. The wind was still whipping furiously, and the snow was piling up. It was dark now and the pathways that had been shoveled out earlier were quickly filling in. No one would be back out again until the morning, so Scott and Emma could only go out a short distance from the entranceway.

Scott felt a little better because if the creature was around, they would be able to see its tracks and quickly get back inside. Knowing nothing about that potential threat, it broke Emma's heart to see how much worse the storm had gotten, and to know that Callie was out in it somewhere and she could do nothing for her.

They only stayed out a few minutes. There was no sign of Callie and no way she could hear them call to her over the howling wind.

"Oh, my," Emma exclaimed when the door opened too easily in her hands and she almost fell back into a snowbank. She'd been looking down, trying to keep the blowing snow out of her face and eyes and hadn't seen John Hubbard pushing the door open for her.

"Hi, John, I didn't see you."

"Sorry about that, Sally needs a quick trip out before we settle in for the night. Where's Callie?"

Emma couldn't find the words to say out loud, so Scott stepped in to help.

"She took off this morning and we haven't been able to find her."

"Oh, damn, I'm so sorry," he mumbled. "I'll be sure to keep an eye out for her when I'm out with Sally."

"Thanks," Scott replied. "Be careful, I wouldn't go far if I were you. That blizzard's really raging, and the snow is piling up fast."

"Will do, take it easy. I'll let you know if I see anything."

"Thanks," Scott replied, and Emma gave John a tremulous smile before they turned and walked down the hall.

Once back in Emma's room, she swallowed her tears and tried to not dwell on what might be happening to Callie.

The two of them peeled off their layers of winter clothing and got comfortable against the headrest of the bed, holding hands, their bodies resting snugly against one another.

Scott put his arm around Emma and pulled her head over against his chest. The slow rhythmical beat of his heart calmed her down and somehow gave her hope.

"You okay?" he asked, stroking her hair, knowing that she was struggling to keep her emotions in check.

"I guess so, I'm just really glad that you're here with me." She put her arm around him and snuggled her head more comfortably against his chest.

"I only wish there was something that I could do to help."

"You do help, just being here with me helps me to be stronger and it means so much that you care about what happens to my Callie. It really does. It's funny, though, we've been together now, what, two days and haven't really talked about where we've been or where we want to go. My melodrama with Callie seems to have taken away from our reunion. It certainly isn't going the way that I had envisioned."

"Me either, but then, life rarely does." He continued stroking her hair. "We have all the time in the world to get to know each other again. There's no rush."

They just held each other quietly for a few minutes.

"So, do you see something developing between Skylar and Tim?"

"I don't know, he can be a little awkward with women. He lives in his head too much and doesn't get out and socialize enough. He'll probably end up scaring her away. That's what he usually does."

"Doesn't he date?"

"A little bit here and there, but nothing serious. We all have needs you know."

"What about you?"

"What do you mean?"

"Based on my experience, you are very good at socializing, particularly with women. So, what about your needs while we were apart?"

Scott was silent for a few moments and Emma felt her heart start skipping nervously around her chest. She suddenly wanted to kick herself for opening this particular can of worms.

"I wasn't celibate, if that's what you're asking. But, I didn't care about any of them."

"Any of them? How many?" Emma's stomach was doing flipflops now, but she couldn't stop herself from asking the questions. She continued to rest her head against his chest, she didn't want to look into his eyes, afraid of what she might see.

"I don't know, Emma, I didn't count. When it happened, it happened. You sure as hell can't be jealous."

"Why can't I?"

Scott sat up straighter and moved her away from his chest so that he could look at her. His dark brown eyes were so intense that Emma wanted to look away but found that she couldn't.

"You have no right, that's why. How many times did you have sex with your husband; or wake up next to him in the morning and share a quick kiss; or smile at him across the dinner table. All of those small, seemingly inconsequential things ran around in my head constantly for two years. I couldn't not see them. So, if I wanted to have mindless sex with someone that I barely knew, someone that might help me lose those images for just a little while, that's what I did."

Emma didn't respond for moment, still caught up in the intensity of his stare and the pain in his voice.

"It may have been like that a long time ago, but never after you and I met, Scott. Jeremy and I barely tolerated each other. We both hurt each other so deeply that it was almost impossible for our marriage to work, but we stayed civil to each other and we tried to give the relationship a chance, because of the children. Ultimately, we both knew that it was just a matter of time before we wouldn't be able to pretend anymore."

Scott gave a little laugh, stood up and started pacing around the room, running his fingers roughly through his hair. His emotions were painfully bubbling up to surface and he needed some sort of release. *"Why the hell did she have to stir all of this up?"*

"That doesn't make a goddamn bit of difference to me, Emma. It really doesn't."

"Scott,"

"No, I can't deal with this right now, Emma. I think I still have issues that I need to work through, so, maybe I was right in the beginning that we should take this in baby steps. I need to be alone for a little while."

"Will you come back, or should I come find you?"

Scott just looked at her and Emma could see the pain and the confusion in his eyes. And she was suddenly petrified that she could be losing him. *"What have I done? How did things turn around so quickly and so completely?"*

"Scott?"

"Don't worry, it's not like I can just take off and leave you here, right? I'll talk to you later."

CHAPTER 7

There weren't a lot of options, so Scott made his way back to the bar and ordered a draft beer. It was pretty quiet, there weren't very many people in the bar area, although there were still quite a few hanging out in the main lounge.

Which is why Scott was less than enthused when a tall, sun-tanned young man walked in a couple of minutes later and sat on the stool right next to him and ordered a beer with a whiskey chaser.

After downing the shot and motioning the bartender to bring another, he turned to Scott. He had bleached blonde hair and the fleece pullover and cargo pants couldn't hide his lithe, athletic body.

"Damn," he said, giving Scott the once-over, "you look like I feel. Don't tell me, woman trouble, right?"

"I guess you could say that."

"It's always a real headbanger when you find out, yet again, how easy it is for them to eviscerate you, and to know that you let them do it, over and over and over again."

"Well, I'm not so sure that our woman problems are exactly the same, after all," Scott replied, sipping his beer. "Sounds to me like you need to make a change."

"Yeah, that's what I keep telling myself, too. And what do you need?" he asked, his bright white teeth standing out in stark contrast to his deeply tanned face.

"What do I need? I need a change too, actually. But, I think I need to dump some baggage first and I haven't quite figured out how to do that."

"I hear you," he agreed. "By the way, I'm Christian Hebel, resident drone pilot."

"Scott Devereaux. What the hell is a drone pilot?"

"I am, or more accurately, used to be, on the pro skiing circuit. I tore up some cartilage in my knee so, now, I just travel from slope to slope and check them out. I can use my drone to video people skiing, or to check on conditions. It's pretty cool, particularly when there is the threat of an avalanche, the drones can come in really handy."

"So, you're like a contractor, people hire you to use the drone for whatever they want to see?"

"Pretty much, if this storm ever stops, I'll give you a demo. My drones are top notch. They are weather resistant, but I wouldn't risk them out in this storm, that would really be pushing the envelope, so you'll have to wait a couple of days."

"I'd like that, I've never seen one in action. It just shoots video?"

"I can do that or use infra-red thermal imaging to try and find heat sources, like people buried in an avalanche."

"How far can they go?"

"Mine can travel up to fifty miles per hour and the batteries last about forty-five minutes. Once the battery gets down to fifteen percent, mine will automatically return, so I don't have to risk losing them in mid-air. Using them on the slopes like I do, I'd never find them again in the snow."

"Sounds really interesting," Scott replied.

He thought that he heard Tim's voice just then and turned to see him and Skylar getting up from a couple of comfortable looking chairs positioned in front of the fireplace in the lounge. They seemed to have gotten quite cozy together and were now headed down the hall in the direction of Tim's room.

Scott smiled to himself, hoping a little extra-curricular activity would help improve Tim's overall attitude. His smile faded when he glanced over at Christian and discovered that, for some reason, he was also staring intently at Tim and Skylar as they walked away

"You know," Christian said, turning back to Scott, once they were out of sight, "I think you're right about making a change, a big one. I thought I found someone who was, 'the one', and gave it all I had. It's the only reason I came to this Podunk little ski lodge. But, she likes to play games, can pretty much have any man she wants, and she likes to be sure everyone knows it, particularly me."

"Uh, oh," Scott thought, *"looks like Tim might have gotten himself right in the middle of something about to go south."*

"Maybe she's too young and doesn't want the same things that you do right now."

"She should say that to my face then, not pretend to agree with everything I say, and then cut my legs out from under me." His voice was beginning to sound very bitter.

"Could you ever trust her again?" Scott asked.

Christian stared down into his glass, trying to find an honest answer.

"Probably not," he finally responded, pursing his lips as he looked back over at Scott. "But, I don't like to lose, so I think I'll play a little longer. And when I've reeled her all the way back in, just when she least expects it, I'll show her exactly what it feels like when the shoe is on the other foot."

"Doesn't that make you nothing more than kind of a douche?"

"So, what?" Christian asked, his pearly whites flashing again at the thought of the revenge that he would take on 'the one', once she came back to him. "And what about you, your girl cheat on you, too?"

"In a manner of speaking."

"Cut her down to size, man. Do whatever you have to, so that she feels even worse pain than she caused you. It's the only proper payback and the only way to get yourself back where you were before she stomped on you."

Scott just stared at him, the thought of deliberately bringing Emma as much pain as he had felt over the last couple of years was totally inconceivable to him. No matter what they had experienced during the time they'd been separated, neither of them would ever deliberately hurt the other.

Scott was disgusted that this man could be positively gleeful about the thought of doing that to the woman he supposedly loved.

"Your momma must have done some real twisted stuff to you when you were a kid," Scott said, disgust oozing out of his words. He threw his money down on the bar and walked away. Christian's smile faded, and his eyes narrowed as he watched Scott leave.

*   *   *

Emma paced slowly around her room, trying not to panic, trying not to cry, trying to give Scott the benefit of the doubt and know that he would understand after he had a chance to think things through.

Her heart was racing and her stomach was doing flipflops, she was a mess and couldn't seem to get her emotions under control.

But, she forced herself to take an honest look at the situation. She and Scott had met during a time when Emma just found out that her husband cheated on her and she was emotionally crushed.

Not only was she vulnerable at that time because of Jeremy, but Scott and Tim were saving her and her entire family from the demon that was terrorizing them. Both she and her children had been hurt and tormented and were barely able to escape the house with their lives.

That was when the Devereux brothers arrived to save the day. That was when Emma discovered that Scott was not just handsome and charming, he was also strong and brave. He was her hero, so her emotions ran even higher and more intensely towards him than they might have, had they met under different circumstances.

Emma never doubted the depth of their feelings for each other, but they were only together a very short time, much more time had passed since then, while they were separated. Emma realized that she really didn't know Scott very well, and he didn't know her either.

Emma barely knew herself any more, but she did like who she was becoming since all of that happened and intended to continue her journey of self-discovery.

"Maybe, I'll just have to make that journey alone," she thought sadly. She hoped not, just the possibility of it made her heart hurt, but, as always, Emma would do what she had to do.

Her body froze when there was a sharp knock on the door. She took a deep breath and steeled herself, hoping she would be strong enough for whatever was about to come to pass.

Scott stepped through the doorway and Emma noticed then how his very presence seemed to take over the room, how everything about him filled her senses and threatened to overwhelm her. Her head started to spin and she felt dizzy. Stepping back away from him, she walked over to the edge of the bed and sat down.

"I have issues," Scott said, bluntly. "There are things that have consumed me for so long that I can't just turn them off or pretend that I didn't feel them then, or that I don't still feel them now."

Scott stopped talking and walked over to Emma. As he stared down into her brilliant emerald eyes, she reminded him of a deer in the headlights, unsure of which way to turn and run. But, then her face changed, she never turned her eyes away from his, but inhaled deeply and seemed to be reaching down deep within herself for an appropriate response.

"What do you want me to do, Scott? I'm sorry that I hurt you, I'm sorry I wasn't there for you and I'm sorry that I put you through so much. But, I'm not sorry for the decision I made. I had to do what was right for my children, and it would not have worked out for us in the long run then, not if I thought I was choosing you over them and hurting them in the process. I would have hated myself.

I can't change the past. I can only be here for you now. I can only love you with my whole heart, the way I've wanted to since the day I met you. Is that enough, or is what you went through too much to get past? If it is, you have to tell me now, before we get any more deeply involved, because I can't pretend with you. It has to be all or nothing."

Scott was a little surprised at her reaction. She had changed. When they first met, Emma was a giver, she would do anything to make sure everyone around her was happy regardless of the cost to herself. Which was exactly why they ended up apart for so long.

Emma was stronger now, and she wasn't going to let anyone, not even him, make her feel guilty for the choices she made in her life. Scott respected that and had to look deep within his own self, so that he could answer her honestly. She deserved no less.

Scott grabbed Emma's hands and continued to stare deeply into her luminous eyes.

"I love you." Scott shrugged and gave her a boyish smile. "I have since I met you and, although sometimes, I still can feel those arrows that kept piercing my heart when we were apart, those feelings are starting to fade a little. To have you back again, to feel you in my arms, to listen to your sweet voice and look into those beautiful eyes, I couldn't ask for anything more in my life. It's all I want, all I need.

If you can be patient with me, eventually the crap in my head will fade away completely. If it does rear its ugly head again, which it most likely will, I think I'll be okay if you just look at me like you are right now and tell me how lucky we are to be together. Then kiss me and together we'll make it go away. Are you willing to live with that, because I'm all in?"

Scott's heart stuttered in fear for a moment as Emma pursed her lips and pulled her hands away from his. She stood then, directly in front of him, staring back into his deep, dark eyes, as if her answer lay somewhere within them.

Time stood still for a moment, until Emma finally replied, "Yes, I am. Now, come here and love me like only you can."

Scott's heart started doing backflips in his chest. He took her hands in his and pulled her up hard against his body, more than happy to comply with her request.

*   *   *

Needless to say, Scott and Emma spent a very pleasant night together and Scott was still smiling the next morning while waiting for Emma to finish up in the shower.

He was restless and wrote a quick note, letting her know that he was running outside for a few minutes to check and see if there was any sign of Callie.

They still had a lot of things to work through and he knew it would take time before they got to where they needed to be, but if they could get the dog back, it would be one more step in the right direction. Scott didn't think it was likely, but he chose to believe the possibility existed, the same way that he had chosen to believe that he and Emma would end up together.

That scenario had seemed unlikely too, but it came to pass, so he wasn't going to give up on Callie either. Throwing on his coat and gloves, Scott headed out the front door.

"Gabriel, is that you?"

The skinny hooded figure shoveling off the outside entrance way could be no other, although his face was wrapped in a scarf and he was wearing a wool cap, so Scott couldn't be absolutely sure.

There was another employee, also bundled up so completely that he was unidentifiable, however, that employee got to use the snowblower and knowing how much the manager disliked Gabriel, Scott made a correct assumption that he got the short end of the stick, or the shovel in this case.

The boy stopped and turned to him, only his eyes were visible as he nodded but, somehow, Scott knew that Gabriel was smiling under the scarf.

"Is there anything they don't have you doing?"

This time the boy shook his head in the negative and Scott was positive that the smile got bigger. The snow wasn't quite so deep under the carpark roof, but the wind was still whipping furiously and most of the snow blew right back where Gabriel had just shoveled it from.

"We still can't find Emma's dog, have you seen any tracks?" Scott had to raise his voice as the wind howled even louder.

Gabriel shook his head and let his eyes express his sadness at the news.

"Thanks, dude, I'm going to go check around the building."

There were paths shoveled outside each of the doors but, in between them was rough going. Scott struggled through the mounds of snow collected around the outside of the building. The icy snow pellets attacked him as he walked, even with the sunglasses on, he had to keep his eyes focused down towards the ground to protect them. His gloved hand held fast to his hat so that it didn't get blown off his head.

It was a brutal little trip and he was starting to regret taking it, but knew it was worth the trouble if he found any sign of Callie.

It took a while and Scott's jeans were soaked, and he was tired and cranky by the time he circled the building completely. He was even more frustrated because he had seen no tracks and realized that it was snowing so hard that they would have filled in very quickly. Callie could have been there five minutes before and he probably wouldn't be able to tell.

Rather than make his way back around to the front of the Lodge, he decided to go in by one of the side doors. That pathway had been shoveled earlier, but was already filling back in. Fortunately, it was still passable, and the door was unlocked.

Once inside, Scott shook the snow off his hat and out of his hair and wiped the wetness from his eyes and cheeks. Better able to focus now, he froze at the sight of what looked like a bloody handprint, high up on the glass of the doorway, the inside of the doorway.

Scott slowly withdrew the pistol from his pocket and turned down the hallway, there were streaks of red on the walls in spots along the hallway, so he moved forward cautiously.

He tried the doors along the way, but found each of them locked, until he reached the room that the newlyweds were in, the one that had originally been his and Tim's.

Scott could see that the wood was splintered around the lock and the door had obviously been forced open.

He quietly pushed it open with his left hand, while holding the pistol tight in his right. The smell almost knocked him off his feet, the room reeked with the stench of blood and death, but something even more rancid and nauseating was able to overpower that.

And there was blood everywhere, along with bits and pieces of Lauren and Craig Jeffries. There wasn't enough of either of them left to even check for a pulse, it was the most brutal killing that Scott had ever seen. He held his hand to his nose and started to back out of the room when heard something and stopped dead in his tracks.

"Callie, is that you, girl?"

The dog slithered out from under the bed, whining pitifully, looking weak and possibly injured. She had streaks of blood woven into the black hair along her side, but Scott didn't know if it was her blood or not.

"Come here, girl, good girl." Callie continued to whine as she approached him, and her tail started to move back and forth a little more zealously when she realized who he was. Scott squatted down in front of her and she rested her head on his thigh.

He patted her head and then reached along her side to see whether or not she was cut, she winced a little but, other than being sore, she didn't appear injured.

"Come on girl, let's get you back to Emma." He headed out, shut the damaged door as tightly as he could and placed the Do Not Disturb card on the handle. He didn't want anyone discovering the scene until he had a chance to talk to Tim.

*   *   *

"Oh, my God!" Emma exclaimed when she opened the door and Callie rushed over to greet her.

Emma's face immediately scrunched up in disgust. "Hey baby, you smell really, really bad. Where was she?"

"It's a bit of a story, let me grab Tim and tell you both together. The phones don't seem to be working, so I'll have to run down to get him. We'll be back in a few."

He stopped and turned towards them. "You might want to think about a quick bath for her or we won't ever get the smell out of this room."

"Good thinking, I'm on it. Come on girl, time for a bubble bath."

Scott hurried down to Tim's room, smelling the chlorine from the pool long before he got to the door. Using his own keycard, he opened it and stopped abruptly just a foot inside the room.

"Damn, sorry about that," he said, casting his eyes down to the carpet, trying to unsee what he had just seen Tim and Skylar doing.

"Couldn't you put a sock on the door, or something, so I knew not to come in?"

"Excuse me, but I thought you might be busy yourself. You weren't exactly my first priority. Can you just get out of here, please?"

"We need to talk, right now, so finish up and get down to Emma's room. Seriously, Tim, now."

Tim frowned at the tone of Scott's voice and knew he wasn't kidding around, so he did exactly what he was told and finished up. After all, it wouldn't have been right for him to leave Skylar unsatisfied. Once that was accomplished, he threw on some clothes and headed out the door.

"Hey, you coming down for a massage this morning?" Skylar called to him as he was closing it behind him.

Tim stuck his head back in, the sheet barely covered anything as Skylar held it demurely in front of her and he admired the view for a moment before responding.

"I'm not sure what's up, but I'll definitely be checking in with you later on."

By the time Tim arrived, Emma had given Callie a quick bath and now the room smelled more like wet dog and a little less like the stench from Room 107. Emma was calmer, but Callie was definitely not behaving like herself. While giving Callie the bath, Emma had checked her over and hadn't found any wounds, but the dog was sore and scared, and completely wiped out.

"Tim, come on in." Scott checked the hallway, saw no one else in the vicinity and closed the door behind him.

"You got the dog back, great, where was she?"

"We have a problem, a big problem," Scott said, his voice calm and level, but filled with concern, and they both looked at him curiously.

"Emma, there is something I didn't tell you that you need to know. When we were outside looking for Callie yesterday, I saw tracks, big tracks, and it looked like Callie's paw prints were following it."

"What kind of tracks, and why didn't you tell me then?"

"They were made by something very large that was walking upright, I don't know exactly what it was."

"I don't understand, wasn't it a person?"

"Definitely not a person, I can't say for sure, but I think it was similar to what Tim and I killed at that cabin."

"So, you think there is one of those creatures in these woods, too? Why were you afraid to tell me that?"

"I was afraid that it would kill Callie, and I thought I'd save you worrying needlessly, until we knew for sure."

Emma walked right over to him, her face just inches below his. "You won't ever lie to me again, agreed? Not even to keep me from worrying. I can't have lies, I can't have you being dishonest with me, Scott, that's a deal breaker. You have to have faith in me and I have to be able to trust you, unconditionally."

Even Tim was impressed at how much more assertive she'd become. When they first met her, he realized how stubborn she could be, and not always for the right reasons. But, now, it was more than that, she had become someone that would not take any shit from anyone, ever again. He liked it and couldn't wait to watch how it played out with Scott.

"Agreed, and I'm sorry." Even with this horrific situation now on their hands, his heart swelled, and he just wanted to take her in his arms. Instead, he leaned down, kissed her lips briefly and stepped away while he still could.

"Okay, then," Emma said, not quite understanding his reaction, "Callie is alright, so as long as we all stay inside, there shouldn't be any further problem, right?"

"Wrong," Scott replied, getting serious again. "I came in from the parking lot at the side door and there was blood on it. I followed a trail of blood streaks along the walls of the hallway. I checked all the doors and finally found one that had been kicked in, and that's where I found Callie, along with two dead bodies."

"What?" Emma couldn't restrain herself and popped up off the bed that she had just sat down on. "Did you call the police, what killed them? Why was Callie in that room? I don't understand."

Scott realized that she wasn't used to having conversations like this, not like he and Tim were, so he walked over to Emma and wrapped her tightly in his arms.

"We are trying to figure out what happened, Emma, and what's going on. I need you to stay calm, okay?"

She nodded her head against his broad chest and he slowly stepped back away from her, lifting her chin with his finger, he asked "Are you alright, would you rather that Tim and I went somewhere else to talk this out?"

"No, please, stay here with me. I am okay, it was just such a shock. Are they really dead?"

"Yes, there is no doubt about that."

Scott took a deep breath, grabbed her hand and sat her back down while he paced around the room, running his fingers roughly through his hair and leaving strands sticking out helter-skelter, as if they shared his frustration.

"Whatever it was, it tore them apart, and it stunk bad, worse than the one at the cabin. Bad enough to make you want to retch."

"Do we have enough ammo? We better take a look around the Lodge, make sure it didn't get anyone else."

"I agree, but I think it left, that's why there was a bloody handprint on the exit door. And, I have extra ammo for our pistols, but we are definitely gonna need bigger guns than these. And there is something else that we need to keep in mind."

"What?" Tim asked in confusion.

"The one we killed had your scent all over it, didn't it?"

"Probably, after the bear hug it gave me, why?"

"That couple was in our original room. You were in there when we first checked in, right? You and your stuff?"

"Yes, for a little while, not long. I asked for a different room, one closer to the jacuzzi and got the hell out of there."

"There were other occupied rooms between the door and Room 107. Why did it just walk past those rooms and only attack the people in 107? I'm wondering if it has your scent somehow."

"And it's here for revenge? That's crazy."

"I know, but I have no other explanation. And, I definitely do not know what went on with Callie and that creature either, or why it brought her back to the Lodge. None of this makes any sense."

"So, what do we do now?" Emma asked, unable to escape the feeling that she was in an episode of the Twilight Zone.

"We're going to have to talk to the manager, see if they have any security footage, maybe we can actually see the critter coming into the building. We've got to check each room, make sure everyone is okay and that it isn't still in the building somewhere. And we need to go back out to the car for some serious weaponry."

"I'll take the run to the car, you go try to find the manager," Tim said, heading towards the door. "Emma, we don't want anyone else to know Callie was with that creature or that she was in that room, okay? At least, not unless they have security footage of it. You should probably stay here with her."

"Not a chance in hell," Emma replied. "She stays with me, and I stay with Scott."

Tim looked over at Scott, expecting, and receiving, a nod confirming that would be exactly what was going to happen.

CHAPTER 8

"Gabriel, Gabriel," Emma called, when she spotted him in the lobby.

"Yes, Ma'am, do you need something?"

"We need to speak with the manager, do you know where he is?"

Gabriel furrowed his brow and squinted his eyes as he thought about that for a moment, then shook his head.

"Nope, haven't seen him for awhile. Just came in from shoveling. Did you check his office?"

"Where is his office?"

"There's a little hallway that leads to it, back behind the service desk. I can take you there."

"Please do."

A few moments later, Gabriel delicately knocked on the manager's door. "Mr. Noffsinger, these guests need to talk to you."

"Give me a minute," came the brusque reply, and Gabriel smiled nervously at them.

"He doesn't like to be disturbed."

"Really," Scott said, "well, if he doesn't get his ass over here and let us in, I'll be doing more than just disturbing him."

Gabriel liked the thought of that and smiled broadly but wiped it quickly from his face when the door was swung open.

"What do you need?"

"A little common courtesy to start with," Scott said, pushing the door open wider and walking into the office, followed closely by Emma and Callie. Gabriel stood at the doorway, not sure what he should do.

"Gabriel," Scott said, "you better join us, I think I'm going to need your help."

"Just a damn minute, Mister," Noffsinger began, his cheeks starting to flush at Scott's impertinence.

"Mr., what is that, Noffsinger," Scott said, looking closely at the man's name tag. "We have a problem, a potentially very big problem. My brother and I can take care of it for you, but we need your help."

"What are you talking about, what kind of problem?"

"Two of your guests have been killed and we aren't sure what kind of," he hesitated, "animal, did it. Somehow the creature got into the building and broke into their room."

All of the blood drained from Gabriel's face and he looked as if he might pass out. Emma grabbed his arm and helped him sit down in one of the office chairs while he whispered what sounded like, "Holy flaming shit balls".

Mr. Noffsinger sat down heavily in his own chair, as if his legs had suddenly given out on him.

"That can't be," he muttered in disbelief.

"It's a fact, Mr. Noffsinger, what the hell kind of name is that anyway? What's your first name?"

"Jerry."

"That's much better, so, Jerry, this is for real and we need to deal the situation right now."

"But how could this happen? I don't understand. Are you sure that they're dead?"

"No doubt about it."

"How do you know about this?" Noffsinger asked weakly, rubbing his hands rapidly back and forth on his pant legs, trying to relieve the anxiety that was threatening to overwhelm him. The storm, among other things, were bad enough, this bit of information was almost more than he could handle.

"How is it that your staff hasn't noticed the blood in the hallway, or the stench coming from that room? It's pretty obvious."

Noffsinger's demeanor changed, he was beginning to overcome his shock and moving into self-preservation mode. No way was he going take the fall for this when he couldn't possibly have prevented it.

"My staff is down to next to nothing, we don't have enough people to check everything. I asked to keep more staff on when we first heard about the storm coming, but corporate refused to listen. Which room did this happen in? And how did the animal get in?"

"I don't know how it got in, but it happened in 107. I put the Do Not Disturb sign on the door, but we have to get the bodies out of there and the blood cleaned off the outside door and the walls. Do you have security cameras in the hallways?"

"We've shut most of them down, per upper management's directive," he added. "Gabriel can take you to our security booth. Cliff's the only security person I have on right now, he can help you with those."

"You okay to do that, Gabriel?" Scott asked, noting his pale face and wide eyes. The young man just nodded nervously, his mouth hanging slightly open.

"What do we do about this animal?" Noffsinger asked, his voice was still weak, but he was eyeing Callie suspiciously.

"We'll check each room and make sure it isn't still in the building. If not, we have to think about how we can block off the exterior doors, so it can't get back in."

"Yes, yes, of course. Are you police officers, then?"

"Something like that," Scott replied. "You need to try to reach the local police though and get them out here as soon as they can make it. Someone said something about Yurts being used here. Are all those people inside now, or do you still have some staying out in those things?"

"We have two in use, very high paying customers, I tried to convince them, but they refused to come inside."

"We'll have to check on them and insist they come in, but not yet. Get your staff together and get a bunch of them over to 107 to get it cleaned up, also the walls and that exit door. It's not a pretty picture in there, you'd better give them some advance warning about what they are walking into. And, for God's sake, at least make sure the outside doors are locked Give me a key so we can come back in after we check those damned Yurts."

Noffsinger nervously rifled through a drawer and came out with an extra keycard. "This is like a skeleton key, it will open any door in the Lodge."

Scott grabbed it and started walking out the door. "Come on, Gabriel, take us to see Cliff."

"You're the only security person here?" Scott asked dubiously, a few minutes later.

"Yes, sir," Cliff Lawrence replied, becoming slightly offended when he noted how skeptical Scott seemed to be about him. "I'm a little long in the tooth, but I can handle myself just fine. What do you need?"

"There's been an animal attack in one of the rooms and two of your customers were killed."

"Son of a gun," Cliff replied, trying to wrap his head around that. The biggest crimes they ever had at the Lodge involved petty thefts and this was way out of his comfort zone.

"What can I do?"

"We just need some information right now."

Cliff was rattled and suddenly felt suspicious of everyone. "Who are you and why would I want to provide you with any information?"

"My brother and I are law enforcement." Scott never hesitated as he bluffed his way through the conversation. "We're here on vacation, but we can take care of this situation and, hopefully, you can help us do that."

Gabriel looked like he was about it say something, and Scott gave him a quick shake of his head and glared at him, hoping the boy would know enough to keep his mouth shut.

"What kind of animal? And how do you know it was an animal, not a person?" Cliff asked, still a little skeptical about Scott.

"I'm not sure exactly what kind of animal. If you have doubts, I'd suggest you go check it out yourself. I'm pretty sure you'll come to the same conclusion as I did. They are in Room 107 and it ain't a pretty sight."

"That's alright, I'd better see it for myself. What do you need in the meantime?"

"I'm not sure what we're dealing with, do you have any security cameras in the hallways?"

"Which floor?"

"First."

"No, nothing there. We only keep them operating in the upper floors, that's where the big money people stay."

"Damn, how about the parking lot or doorways."

"No, budget cuts, all we ever got from them was fender bender photos that the insurance companies wanted. Wasn't worth it for us, and we don't have enough guys to monitor the screens we have right now."

"Oh, hell," Scott said, running his fingers through his hair. "Thanks for your help, Cliff, we may need you shortly, so stay ready."

"I'll think about that, once I've seen what's happened with my own eyes."

"Understood. Come on, Emma, let's go find Tim. Gabriel, we may need you to show us around. It could get a little dicey, are you game for that?"

"For sure, just tell me what you need me to do." His color was back, and he seemed much more confident, almost eager for the adventure. Scott could only hope that the young man would live through it.

"For now, come with us while we find my brother. Emma are you sure you want to bring Callie with us?"

"I think so, if it's in the building, she'll let us know. Most likely, well before we are anywhere near it. I do have to stop back at my room first, okay?"

*   *   *

"You have a gun?" Scott asked in surprise, when they returned to her room and she rummaged through her bag, pulling out a little pearl handled pistol.

"Of course, I knew I'd need one if I met up with you again, so I took a class, got my permit and I've been practicing. It's legal and I can hit what I'm aiming at," she added, seeing his skeptical look.

"Let me see it." He took it out of her hand and looked it over, it was clean and oiled, so she might have learned a little bit about guns after all. ".38 Smith and Wesson?"

She nodded proudly.

"Hammerless?" He looked at her quizzically.

"They told me that I had to be careful not to catch the hammer on anything in my bag or I could end up shooting myself, so that seemed like the smartest way to go."

"So, you've got yourself all ready for a life of adventure, have you?"

"Yes, I have. I got rid of the mini-van, too."

"And replaced it with?"

"Cherry red Ford Mustang, eight cylinder. She can move like nobody's business."

"Well, aren't you just full of surprises," he responded thoughtfully.

"You ain't seen nothing yet," she whispered in his ear, opening the door and leading Callie down the hall to Tim's room, leaving Scott and Gabriel to hurry along behind her.

The smell of chlorine hit them again, before they even got close to his door, and Scott realized that smell may have prevented the creature from detecting Tim's scent, if Tim was even what it was after. That still seemed like a stretch, but nothing else made any sense.

Tim opened his door for them and went back to loading some of the heavier weapons that he had laying out on his bed. Scott grabbed one of the shotguns and a handful of shells for it, to bring along with his pistol.

"You guys ready for this?" Scott asked, looking intently at Emma and Gabriel. They both nodded, Gabriel a little more eagerly than Emma.

"Do I get a gun, too?"

"No!" Scott and Tim both shouted to Gabriel at the same time.

*   *   *

Scott, Emma and Callie headed in one direction and Tim got the pleasure of taking Gabriel with him to start the other way.

"Let's meet up back at the lobby once we have all of the first floor covered. Then we can go together to the next one and so on. How many floors are there, Gabriel, just three, right?"

"Right, plus the basement."

It was a little easier for Scott and Emma because they just had to allow Callie a few steps into the various rooms. If she didn't have any reaction, they knew it was clean.

Some of the guests were already familiar with Emma and Callie and had no problem buying their story about a possible wild animal that might be loose in the Lodge. Seeing Scott carrying a shotgun over his shoulder did make more than a few of them uncomfortable though, and they were a little hesitant about letting him in any further than the threshold of the door.

John Hubbard answered the door when they knocked. "Fantastic, Emma, you got Callie back, that's great news."

"Thanks, John, I'm so relieved, you have no idea. Sorry to bother you, but we think there may be a wild animal loose in the building and we're just checking to make sure everyone is alright. I'm sure Sally would let you know if anything got in your room, right?"

Sally and Callie greeted each other, but this time a little more stiffly than they ever had in the past. The Lab knew something was different about Callie and it was upsetting to her.

"Yes, she would. Hey, girl," John said, surprised to see Sally bracing and the hair along her back rising, "be polite, what's up with the attitude? That's not like you, now go lay down, Sally."

"And rest you in my arms," Scott added, unable to help himself.

"Seriously, no one has ever said that to you before?" Scott asked, as John just continued to stare at him in confusion. "Eric Clapton ring a bell?"

"No, why?"

"Never mind," Scott replied with a heavy sigh. "If you do see or hear anything unusual, let us know, alright?

"Certainly."

"Come on Emma, let's check out the next one."

93

They continued on and, if no one answered, they used the pass key to open the door and let Callie take a couple of steps inside. If she had no reaction, they left, closing it tightly behind them and moving on to the next one.

The only time that Callie did get agitated and start to whine was when they approached room 107, where Scott had found her.

As they walked past it, Scott could hear gagging sounds coming from inside and was relieved that Noffsinger had actually done what he'd asked and sent in a cleaning crew. Scott was surprised about that, he didn't have much confidence in the man.

It didn't go quite so quietly and easily for Tim and Gabriel. With the size and the smell of the creature, it wasn't like it would be hiding under the bed, so just a cursory check was enough. But, they still had to get into the rooms and, although, most of the guests were familiar with Gabriel, they were still a little uncomfortable with the intrusion, especially from a stranger carrying a loaded weapon.

They didn't have a passkey, so they had to spend a little more time knocking to make sure someone wasn't in the room. If not, Tim just tried to smell the air around the door. If the stink monster was inside, Tim was pretty sure he would at least get a whiff of it.

Gabriel was getting more and more nervous as they continued on and Tim was beginning to worry about him.

They were standing in the hallway, about halfway done, when Tim decided that he needed to say something. Gabriel had been knocking on the doors and Tim could see his hand shaking uncontrollably as he extended it and his lip quivering when he tried to speak. It seemed to be getting worse with each door they approached.

"Gabriel, there is nothing for you to worry about. If it is in one of these rooms, it isn't going to answer when you knock. We're pretty much just making sure that everyone is okay, and that it isn't hiding in an empty room."

"Right," Gabriel responded nervously, looking down at the floor, unable to meet Tim's eyes.

"If no one answers, you just step back and I'll check things out around the doorway. Nothing is going to happen to you."

"Right," he repeated. "I know".

"Alright, let's finish with this floor." They started over towards the next door, but Tim stopped again and turned to look down at Gabriel. "There's something my father told me when I was young that I think might be of help to you."

"What's that?"

"A coward dies a hundred deaths and a brave man only one. So, don't be afraid when there is nothing to be afraid of, stand strong, okay?"

Gabriel looked at him in gratitude and nodded, but try as he might, he couldn't keep his hand from shaking as he knocked on the next door.

The only real problem that they ended up running into was with a person, Christian Hebel, to be exact. It was late morning, but he was still sleeping and was not happy to be disturbed.

His mood got even uglier when he recognized Tim standing at his door and realized that he was Skylar's new boy toy.

Tim noticed the ugly scowl on the man's face, but he'd never seen him before and had no idea why the guy would instantly dislike him. Tim didn't particularly care, but he didn't need any issues with him right now.

"What the hell do you want?"

"I'm sorry that we woke you." Tim decided to try and be as pleasant as possible, but he only had a limited amount of patience and hoped this guy didn't push him too far.

He could smell the alcohol that the man must have been sweating out overnight and knew he wouldn't be in the best frame of mind. "We are checking everyone's room, it'll only take a minute, if you don't mind."

"I do mind." Christian stayed in the doorway, blocking their entrance and their view.

"It'll just take a minute, we need to step inside and make sure there are no problems."

"What exactly are you looking for?" Christian was only wearing a pair of shorts and he puffed his muscular chest out, wanting to make sure Tim saw exactly how fit he was.

"We think that an animal may have gotten into the building and we just want to make sure it isn't hiding in anyone's room."

"What kind of animal?"

"Look, buddy," Tim was beginning to get annoyed now, "I just need to step inside briefly. It's for your own safety."

"Go to hell, I don't need anything from you and I can take care of myself, thank you very much. Why don't you get back to having fun with your co-employee? Or did she send you here just to mess with me? I bet she did, didn't she, that damned minx?"

"What are you talking about?" Tim sincerely had no idea what Christian was saying and thought maybe he was still drunk.

Christian had to look up to meet Tim's eyes. "You can tell her that her little games aren't working, and she doesn't get a free peak into my room to see if I hooked up with someone else. If she wants information, she knows where she can find me."

He stepped back into his room and slammed the door in Tim's face.

"What the hell?" Tim asked the door.

Gabriel cleared his throat nervously, not sure how angry Tim was, or how he intended to deal with that anger, but felt he should give him an idea of where Christian might have been coming from.

"Um, I saw you guys having dinner with Skylar last night. Did you, maybe, hook up with her?"

Tim looked at him with a mixture of anger and disbelief. "What the hell does that have to do with anything?"

"Oh," he said a second later, after connecting the dots. "Is Skylar the she that this guy was referring to?"

"I think so, I used to see them together a lot, right up until a few days ago."

Tim gave the closed door a scorching look. "Well, I think he'd give Mr. Stinky a run for his money if he did stop by, so I guess he's on his own. What's his name?"

"Christian, I don't know his last name. He's some kind of pro skier, I guess."

"Yeah, well, good for him." Tim said gruffly, turning and heading over to the next door.

"Who's Mr. Stinky?" Gabriel asked, when he thought it was safe to do so. They'd knocked several times, but there was no answer and no sound coming from inside the room, so it looked like this one was clear.

"That's just a nickname for the crea, uh, the animal. It really stunk up that room, so that's what I started calling it. If you do smell anything, anywhere, that is really rancid and strong, let Scott or me know right away, okay?"

"Sure," he replied, his scraggly beard scrunching up as he pursed his lips and tried to envision what kind of super stinky animal they might be looking for.

"That looks like the last of them on this half of the floor, let's get back to the lobby and see if Scott and Emma are done yet."

The four of them met up and headed to the upper floors. They had a pass key and were able to open all the doors and check each room. Once Tim unlocked and opened it, Scott led Callie a few feet into the room. There was no smell or creature in any of them and Callie gave no indication that there ever had been, so they headed back downstairs.

Scott and Tim made a quick trip to the basement with Callie, but that was all clear, as well.

CHAPTER 9

"Gabriel, can you take us outside and show us which of the Yurts has guests?"

"Sure, I'll meet you out by the front desk in a few minutes. I can double-check with Mitzi on which ones are still being used. You better wear high boots, I don't think they shoveled the paths to the Yurts yet."

"Great, thanks. We'll meet you there in a few." Scott replied, then looked at Emma as if he was contemplating having to do battle.

"Emma, Tim and I need to go convince those people that they have to come inside and stay. I need you to go talk to Hoffnagle, or whatever the hell his name is. Let him know this place is clean, but that we are bringing those guests in, so he'd better get some rooms ready for them. You okay with that?"

Emma nodded hesitantly. "Sure."

"Really?" he asked.

"Yes, Scott, and although I do feel better when I'm with you," she answered quietly, "I'm not stupid. You don't need me out there, but you do need me in here while you're gone. I get it."

"You're adorable," Scott replied, one his special mega-watt smiles lighting up his face.

"Tell the manager to have Cliff go around and make sure all of the exit doors have been locked. We'll be going out the side door by the Yurt path. Man, that just sounds so silly when I say it out loud, anyway, have them leave that door unlocked for now."

"Okay, please be careful." She rose on her tiptoes and kissed him lightly on the lips. "I mean it, all of you, don't make me have to come out looking for you."

"We'll be fine, go talk to the manager."

*   *   *

Emma knocked hesitantly on the door to Mr. Noffsinger's office, which was slightly ajar. When there was no response, she started to slowly push the door open the rest of the way, stifling a scream when he came around from the back side of it and scared the daylights out her.

"What do you want," he asked brusquely, and just then Callie let out a low growl and Emma had to pull back a little on her leash.

"Sit, Callie." She said nothing more until the dog obeyed and by then Noffsinger had made a broad swath around the two of them and was standing safely back behind his large oak desk, staring at Callie suspiciously.

"She won't hurt you." Emma felt like she needed to reassure him, he was the manager after all, and she couldn't have him putting any restrictions on Callie while they were at the Lodge. "You startled the two of us and she was just protecting me."

"I don't care," he said, still keeping his eyes trained on Callie. "That was not acceptable behavior for any dog allowed in our Lodge."

"She did nothing wrong, you came around and startled us both. What the hell were you doing hiding behind the door, anyway?"

"I wasn't hiding," he insisted, but his face was turning an interesting shade of red.

"Whatever you say," she replied. He did finally raise his eyes to hers when he heard the doubt in her voice.

"This is my office and what I do in it is none of your concern. What do you want?"

Emma was glad that he now seemed much more worried that she might spread the word that he was hiding out in here, than he was about Callie. She thought it best to hurry up and gave him the message and get out before he started to dwell on the dog again.

"I just stopped in to let you know that we checked all the rooms and everyone else is alright and we couldn't find any evidence that the animal in still anywhere inside the Lodge."

"Oh, that is good news. Thank you." He pulled a handkerchief from the pocket of his suitcoat and started patting at the moisture forming on his forehead.

"Have you been able to get through to the police yet?"

Noffsinger looked guiltily at the phone and Emma wondered suspiciously if he had even tried to call them at all.

"No, all circuits are busy still, must be because of the storm."

"Please keep trying, it's imperative that we get some help out here. Scott also asked if you could please have Cliff make sure all of the outside doors are locked, all of them except the side door leading to the Yurts. They are going out and making sure that both those couples come inside. It's the only way we can be sure they are safe. You can provide rooms in here for them, can't you?"

"Of course, I can," he replied, suddenly filled with self-importance. "You get along out of here, and if there are any more incidents with that dog, just know that there will be repercussions."

"Mr. Noffsinger," Emma replied, her eyes narrowing in anger, "you couldn't ask for a more well-behaved dog than my Callie and there will not be any incident. But, don't you ever threaten me, or my dog, again."

Emma turned and walked calmly out of the room, with Callie heeling obediently at her side.

*   *   *

Emma went to the bar, where she waited impatiently for the three of them to return. She kept Callie with her and sat at one of the booths in the corner.

"Excuse me, Miss?"

"Yes," she replied, looking up at the devilishly handsome young man that had wandered over to her table.

"Can I get you a drink?"

"Thanks, but I'm fine."

"Sorry, I'm not trying to hit on you, I just wanted to talk to you and try to find out what's going on. I've seen you with one of the guys that came to my room to check it out a little while ago. I was wondering if you might impart a little information. The explanation they used was a little hokey, I didn't buy it."

Emma hesitated, not sure what she should say. "Please, have a seat, I'm Emma Draper and those men are my friends."

"Thank you, I'm Christian Hebel." His magnificently white teeth almost glowed in his well-tanned face. He wore a tight V neck sweater and held himself almost as if he were posing, making sure she had a good view of his muscular physique

"So, what gives? I've been up here skiing ever since the season opened and there haven't been any problems until this storm hit. Does that have anything to do with it? Or was the visit some kind of a practical joke?"

"Definitely not a joke," she replied, confused as to why he might think that. "And I really couldn't say if it has anything to do with the storm."

"What then? Why would they need to see my room?"

"We think there is some kind of an animal loose, that it might have gotten into the Lodge somehow. It could be dangerous, so we just wanted to make sure that everyone was safe."

"Rabies, right?"

"What?"

"Someone found a rabid animal and now the Lodge is worried that it spread to other animals. They're worried about lawsuits if someone gets bit."

"How did you know?" Emma asked, surprised at how easily she could lie to this smug, young man.

"Seriously, you can't get much by me. I've been around, and I know how people think."

"You said that you've been here all season, have you noticed any strange tracks or smells?"

"Like what?" he asked.

"I don't know, anything unusual."

"I stick to the main trails, so I haven't seen any weird tracks. I did go out just before the storm hit for one last run and up towards the top of Mount Piler, I did smell something major league funky. I figured something had died and was rotting, why?"

"No reason, just trying to rule everything out. Did you mean Mount Pelier?"

"No, Mount Piler, it's the only difficult trail at this resort. The only one I find even remotely challenging. They call it that because there are a few spots that can be especially brutal, if you don't know what you're doing."

"Everything okay here?" Emma could hear the edginess in Scott's voice and, even though it wasn't necessary, she kind of enjoyed his jealousy.

"It's fine, have a seat. This is Christian, sorry I can't remember your last name."

"Hebel," he stated, extending his hand towards Scott, "and I do believe that we've already met. Is this your lady friend, Scott?"

"Yes, it is, you trying to play your games with her? I wouldn't bother if I were you, she's way out of your league."

Christian's dark blue eyes met Scott's dark brown ones and Emma wondered what could possibly be causing the uncomfortable undercurrent she felt between them.

"Yes, well, I was only trying to get a little information from her, and no worries, I won't mention anything about the possibility of rabies."

"Good, thanks," Scott replied, nothing on his face giving away the fact that he had no idea what Christian was talking about.

"I'll leave you two alone, let me know if there is anything I can do to help."

"Thanks," Emma replied.

Once he was far enough away, she turned to Scott and grabbed his arm. "Where are Tim and Gabriel? It was in the Yurts, wasn't it?"

"Yes, how did you know?"

"Look at Callie. She went crazy sniffing your pant leg and now she's cowering under my chair. That thing must have scared the crap out her, and it takes a lot to scare my girl. I couldn't wait for that guy to get out of here, so I could talk to you about it. And, by the way, he smelled something rotten at the top of one of the ski trails a couple of days ago, but I don't think that matters much now. What did you find?"

Scott was quiet a moment, he looked down at the beautiful, black shepherd, visible enough under Emma's chair that he could see the dog's hind legs shaking as she whimpered periodically.

"It's okay, girl, we won't let it get anywhere near you aga n."

"So, was everyone alright?"

Scott shook his head and stared down at the table, he couldn't get the sight out of his mind, and didn't want Emma to know how horrible it had been.

"One of the Yurts had its door torn off and, well, it didn't leave any survivors."

Emma reached over and put her hand over his. "Talk to me Scott, let me be there for you, please."

He raised his eyes and met hers. Emma could see the anguish in them and knew it must have been horrible to affect him so deeply.

"There's nothing that you can do, Emma, but I appreciate the thought. It was something that I'll never be able to forget. They were torn to shreds, even worse than the couple in 107. The entire place was just bits and pieces of body parts, and blood, lots of blood. Between seeing what I saw and the stench of it all, I feel like I need to take a hot, hot shower and scrub myself with a brillo pad to get it off me."

There was nothing Emma could say in response, she just continued to hold tightly to his hand so he knew that she was there for him.

"I am so glad that you didn't come out with us."

"I am, too. Do you know who they were?"

"I'm going to check with Mitzi and see what information she can give me on them. We did get the couple out of the other one and brought them in, forcibly. No way we were taking a chance of leaving them out there with this thing around."

"Tim hasn't been out to the Yurts before, so, it must not have been looking for him after all, right?"

"I don't know, if this had been done by a person, I'd say it was someone in a mindless rage, everything was just torn to shreds and the place was totaled, not one item left undamaged. It reminds me of the condition of that cabin after the creature was done tossing it."

"But, you didn't actually see the creature?"

"No, it happened hours ago."

"What now? And where are Tim and Gabriel?"

"Gabriel is probably still getting sick. It wasn't a pretty sight and he didn't do too well with it. Tim was checking in with the manager and making sure the doors are all locked tight."

"Is that good enough?"

"I don't know, if this thing wants in, a locked door isn't going to stop it. I'm not sure how much we should be telling everyone. We don't want a panic, but people should have an idea of the danger they might be in. It's a real conundrum."

"When I spoke with Mr. Noffsinger earlier, he still hadn't been able to get through to the police. Has he had any luck since then?"

"Not that I know of, apparently all the phone lines are dead, for some reason. I thought they buried the phone cables underground, so service wouldn't be disrupted by bad weather, but I guess that's not the case up here."

"How about cell phones?"

"I know the service has been spotty here at the Lodge, apparently the mountains interfere with the signals. I'm not sure if the storm is affecting them too, but I haven't been able to get a bar all day. Hey, what the hell?"

The power suddenly went out and the place was as dark and quiet as a tomb. The sound of Callie whining quietly under table did nothing to calm Emma's nerves.

"Bartender," Scott yelled out into the darkness, "does this joint have a generator?"

"Sure, it does," he replied, as a match hissed and came to life so that he could light the candle in front of him. "Come here, I have a few more of these, then I'll take the flashlight and go check on the generator."

Scott grabbed one of the candles and was heading back over to the table where Emma was sitting when he heard his name being called.

"Scott, you in here?"

"Yeah, Tim, over here, I've got a candle, but we need to find some flashlights. Is Gabriel with you?"

"He's here, says we can get some in the storage room, you coming?"

"I'm coming." He turned towards Emma and tried to hand her the candle.

"Don't even think that we're staying here alone this time. Where you go, Callie and I are going."

Scott smiled for the first time since they'd entered that Yurt and saw the horrific results of the creature's wrath. He couldn't help himself when he saw the look of determination on Emma's beautiful face, which was glowing softly in the candlelight.

"Get a move on then, we better catch up fast, I don't know where we're going."

The four of them, and Callie, made it to the storage room a few minutes later and they each grabbed a flashlight.

Scott was a little concerned that the power hadn't come back on yet. "Where would the bartender have had to go to start the generator?"

"Was it Brad behind the bar?" Gabriel asked.

"Tall guy, maybe fifty, sixty years old, dark hair, mustache."

"Yeah, that's Brad, he's been here forever. The generator is in the shed just outside the kitchen door. He only has to flip a switch, shouldn't take any time at all."

Scott and Tim looked at each other in concern.

"Tim, give Emma the key to your room. Emma, I need you to take Gabriel and Callie and go back to his room and wait for us."

"I told you," she began, but was abruptly interrupted.

"Tim and I have to go check on Brad and the generator. I don't know what we're going to find, so I need you to get to Tim's room and stay there, please."

Emma hesitated, she did not want to be separated from him again, but she realized that this was potentially a very dangerous situation, and Scott needed to be able to watch out for himself, and for Tim, so she relented.

"Fine, but if you aren't back in fifteen minutes, I'm coming to find you."

"You're a doll," he said, with a quick kiss to her cheek, "now go."

"You both better be careful," Emma said sternly, as she began to make her way out towards the hallway leading to Tim's room.

"Uh, oh," Tim said a few moments later. They were outside in the blinding snowstorm, standing beside the little shed that Gabriel told them about. The generator still wasn't running and the door was tightly closed.

"What?" Scott had to almost yell to be heard over the howling wind.

"Can't you smell that? It's faint, probably because it's so windy, but it's there, it's creature stink."

They both pulled out their pistols and tried to hold them steady, but the temperature was below freezing and neither of them had taken the time to grab a coat or gloves, so their fingers were freezing up quickly.

They stood to either side of the door, Scott nodded, and Tim yanked the door open. With an earsplitting bellow so loud that it hurt their ears, even in the heavy wind, the creature came roaring forward towards them.

The creature was massive, at least eight feet tall or more, so broad that it barely fit through the doorway. Its dark hair was long and matted with the dried blood of its victims.

With glowing red eyes, it stared back and forth between the two brothers, raising its head slightly, struggling to get a whiff of their scent in the tempest swirling around them.

Its dark fur made it difficult to see in the murkiness of the shed, but once it stepped into the snow, the contrast was fatal.

Scott stood just outside the doorway, no more than a few feet from the monster, and shot it straight in the chest. But, he might as well have been throwing pebbles at it, the bullets weren't hurting it or slowing it down at all, and it was on him in an instant. With a quick backhand from its ape-like arm, it knocked Scott flying several feet away. White clouds billowed into the air as he landed and was swallowed up in a bed of powdery snow.

Tim had to hold his pistol in both hands to keep his grip, his fingers were almost numb from the cold. The creature was staring at him and its eyes blazed an even angrier red color. Tim could have sworn that it seemed to recognize him and, after extending it's big, ugly snout once more towards him, it leaned its head back and let out an angry roar that seemed to go on and on forever. Tim couldn't move, other than to put his hands over his ears and try to stop some of the pain from the deafening noise.

When it did finally stop, Tim barely had any time to react, one long step and the creature was almost on him.

Tim emptied his clip but, although its body jolted at each impact, the bullets did not kill it. It was almost as if its skin was too thick for the bullets to pierce.

His last round went into the creature's face, near its eye, and the creature let out an inhuman roar of pain that brought Tim to his knees. Trying to get back up on his feet as quickly as possible, he looked around, but the creature was nowhere to be seen. It had disappeared into the cold, blowing snow.

Tim knew he needed to check on Scott, but before allowing himself to do so, he reloaded his gun with shaking fingers. It took much longer than normal, but he couldn't let himself be caught unarmed if the creature came back for them.

As soon as he had it loaded, Tim ran over to Scott, pulled him out the pile of snow that he had sunk into and slapped him gently in the face a couple of times to revive him.

"What?" Scott said, coming back to life, suddenly and furiously. He craned his neck, looking all around for the creature. "Where did it go? Did you kill it?"

"No, but I hurt it. Come on, we have to get the generator on and get back inside."

They ran into the shed, Tim held the flashlight while Scott tried to find the ignition switch. Both of them were frozen and shaking uncontrollably, and they sighed in relief simultaneously when Scott found the switch and the generator roared to life.

"Damn," Scott said, looking over in the corner of the shed, "Brad didn't make it."

The two of them ignored their shivering and stared down at Brad. He was bloody and battered but not torn apart like the others had been. Perhaps, the creature hadn't had time before the brothers came out and interrupted it.

"Another wasted life, damn it, Tim, we need to kill this thing before it gets anyone else."

"I know, but it's not like we aren't trying. That thing's got a hide thicker than a rhino."

"We'd better bring Brad inside with us."

"Leave him for now, Scott. There's nowhere for us to put him inside. It's cold out here, he'll keep until we get this situation under control."

It was difficult for them to leave him like that, it felt completely wrong and disrespectful, but, Tim was correct, and they had other things to worry about first.

CHAPTER 10

"Thank God," Emma said, when they walked into the room. "I was just about to come and look for you. Scott, you're bleeding, what happened?"

"We ran into our new friend."

"And?"

"It's still alive, but so are we, therefore, the first encounter is officially a draw."

"Not funny, Scott, what did it do to you? How bad are you hurt?"

"I'm not hurt, it just knocked me flying. I shot it once, Tim shot a full clip at it, and it's still walking." He shook his head in disbelief, wondering how the hell they were going to be able to kill this thing.

"Holy shit balls," Gabriel said quietly. "Is it some kind of supernatural thing? Something that can't be killed? What is it anyway?"

"I don't think it's anything supernatural," Scott replied honestly. "We only had our pistols and I think we probably just need a bigger gun. It's flesh and blood and it can die, and we will kill it, trust me on that, Gabriel."

"Yes, sir," the young man replied, looking at Scott and Tim with eyes filled with adoration. "But, what is it, a bear?"

"Gabriel, you may find this hard to believe, but we think it's some type of a bigfoot creature."

His eyes lit up at the thought of it. "Like the one on that Zapruder video?"

"What the hell are you talking about?" Scott asked.

Ignoring the way that Scott and Tim were looking at him, Gabriel continued excitedly, "You know the film where those guys caught an actual female bigfoot, they even named her, Patty, I think it was."

"Oh, for Christ's sake," Tim said, finally understanding what Gabriel was talking about. "That's the Patterson-Gimlin film. The Zapruder film shows Kennedy being shot."

"Well, whatever, is that the thing you're talking about?"

Scott let out an exasperated breath and wondered why they'd let Gabriel stay with them this long, but he might still be useful, so Scott dug deep and tried to find some patience for the kid.

"Yes, that's the creature that we're talking about."

"How did it know to wait where the generator is? I mean, there are smart animals, but, no way they can understand electricity or generators, or know that we would have to go out to that shed." Tim still couldn't get his head wrapped around what had happened.

"Getting spooky, isn't it?" Scott asked. "Or, it could be that the creature was in the vicinity and smelled Brad when he went outside and went after him while he was in the shed. The door closed behind it and that's when we showed up. End of story, nothing that can't be explained."

"That could work." Tim acknowledged hesitantly, but it didn't feel right, and he needed to be damn sure that they didn't underestimate this creature, not even once, because that could end up being a fatal mistake.

"It's almost dark. Is the place locked up tight?"

"As tight as it can be, according to the manager. But, even if the main doors are locked from the outside, fire code prohibits them from being locked on the inside. So, a guest can venture outside any time they want, and if they don't shut the door tight behind them, anything can come in. I think it's time we have a conversation with all of the guests."

"Gabriel, can you tell Noffsinger that we need to get everyone together, is there a room big enough?"

"Sure, the banquet hall should work."

"Great, let's get everyone there in, say, an hour, okay?"

"Yes, sir," he replied, practically running to the door.

"Scott, what do I do about Callie? She has to go out for a few minutes."

"Tim, why don't you see if you can find any info on this type of creature. Emma and I will be right outside the front door, letting the dog do her business. Emma, get her leash on her first, you can hold the door while I step outside with her."

He ran his hand roughly through his hair as another thought occurred to him. "What are we going to do about the other people here with dogs? We'll have to talk to them individually, after we meet with everyone else."

Tim nodded. "We can try to come up with some idea of how to handle that between now and then. Maybe just a group dog walk, periodically?"

"Maybe, we'll see what the owners have to say. Emma, co you know all the people with dogs here?"

"Yes, there are only three others, so it shouldn't be too big of a deal."

"Alright, Tim, get to work, we'll catch up with you in about an hour."

*   *   *

The noise in the banquet hall was deafening as the three of them approached. Mr. Noffsinger was red-faced and sweating profusely, running back and forth between groups, trying to calm them down but not really having anything of substance to say.

Tim gave a shrill whistle through his fingers and everyone shut up abruptly, turning to stare at him.

"Excuse me," Scott said, raising his voice so that even the people in the back of the room could hear him. "We won't keep you here long, but there is some important information that you need to know."

"It's a goddamn storm, I think we can figure that out on our own, without you having to explain it to us."

Tim recognized the speaker as Travis Benham, the snotty hot tub guy and, yes, there was his wife by his side, her lips pinched together even tighter, if that was possible. And, for the icing on the cake, she was holding the little yap dog in her arms, so they'd have to keep these two behind and have an additional conversation with them about that.

There was mumbling and grumbling from other people in the crowd and Scott decided to try the shock factor, hoping it would shut people up long enough for them to hear what he needed to say. It was imperative that they understand the extent of the danger that they were in.

"Five people have been killed at this Lodge since yesterday."

Benham's mouth opened and closed like a fish, but no words came out.

Gabriel's eyes teared up as he quickly did the math and realized that his friend, Brad, must be one of them, and the manager just looked confused, since he was only aware of the couple in room 107.

The rest of the crowd stood in stunned silence, waiting for more information, and the staff that had been sent to clean up room 107 stared at the floor, knowing that what they saw in that room would haunt them for the rest of their lives.

"Those people were killed by some kind of an animal. We aren't sure what type of animal. It's why we checked all of your rooms today. The creature is no longer in the building and we just want to make sure it stays that way. The doors are locked from the outside, so it can't get in. But, you must not open them and give it any opportunity."

"Have the police been called?" One of the women stepped forward to ask.

Scott looked over at Noffsinger, who nervously shook his head no.

"The phone lines are down, so we haven't been able to get in touch with anyone."

"Can you say radio waves, asshole?" Benham asked. "We all have cell phones and can use them to reach whoever we can, and they, in turn can get in touch with the police. There is always a solution to a problem, if you take the time to think it through."

"Give it a shot, genius. Last time we tried, there was no cell service at all, probably because of the storm. But, hey, if you have a better phone than we do, go for it."

Benham angrily whipped out his cell phone and fidgeted with it for a minute, while his pinched face wife peered over his shoulder and tried to hold their squirming dog still. Then he put his phone back in his pocket and neither of them said anything further.

"And there is no internet service either. Believe it or not, we looked into that, too."

"So, what do we do now?"

"We should be safe enough inside tonight, so go to your rooms and lock yourselves in. Tomorrow, we'll see if the storm is letting up at all and if it is, we can try to go for help."

"We have a good-sized dog and she has to go outside periodically. How do you want us to handle that?" John Hubbard asked.

"I'd appreciate it if any of you that have dogs here stick around for a few minutes and we can figure that out."

There was a large amount of mumbling and grumbling as the crowd dispersed, some stared daggers at Scott and Tim, as if all of this was their fault. But no one approached them or said anything directly to them.

Tim couldn't help noticing the big guy with the bent nose staring hard at them from the doorway. He was just about to walk over and confront him when the man turned abruptly and left the room, leaving Tim feeling even more uneasy about him.

Emma was intercepted by Mrs. Carmichael. Today she was wearing an oversize sweater that was an odd tint of orange and, somehow, she had managed to find a pair of wide palazzo pants with a wild multi-colored pattern that included that particular orangey color, and to finish off the outfit, she was wearing sequined loafers that were a subdued peach tint. The outfit, in its entirety, almost hurt Emma's eyes, and she had to focus on Katherine's face as she spoke.

"My, my sweetheart," Katherine said, in her high-pitched voice, "I hope that we'll all be safe enough here."

"Of course, we will. Scott and Tim won't let anything happen to us." Emma had a hard time taking the woman seriously but felt that she needed to put her mind at ease about all of the safety.

"Are they cops or something?"

"Something like that," Emma replied vaguely.

"I see your man has a bit of a lump under the back of his shirt, is that a gun or is he just happy to see me?"

Emma could only stare at her in disbelief, Katherine obviously didn't understand what the phrase meant, and Emma didn't want to embarrass her, so she just ignored it.

She did look over at Scott and Katherine was right about the gun, he was wearing a long, canvas shirt that was bulging a bit in the back where he had it stuck in the waistband of his jeans. To give Katherine credit, not many people would even have noticed that.

"It is a gun, isn't it?" Katherine asked in a whisper, squinting her eyes at Emma furtively.

"Yes," Emma replied, "but, please keep it to yourself, we don't want to scare anyone too much."

"Good heavens," she exclaimed, "sounds like we have a yellowjacket in the outhouse. Are both of them carrying weapons?"

Emma nodded. "Yes, so, please don't worry, they'll keep everyone safe."

"Seems they're getting a late start, said five people were killed already, right?"

"Well, yes, but we had no idea what going on when those deaths happened."

"I see, well, I certainly am glad the three of you are here, but I best get going and find out where George is hiding himself. You take care now."

"You, too," Emma said, watching Katherine as she walked away, unable to see the woman's face, which was now scrunched up in concentration as she mulled over these new developments.

Katherine had left her uneasy for some reason that she couldn't identify, and Emma watched until she walked out of the room, then pulled her knit duster tight around her body and looked for Scott.

The room had pretty much cleared out and soon there was only the three of them, the Hubbards, the Benhams and one other couple, along with Mr. Noffsinger, Gabriel and Cliff.

Emma walked over to greet the last couple, Wiggy and Ferrin Besaw. She had spent some time with them before Scott arrived, but hadn't seen much of them in the last few days. Wiggy was holding their little Morkie-poo, Simba, protectively in her arms.

They were in their early thirties and got the pup to practice their parenting skills before taking on the much bigger task of having their first child. If their dog raising was any indication, then their children were going to turn out to be major-league spoiled brats.

"Hello," Emma said, "are you two doing alright?"

"Not really," Wiggy replied, adjusting Simba in her arms as he tried to wriggle loose and get some attention from Emma.

She reached over to scratch under his chin and he quieted down for a moment. He was a cute little thing, black and white and wearing a little bow tie on his collar. He probably didn't even weigh seven or eight pounds and Emma knew from past experience that he was pretty feisty, and really enjoyed tormenting Callie by humping her leg.

"We'll all be fine," Emma said. "As long as we take proper precautions, it'll be alright."

Scott and Tim walked over to the group.

"I know that your dogs need to go outside and take care of business periodically," Scott said. "I just need you to keep in mind that you shouldn't go far from the doors, stay as close to the building as possible. The doors are all locked from the outside, so always have someone with you on the inside that can open it back up for you when you want to come in. And always, always, be sure the door is closed tightly behind you. If you just follow those three little rules, you and your dogs will be fine."

John Hubbard looked concerned. "My Sallie is old, she isn't always able to do what she needs to do right away. We might have to be outside for a while."

"Don't stay out any longer than you have to, worst case scenario, she makes a mess inside and it gets cleaned up."

Noffsinger cleared his throat and started to say something but Scott turned and glared at him, so he swallowed his words.

"What the hell?" Tim asked, staring down at the miniature little mutt that was going to town on his leg.

"Oh, my gosh, I'm so sorry," Wiggy said, her face red with embarrassment. She had given in and let the little dog run around free and he had bee-lined it straight to Tim's leg.

She hurried over and pulled Simba away, holding him tight as he struggled to get back and finish what he had been doing.

Travis Benham stuck his nose in the air in disgust and started to walk away, with Samantha following close behind, their little Shih Tzu snuggled in her arms.

"Hey, you," Scott yelled, "you clear on what to do?"

Travis stopped and turned towards Scott, looking him up and down in an insulting manner. "I don't know who you think you are to be giving me instructions on what I need to do, but I'm not an idiot, I know how to close a door, and you need to just back off and stay out of our business."

Emma grabbed Scott's arm when he started to move towards Travis, knowing there would most likely be a physical altercation between them, which none of them needed right now.

The two men stared into each other's eyes for moment and then Travis sneered and walked out of the room. The two other couples followed along after them.

Wiggy stopped at the doorway and turned towards Scott and Tim. "We have pee pads that we've been using because we didn't want our little baby to have to go out in this storm, so you don't have to worry about us. We won't be going outside at all."

"Good, thanks," Scott replied, feeling his blood pressure drop a notch or two now that Travis was gone.

"Will you two be keeping an eye on things tonight? To be sure this thing doesn't get in?" Noffsinger asked.

"I know Cliff is your only security staff right now," Tim said, "but don't you at least have some maintenance people, some guys that maybe take care of the slopes, the snow machines, whatever, that can help out to kind of patrol the place overnight?"

"No, the only people I have here now are cleaning and cooking staff, and Cliff."

"I'll patrol if you guys need me to," Gabriel offered.

"Thanks, Dude," Scott replied. "Tim and I can take turns tonight, you get some sleep, we'll need you tomorrow."

He couldn't say for sure, but it looked like relief he saw on Gabriel's face, which wasn't surprising, considering the things he had seen and learned today.

"Me and some of the other guys that work in the kitchen are back in Room 122, if you need me."

"Thanks, appreciate it."

"I have a stun gun, if you need me to take a watch," Cliff offered. The man did not look healthy and neither of them felt very confident in his ability to react quickly should something happen, but they appreciated the offer.

"No, thanks, Cliff, we should be fine. If anything comes up and we do need you, we'll come wake you, if that's okay?"

"Certainly."

"And I'll be sleeping in my office," Noffsinger stated, apparently forgetting the part where he actually offered to help.

The brothers simply nodded at him and turned to each other.

"You go first," Tim said. "I have a couple of other things that I want to check out right now."

"Okay, you sure that it doesn't have anything to do with your new squeeze? She was swinging those hips pretty seductively when she walked out a few minutes ago. I assume that was for your benefit."

"Well, I wouldn't be doing my duty unless I made sure she was all tucked in safely."

Giving Tim a lopsided grin, Scott shook his head. "Just remember to come relieve me at some point tonight. I'm only going to swing around the halls on the first floor. If it comes in above us, there's no doubt that we'll hear it moving around."

"Okay, stay safe, let me know if you need me."

"Will do, Emma, you go back to our room and get some rest, alright?"

"I would rather stay with you."

"I know, but I'll make sure that you're safe. Same as Gabriel, I'm going to need you tomorrow, so you have to get rested up. I think Callie could use a little quiet time, too. It's been kind of stressful day for her."

"I think that might be one of the biggest understatements that I've ever heard."

Scott smiled, it wasn't his usual mega-watt smile, it was tired, strained, and Emma was worried about him.

"Will you be coming to my room when Tim takes over for you?"

"You bet, even if it's just for a couple of hours, I'm going to need an Emma fix."

"Don't worry about waking me up," she whispered, as she stood on her tiptoes and kissed him softly.

*   *   *

Scott wandered the eerily quiet hallways for the next couple of hours, nothing triggered his radar and he was having trouble keeping awake.

As he made his way to the lobby, he heard voices coming from the back hall and wandered curiously in that direction.

Noffsinger's office door was open and Scott stopped a few feet before he got to it, the voices inside were raised so that he could hear them perfectly.

"What am I supposed to do?" Noffsinger asked, his voice sounding whiny and scared.

"Do whatever you have to. This was your bright idea, I do not want the cops here, and I want those two men, whoever the hell they are, to keep their noses out of my business. Make that happen or you'll regret it." The man's voice seemed familiar, but Scott couldn't place it.

"How? I can't control what they do."

"This is your Lodge, you make the rules, not them. Keep them away from our stash. If they find it, you'll leave me no choice but to have to take care of them myself, and you won't like the mess I make."

"But, but, what about this animal, they're helping with that."

"I think this 'animal' threat is bullshit and they're using it to flush us out."

"You think they might be feds?" Noffsinger's voice went up an octave when he asked.

"It's possible, fix this, and quickly, understand?" Scott noticed that the voice and the footsteps were getting closer so he stepped quietly into a broom closet. He left the door open a crack, but the man walked by quickly and his face was cast down towards the floor, so Scott couldn't get a good look at him.

He was wearing a suit though, a very nice, very expensive suit, as far as Scott could tell from his quick look through the crack of the door. Not many people were walking around the Lodge in expensive suits, so they should be able to figure out who he was quickly enough.

Scott debated going in and confronting Noffsinger but thought better of it. They needed more intel about what was going on and who this guy was before doing that and exposing what little knowledge they did have.

He couldn't follow the man since all of the other guests were in their rooms and it would be really obvious if he tried to tail him right now.

Having no other options, he headed for Tim's room and woke him up.

"What the hell could they be doing?"

"Don't know, all I do know is they have a stash of something here that they don't want anyone finding, and that they are afraid that we're feds."

Both men were silent for a few minutes, trying to figure out what could possibly be going on, but they came up empty.

"I got nothing," Scott said. "We checked the whole Lodge when we were looking for McStinky, so how come we didn't see anything that didn't belong?"

Tim shook his head. "No clue, since we don't know what it is, it could have been sitting right out in front of us and we wouldn't have even noticed."

"Maybe, tomorrow morning, or hell, this morning now, let's grab Gabriel again and check out some of the areas that aren't guest rooms and take a little closer look at what's in them."

"That works, go get a couple hours of sleep, I'll wake you for breakfast and we'll talk more."

*   *   *

"Damn, your feet are cold, Scott."

"I know," he said, rubbing his bare feet up and down Emma's legs as she squirmed, and he held her even tighter in his arms.

"You are such an asshole," she whispered, wriggling against him and feeling more than just his cold feet rubbing against her.

"I know," he replied again, just before capturing her lips with his own and pulling her on top of him, savoring the feel of her against his bare skin.

The light was dim in the room, but she could see the sparkle in his eyes and, even with the horrific events that were going on, she was so happy to be with him again.

"Scott," Emma said quietly, tracing his lips with her finger, "since the first time we met, it's always been you."

Scott planned on taking his time with her and enjoying every inch of her body, but that was not to be. Her words sparked a longing deep inside him and he pulled her down tightly against his chest and kissed her thoroughly.

Both of their bodies were burning with a passion that needed to be satiated and it was over much quicker than Scott had intended, but with an intensity that neither could have imagined possible.

They held each other for a few moments afterwards, trying to catch their breath and get their hearts back to a normal rhythm.

Emma smiled contentedly, snuggling her head against Scott's broad chest, feeling the steady rise and fall of it, as he fell into a deep, exhausted sleep.

CHAPTER 11

Scott noticed that Tim looked very distracted that morning at the breakfast table.

"Other than the obvious, what's going on with you, Tim?"

"Either of you ever see that guy before, the one standing in the doorway?"

Emma and Scott turned to see who he was talking about. The man had a short, trim haircut and his sweater fit tightly against his broad chest. As if sensing their interest, he turned to stare directly back at the three of them sitting in the center of the room.

His features never changed, but his eyes seemed to harden as he looked them over. Apparently seeing what he needed to see, he turned and headed over to the buffet.

"No, why, what's up with him?"

"He was in the gym the other day, something's a little off with him, I'm not sure what."

"Think he could be one of our bad guys?"

"Maybe, he's alone, doesn't really seem like a skier, does he?"

"What are you guys talking about now?" Emma asked, always feeling like she was playing catch up with these two.

Scott smiled at her, noting the frustration in her voice. "Sorry, we had a new development last night, and you didn't give me a chance to tell you about it when I got back to the room."

"I didn't give you a chance? It was you that..."

"Stop, Emma, before I hear something that I really don't need to know. Let's just skip to the chase. Scott overheard the manager with someone last night and there is something going on here that's not on the up and up and is most likely very illegal."

"And someone is afraid that they are going to get found out because of the creature thing happening," Scott added.

"I don't understand."

"We don't either," he said, frowning in concentration while his fingers rifled through his hair. "They've got something stored, or hidden, here at the Lodge and don't want the authorities, or anyone else, to find it. Somehow, Hassenfeffer is involved."

"Do you mean Noffsinger?"

"Whatever," Scott replied impatiently.

"But, this guy from the gym, how did one of us not run into him checking the rooms yesterday?"

"I don't know," Scott said thoughtfully, searching for the man in the sea of diners and locating him in a corner, with his back to the wall so that he could watch everything that was happening in the room. "Maybe, he just wasn't in his room when we went by. There were at least two or three that we used the passkey on because no one was home."

"Now that you mention that, we didn't see anyone wearing a fancy suit, either," Tim said, his eyes scanning the crowd.

"Why were you looking for someone in a suit?" Emma asked, now completely bewildered by their conversation.

Scott reached over and took her hand in his. "Sorry, we aren't really explaining this very well. It's going to take us a little while to get used to having someone else in our little posse that we need to keep in the loop.

I only got a quick glance at the guy who left the manager's office and I couldn't see his face, just what he was wearing, and it was a very expensive suit."

Tim joined in then. "We figured he would stand out like a sore thumb dressed like that, but neither of us have seen anyone like that. Have you?"

Emma shook her head. "No, not even before people started leaving because of the storm."

"Come on, Tim, let's find Gabriel and take another look around this place. We'll have to check to see if we missed something. Depending on what we find, we may want to have a conversation with the manager, or maybe with our new friend. Maybe he knows who the suit is. Hell, maybe it's him."

"And what about me, are you just going to leave me out of this?"

He gave Emma's hand a quick squeeze and smiled at her. "For now, there's nothing for you to do. We still have to grab Gabriel, and the less of us that there are, the less conspicuous we'll be."

"Fine," she said, but it was clear that she wasn't thrilled about it.

*   *   *

They found Gabriel shoveling out one of the side doors, the wind whipping his red hair around his face and into his eyes, and he was more than happy to quit that particular job for a little while and help them out.

"Brutal out there today, isn't it?" Tim asked, once they were all inside.

"Yeah, but I hardly notice because of my socks."

Scott shook his head and knew he shouldn't ask, but he couldn't help himself. "Your socks?"

"Yeah, man, check these out." He was wearing sweatpants that were tight to his calf and he had a little trouble pulling the leg up almost to his knee, revealing a scrawny, very pale leg almost covered by a long wool sock with a battery pack attached to it. "I swear it keeps my feet so warm, I don't feel the cold at all."

"Awesome, Gabriel, you are the definition of high-tech, my friend."

"Thanks, Scott." He positively beamed at what he could only assume was a compliment. "What exactly do you need to see?"

"Are there are any rooms, storage rooms, places like that, not guest rooms, that we might have missed?"

The blood drained from his face under the ruddy windburn on his cheeks. "Is it back in the building?"

"No, it's not," Scott reassured him. "We think there might be something else going on."

Tim looked at Scott in frustration, wondering why he would share that information with Gabriel. He was a good kid but hadn't exactly proven his trustworthiness yet. As far as Tim was concerned, certain things should be left unsaid until they were certain of what they were dealing with and who might be involved with it.

They had been burned in the past and Tim had some serious trust issues. His mother and brother were the only two people in the world that he would share everything with. No one else had earned that right and he would only share what he had to, in order to obtain what they needed to get their job done.

"Like what?" Gabriel asked, his voice an octave higher than normal.

"To be honest, I'm not sure. We think someone may be hiding something here illegally."

Gabriel looked from one of them to the other, wondering how they had come by that information, but knowing they'd never share it with him. He was in awe of the two brothers, they were everything he felt that he was not. Without hesitation, Gabriel would follow their lead, regardless of whether or not he had a clue of why he was doing it.

"Something big?" he asked, as he mapped out the floor plan of the Lodge in his mind.

Scott shrugged his shoulders. "We don't know yet."

"The upper floors are all guest rooms and storage closets. We checked all of them, right?"

"Right," Tim acknowledged.

"There's a walk-in freezer in the kitchen and a pantry."

Scott shook his head. "Nope, we checked both of those out. Of course, it probably wouldn't hurt to take a closer look, but I think they get a lot of traffic all day long, so it probably isn't the right place to hide anything."

"What about the wine cellar?"

"The what?"

"Wine cellar, it's down in the basement."

"We checked the basement," Scott said, "but there were just basic utility items, furnace, hot water tank, washing machines, things like that. No wine cellar."

"It's off to the side and the door's kind of hidden, they need to keep it closed so the temperature stays constant for the wine. Mr. Noffsinger doesn't let me go down there because I might break something. They showed it to me when I first started working here, before they knew what a klutz I was," he added, with a lop-sided grin.

"Lead the way, let's check it out," Tim said.

*   *   *

Emma was bored and frustrated and didn't know what to do with herself. She wandered around the hallways, which were virtually empty, thinking about this new twist. She couldn't imagine what someone would want to hide in the Lodge, it made no sense.

"No dog today?" Mitzi asked, as Emma walked over to the main doors in the lobby to look out at the storm, which was still roaring furiously.

"Good morning, Mitzi," she replied. "Not right now, I took her out earlier. Doesn't look like this has let up at all, has it?"

"It tapers off for a little while and then starts blowing again, even more furiously. I'm not sure if it is continuously snowing or if it just looks like it because the wind is so strong."

"Will it stop soon?"

"I don't think it will for awhile. I haven't seen it storm like this in a long, long time. My Gram says if something this brutal is happening then the end must be nigh." Mitzi laughed, although nervously, as she stared at the storm raging outside the large double doors.

She looked young enough to still be in high school, but Emma was sure she had to be in her early twenties, or maybe even older than that. She was a tiny thing, with brown curly hair that she was constantly trying to smooth into submission. and was wearing her daily uniform of black slacks, white blouse and a maroon blazer.

"Let's hope that your Gram isn't correct," Emma said thoughtfully.

"After hearing about that creature killing people here, I'm starting to think that she might be right."

"Oh, Mitzi, please don't worry, Scott and Tim, my friends, they'll take care of us."

"I hope so, Emma, but I'm not sure if I'll ever be able to really feel safe here again." She stared out into the storm, as if trying to see what might be hiding in it, then shook her head and turned back towards Emma.

"It's almost like I'm inside a snow globe and I think I might be getting a little claustrophobic, or maybe even full blown chionophobic, staring out at all the whiteness constantly."

"What does that mean?" Emma asked curiously.

"Fear of snow," Mitzi replied absently, her eyes returning to the swirling snow outside of their own volition.

"I did not know that was a thing. But, I guess I can understand how it might happen."

"Is there anything I can get you?" Mitzi asked, shaking herself out of her reverie and turning towards Emma.

"No, I'm fine, thanks."

"Okay, I'm going to go help out with the other staff, there isn't much for me to do here right now. It's not like we're getting a lot of new customers."

"I'll see you later then." Emma took her time staring out the doors until Mitzi was gone from the Lobby, then she turned and started slowly down the short hallway towards the manager's office.

Emma had no idea what pretense she would use, but she wanted to see if she could glean any information from him about what was going on.

"Mr. Noffsinger," Emma called, rapping softly on the door and pushing it open. "Mr. Noffsinger are you in here?"

There was no one in the room, but there were papers strewn all over the desk and Emma bravely sauntered over and rifled through them, looking for anything that might give her a clue about what was being hidden here, and why.

All of the paperwork seemed to be directly related to the Lodge itself and was not of any use, until she found of couple of racing forms from Hialeah Park that had notations written in the margins next to certain horses.

Setting the racing form back down on the desk, she noticed some newspapers with all of the upcoming professional sports events listed. Certain teams were circled and odds were written in the margins alongside of them.

"I do believe our friend, Mr. Noffsinger, may have a bit of a gambling problem."

"What are you doing in here," Noffsinger asked abruptly startling Emma and making her jump and flush guiltily.

"Oh, I, um, Scott asked me to look for you and see if you've had any luck getting ahold of the police yet."

She looked him straight in the eye, but knew she wasn't a good liar and could only hope that he couldn't read the deceit on her face.

"What's that got to do with my personal papers?"

"I'm sorry, I didn't mean to pry, I saw a newspaper and it's been days since I was able to catch up on what's going on in the world. I just couldn't help myself. Forgive me?" She smiled prettily at him and he started to thaw a little.

"The papers are old, they won't be much help to you." He swept them into a drawer and sat down in the large swivel chair behind the desk.

"I don't know what I was thinking, well, I'm sorry I bothered you." Emma started walking towards the door but stopped abruptly when he called out to her. Taking a deep breath she turned back towards him with another brilliant smile.

"Yes?"

"I still haven't been able to reach the police, or anyone, for that matter, if you'd like to let Scott know."

"Of course, I'd forget my head if it wasn't attached, thanks." Emma hurried out the door, her face flushed and her heart pounding furiously in her chest.

Turning the corner quickly back into the Lobby, she ran straight into the tall, muscular man that Tim had pointed out at breakfast that morning. His chest was a like slab of concrete and she bounced back slightly after hitting him.

He grabbed her arm roughly and looked around to be sure no one was watching them. "Come with me, I need to have a conversation with you."

Emma tried to get her arm out of his grasp, but he was too strong. He wrapped his other hand around her mouth so that she couldn't scream and pulled her along effortlessly to his room.

There was no one out in the hall to see what was happening or to help her escape from him.

*   *   *

Gabriel hesitated at the door to the wine cellar. "It's locked, guys, it's never locked. I don't understand."

"Stand back," Scott ordered, grabbing a piece of pipe laying off to the side of the room.

He smashed at the padlock until it broke free.

Scott and Tim took their pistols out, just to be on the safe side, and they slowly entered the murky wine cellar. "Where's the light, Gabriel?"

Gabriel went over to the far wall and fumbled around for a moment before flicking on the switch. The lighting was dim, but they could see what they needed to see. There were wine racks placed all around the room, which was surprisingly large, some of them were empty, some full. It was cool in the room due, no doubt, to some type of refrigeration unit.

Scott and Tim wandered around the wine racks while Gabriel stayed near the door.

"Scott, come see this," Tim said, as he reached the end of one of the long racks on the far side of the room.

"What is it?"

"Cases and cases of alcohol, look, Gin, Whiskey, Vodka, a little bit of everything."

"Gabriel," Scott called out, "come here."

"Is this normal, do you keep this much alcohol down here along with the wine?"

Gabriel stared at the cases in confusion. "No, there's a storage room upstairs, right off Noffsinger's office, that we keep all the actual liquor in. He likes it close by, so he can keep track of it and make sure the employees aren't stealing it."

Scott and Tim looked at each other.

"What then? He's stealing liquor?"

"More likely, they're bootlegging."

"What are you talking about, Prohibition has been over for a long time, right?"

Tim shook his head in disgust at his brother. "Don't you ever read? It has nothing to do with Prohibition, you nimrod, it has to do with tax evasion. They smuggle the alcohol from one state to another, skip the distributors and the taxes, and make millions. This is big business, Scott. But, what's Noffsinger's part in it? I wouldn't think he would be smart enough, or gangsta enough, to have anything to do with something like this."

"Maybe we better ask him."

"I agree, let's go see what he has to say for himself." Tim said, as they made their way back into the main part of the basement. "Wait up a minute, I need a closer look at this, because I really hope that I'm not seeing what I think I am."

He pulled Scott over to one side of the room where there were all kinds of cables and wires.

"I think this is the phone cable, and it sure as hell didn't go out because of the storm." He held it up to show Scott that it had obviously been cut. "And I imagine these other cut lines are for cable, internet, all the means of communication out of this place."

"What the hell," Scott said. "I'm going to find whoever did that and, right after I kick their ass, I'm going to make sure they understand that they are responsible for every death that's happened here so far, and every one that might still happen."

His jaw tensed, and his eyes narrowed as he envisioned exactly what he would do to the person who had sabotaged their only means of communication, and their only possible hope of getting everyone out of here safely.

Gabriel cleared his throat nervously and started moving towards the door. He admired Scott a great deal, but was still a little afraid of him, particularly when he was angry, so he decided he'd better just be quiet and stay out of the way for now.

The door to Noffsinger's office was locked and no one answered, regardless of how long and how loud they banged on it.

"Gabriel, you better get back to work, we'll come find you if we need anything else, okay?"

He took a deep breath and nodded, his lips pursed in concentration, which made his thin, little goatee stick straight out. "Want me to let you know if I see anything suspicious?"

Scott forced himself to keep a straight face. "That would be real helpful, Gabriel, thanks."

"No problem, I'll catch you guys later."

After he walked away, Scott finally relented and smiled broadly. "You know, I like the kid, he is kind of, what did Creamsicle call him that first night?"

"You mean Noffsinger?"

"Of course."

"I think he called him a dipstick, didn't he?"

"That sounds right, anyway, even though Gabriel really is kind of a dipstick, I'm starting to like him. At least he's trying to be helpful, which is more than I can say for the other dickheads left in this place."

"Yeah, he's kind of like that dumb little brother that we never had."

"Speak for yourself," Scott replied with a grin.

After ducking to avoid the punch Tim threw in his direction, Scott checked his watch. "It's close to lunch time, why don't we meet at the dining room in, say, half an hour? We can figure things out then. You aren't going to bring your new squeeze, are you?"

"Her name is Skylar, and yes, I did plan on going to see if she wants to join us, why?"

"We don't know who's involved with this bootlegging thing, Tim, could be any number of employees getting their hands dirty with it. We won't be able to talk about that part of what's going on, that's all."

"That didn't keep you from letting Gabriel in on it, and I know that Skylar wouldn't be involved in something like that but, if it makes you feel better, we won't talk about it until later."

"You're right, we won't. I've got to find Emma, we'll see you there in thirty."

"Fine, we'll meet you then." He had no idea if Skylar would be able to join them, but thought he'd throw in that last jab, just for fun, since Scott was being such a hard-ass about her.

CHAPTER 12

Even the best laid plans get screwed up occasionally, and Scott could not find Emma anywhere. After checking her room and the common rooms on the first floor, she was still nowhere to be found. He knew she hadn't disappeared outside because Callie was still in her room.

Mitzi, the girl behind the check-in desk, was the only one that had seen her, but that had been quite a while before and she had no idea where Emma had gone after they spoke.

Scott was at a loss and was beginning to get very worried. She wouldn't have just disappeared without at least leaving him a note letting him know what she was doing, besides, there was nowhere for her to go.

All Scott could think about was the guy in the suit threatening to take things into his own hands and was concerned that he may have started with the easiest target, while she was alone and unprotected.

Scott was starting to get himself all worked up, his heart was racing and his palms were sweaty. He realized that if he was going to be any help to Emma at all, then he needed to calm down and get focused. He wouldn't be able to do anything productive in his current state.

He forced himself to stop in one of the long hallways and take several deep breaths. While he fought the urge to punch out one of the walls in his frustration, Scott tried to figure out what needed to done next. When he felt a little calmer, a little more under control, he headed for the dining room again.

Tim was there by now and had, thankfully, arrived alone, so Scott went over and sat down with him.

"Emma's missing," he said, running his hand roughly through his hair.

"What do you mean?"

"Tim, what don't you understand? She's not in her room, she's not anywhere. She's missing."

"Did it get her?"

"I don't think so, there's no indication that it got inside today and Callie's in the room, Emma wouldn't have gone outside without her."

"Then she's got to be here somewhere, where could she go?"

"Exactly. Hey, there's Nutslinger, looks like he's heading towards his office. Let's go have a chat with him. If his bootlegging buddies are responsible for this, and they hurt a hair on her head, there's going to be hell to pay."

"Calm down, Scott, we don't know anything yet. We'll find her, but, go easy for now."

"Go easy, you're kidding, right?"

"You know what I mean."

They hurried down the short corridor after Noffsinger and Scott stuck his foot in the door just as the manager tried to slam it shut. Instead it bounced back and hit the manager in the face.

"Hey, what the hell is going on? Get out of my office," Noffsinger yelled, putting his hand up to his nose, checking to make sure it wasn't bleeding.

"Not a chance." Scott walked slowly towards the man, who began to sweat profusely. He backed up into his chair, almost falling into it, then grabbed a linen handkerchief out of his pocket and began dabbing at his moist forehead, his eyes darting back and forth constantly between the two of them.

"What do you want? Is it back?"

"No, but we need to talk to you about our friend, Emma."

"I don't know what she thought she saw, but it was nothing, just some old newspapers."

"What are you talking about?"

"The papers that she saw when she was snooping around my office earlier."

"What papers?"

"I told you, they were garbage, old newspapers that just got left lying around."

Scott took a couple more steps toward him, his face was devoid of emotion, but angry sparks shot from his dark eyes as he stared down at Noffsinger.

"Let's try again," he said quietly. "And this time, tell me all of it, and tell me the truth or I'll start breaking your fingers, one by one, knuckle by knuckle."

"Tell you all of what?" His voice went an octave higher and Scott could smell the fear coming off him.

"How long ago was Emma here and what was really in the papers that she saw?"

Noffsinger hesitated, but when Scott started to move forward again, he answered quickly. "She saw some old racing forms, maybe some odds written in the margins of the sports section, that's all."

"Is that what they have on you? Are you into them for gambling losses?"

Noffsinger wiped his forehead again as he looked guiltily down at the desk. "I don't know what you're talking about."

"Who's the guy you met up with in the middle of the night last night? The bootlegger you're working with?"

Noffsinger's ruddy cheeks completely drained of blood and went as pale as the white sheets of paper on his desk.

His mouth opened and closed, but no words came out.

Scott was out of patience and grabbed the collar of his shirt, twisting it and cutting off his air. "Emma is missing. Who is the man that you are working with?"

Noffsinger tried to answer but could only make desperate, gagging noises because Scott's tight grip was cutting off his air.

"Give the man a chance to answer," Tim said, as he grabbed Scott's arm and tried to loosen its deadly hold.

Scott reluctantly released Noffsinger's collar and took a step back.

"So, talk, who is he?"

After a brief coughing fit, he responded, "The man I'm working with isn't here, he sent some lackey to check on things before the storm hit and the guy got stuck here."

"What's his name?"

"I don't think it's his real name, but he told me it's Lottridge."

"What room is he in?"

"I don't know, Mitzi just handed out room keys, didn't note who got which ones, we've got staff and everyone else staying here, she just tried to find a room on the first floor for everyone."

"What does he look like?"

"Kind of non-descript. An older guy with a receding hairline. I've only met him a couple of times, but he always wears a nice suit."

Scott and Tim tried to picture of all the people they'd seen since arriving and still couldn't recall anyone walking around in a suit, expensive or otherwise.

"So, has he just been hiding out in his room?"

"I don't know, he's only been here a few days and only comes to see me at night, after most people have retired. And I don't get out and mingle with the guests that much."

"How the hell do we find him?"

"I don't know, I really don't."

"If anything happens to Emma, anything at all, you're gonna wish you had a better answer than that. Were you involved in taking out the phone system? Because, if you did, whether or not you see the inside of jail for the bootlegging, I'll make sure you get aiding and abetting a murder for those people that have lost their lives here."

"Hey, no, wait." Noffsinger hurried around his desk as Scott and Tim strode out of the room. "I didn't know about that. I didn't, I swear. I'll help you anyway that I can. I haven't done anything wrong."

He stopped abruptly as the door slammed shut, just mere inches from his already throbbing nose.

*   *   *

"This is getting really ridiculous. You can't keep me here forever." Emma said the words as forcefully as she could muster.

"You'll stay here until you tell me what I need to know."

He was a brutish, scary looking man, with his bent nose, large ears and those piercing dark eyes. His voice was deep and rumbled in his broad chest.

Emma felt uncomfortable being forced to stay in his room, but she wasn't terribly frightened of him. All he'd done was ask her questions, about subjects that she knew nothing about, but he hadn't threatened her in any way.

"I don't have the answers that you are looking for, I swear. Now, please just let me go, we'll find Scott and he can fill you in on what he knows."

"I don't trust him, I want the answers from you."

"Listen to me." Emma stood up, she was getting agitated, and sick and tired of playing games with him.

"I've been stuck in here with you for almost an hour. I do not know anything about any stolen liquor or bootlegging. I came here to meet up with an old friend of mine. We've gotten caught up with some sort of rabid animal that's been hurting people. That is all I know."

"I've seen other men like your friend, Scott, and his brother. Usually, they're with some type of law enforcement outfit, but I don't get that from those two. They have been around the block, though, that's for sure. You can see it in the hardness of their eyes. So, I'll ask one more time, what do they have to do with the bootlegging operation being run out of this Lodge?"

"And I'll tell you one last time, absolutely nothing. I'm done now, I can't possibly answer that same question even one more time. You obviously don't believe me and I'm sorry about that, but it's really not my problem. I don't know who you are or why you care, but if you were going to hurt me, you would have done it already, so I'm walking out that door right now."

He stood and blocked her way, but Emma tilted her head back and stared him straight in the eye. She'd had enough and was actually considering kneeing him in the balls, but he moved out of her way, just in the nick of time.

"Lucky for you," Emma muttered, as she moved around him to get to the door. She stopped just as she was about to exit.

"What do you want me to tell Scott and Tim? Because they will be looking for you, trust me on that."

He stared at her in indecision. Grabbing her had been a spontaneous decision, an unexpected opportunity that had presented itself to him. He was positive that he would be able to intimidate Emma and get her to tell him what was going on, but it just hadn't worked out the way that he anticipated.

She was stubborn as hell, and now he was forced to lay his cards on the table, literally, as he pulled out his wallet and shoved his badge and Federal identification card towards her.

"What is this, who do you work for?"

"Treasury Department, I'm with the Alcohol and Tobacco Tax and Trade Bureau. My name is Kevin McConnell. We got word there was going to be a big exchange here this weekend, but between the storm, your friends, and this mysterious animal, I haven't been able to get a handle on what's happening with the alcohol."

"Then why the kidnapping? Why didn't you just come and talk to us?"

"It's not a kidnapping," he replied irritably. "It was an opportunity and I took it, hoping that you would help me out."

"It would have been a lot easier, and smarter, if you had just asked me, or Tim, or Scott."

"I meant what I said, those men have secrets. I don't know what they are, but I don't feel comfortable sharing information with them."

"Then you're an idiot," Emma said sincerely. "They are the most trustworthy men that you are ever going to meet. They only want to help, so if you need information or some kind of assistance from us, you come and ask for it, civilly. Maybe we can get past this stupid little kidnapping ploy of yours and help each other out."

Emma turned and walked out of the room, her hands were shaking a little, but she was proud of how she had handled him. She just needed to find Scott and let him know what had happened. He'd be going crazy looking for her by now and, somehow, she would have explain but still keep him calm enough so that he wouldn't beat the crap out of this guy, this federal agent.

"He's Treasury?" Scott couldn't sit still, he ran his hand roughly through his hair, stood and started pacing around the room.

"Yes, he showed me his I.D."

"What do you think, Tim? Is he for real?"

"Could be, he has a Fed look to him."

"And what exactly is that?" Emma asked.

"Short hair, well-groomed, physically fit."

"I guess that I'm going to have to kick his ass for what he did to Emma, so I hope he isn't too physically fit."

"No, Scott, don't. He didn't hurt me, he was just looking for information and I didn't have any."

"Information on the creature?"

"No, the alcohol, and I didn't know anything about that. The only thing I learned today was that Noffsinger is a gambler. That's it."

"Yeah, he's the inside guy, but we don't know who the bootlegger is yet. Somebody that walks around in an expensive suit and, other than that, is non-descript."

"I haven't seen any men walking around in suits since I've been here."

"Us either, it's weird," Tim added.

"We checked every room, right?"

"Yes, I don't understand where this guy could be hiding."

"You know, Scott, we went into every room on this floor. But, what if he's hiding somewhere upstairs? All we did was a quick look into cleaning closets and rooms with doors that weren't locked. We didn't open any of the locked rooms up there, we were only worried about the creature, not a person hiding in one of them."

"Alright, let's check out the upper floors again this afternoon."

"Okay."

"Not much more we can do right now," Scott said, turning his gaze to Emma and, with a featherlight touch of his finger, he moved an errant strand of hair off her face.

"I guess that's my cue to get gone. I'll catch up with you later this afternoon."

"Sounds good," Scott replied absently, still not taking his eyes off Emma. Tim could hear her giggling hysterically as he walked down the hall and refused to think even think about what Scott could possibly be doing to cause that kind of a reaction.

*   *   *

"Well, nothing so far," Scott said in frustration, as he shut the door to the room they'd just checked. "What the hell, how come we can't find any evidence of this guy. It makes no sense."

"I know," Tim agreed, unlocking the door to the next room. "Must be a ghost, ah, shit."

"Damn," Scott said, backing swiftly out of the room as soon as he walked in.

The two men stood in the hallway, their faces crumpled up in distaste, their hands rapidly waving the air in front of them, trying to get the smell away.

"Shut the door," Scott yelled, but Tim hesitated, he didn't want to get anywhere near it again.

"Come on, Tim, man up." When that got no response, Scott held his arm over his nose and ran over to the door, leaning in only as far as he had to in order to grab the handle and slam it shut.

"Oh, I could seriously throw up right now. I don't think I've ever smelled anything quite that rancid."

Tim was too busy dry-heaving to respond.

"Come on, Tim, that was the last room we had to check, and we have to make sure there isn't a dead bootlegger in there. Maybe that's why it smells so awful and it's not just the pile of McStinky shit in the corner."

"I don't know if I can go in there, it's putrid and I think I'm gonna throw up. Was there really a pile of shit in the room?"

"Yes, there was and, seriously, Tim, you suck." Scott took off his shirt and tied it around his nose and mouth, hoping it would at least reduce some of the stink. He ran back into the room and searched it as quickly as he could, even pausing to look under the bed. But, he refused to do more than glance at the huge pile of poop that was left in the corner, seeing it in addition to smelling it would have been too much for his stomach to take. It was already roiling in disgust, and he didn't want to take any chances.

Bolting out of the room, he closed the door again and moved further down the hall. Taking in deep breaths of clean air, Scott wiped the moisture off his cheeks, as his eyes finally stopped burning and watering due to the caustic odor.

"Damn, that was nasty."

"No dead guys?" Tim asked.

"Not a one, unless he had already been digested, that pile was almost big enough. But there was no blood, no nothing. Come on, I need a drink."

They sat at a little table in the bar downstairs and quickly pounded down a shot of bourbon, followed by a glass of beer which they consumed much slower.

"How the hell did it get up there without us hearing it?"

"Damned if I know, I didn't notice any broken windows in any of the rooms, did you?"

"No, what is this place? I feel like we are right on top of a black hole that drops off into an alternate universe or something. We got a guy who can hide on us somewhere in this one stinking building, and we can't find him to save our lives. Now, we have a Bigfoot stopping in and walking around the third floor like he owns it. By the way, do you think the turdpile was his way of staking his claim to this place?"

"Seriously, Scott, do you really think that I might actually have a freaking clue about that particular subject matter?"

"Of course not, it was hypothetical, dipstick. But, why didn't we hear it walking around up there?"

"I don't know, it was on the third floor, so maybe that explains it. If it was right above us, I don't think it could have gone unnoticed but, on the third, there's a good chance no one would hear it, and it was a room way back in the corner."

"So, the next question is, what was the point, what did it accomplish by getting in and doing that?"

"Just to see if it could? Getting ready for a full-on assault?"

"That's not a comforting thought, and there are too many stairways for it to use if it chooses to come down and interact with us."

"Interact?"

"Kill us, whatever. But, you really think it could be doing recon, checking the layout of the Lodge and getting prepared for something?"

"I don't know, if it is, this thing is a hell of lot smarter than any animal I've ever heard of. I swear it acts like a human. I wish we'd had a chance to check out the one that we killed a little closer, something's really strange about these creatures, they have too many human attributes."

"What are you saying? That they are part human, part something else?"

"I don't know, no one knows anything for sure about them and there are all kinds of different reports from all over the world. Some people think they might be left over Neanderthals, others that they are part human and part ape, and we know how smart apes can be."

"Those explanations don't really work for me."

"Me either, some people think they are just human beings that have hypertrichosis."

"What the hell is that?"

"A disease that causes humans to have excessive hair growth, like Jo-Jo, the Dog-Faced Boy. He was discovered by P.T. Barnum back in the late 1800's and literally looked like a dog or a wolf, his body was completely covered in hair."

Scott just stared hard at his brother for a moment and shook his head. "How do you keep all these inane pieces of information in your head?"

"I wish I knew. But, I don't think that's the case here either, this creature is way too big to be just a person."

"Maybe it is a cross between a human and a creature of some sort. I guess the speculation about what it is doesn't really matter. It's a killer, and we have to kill it, before it hurts anyone else."

"Agreed, but sometimes if you know what you're dealing with, you have a better understanding of its weaknesses."

"Well, feel free to keep researching and see if you can come up with anything. I think I'm going to go try and find Emma. We'll meet up with you for dinner, alright?"

Scott had an uneasy feeling and, as best as he could tell, it had something to do with Emma. Even though he couldn't put his finger on what was causing it, he was anxious to get back to her and make sure everything was alright.

"There's not much more I can do right now without any internet access, but go ahead, I'll catch you later." Tim replied, watching his brother hurry down the hallway.

He almost called Scott back but decided not to. Tim had something weighing heavily on his mind, but he didn't think it had occurred to Scott yet, and he didn't really want to give his brother anything else to worry about at this point.

But, he couldn't escape the tendrils of fear that were eating away at his peace of mind. If the creature had followed them here, then it had traced their path, including their stop at their mother's house. And with no way to communicate, Tim wasn't able to call her and reassure himself that she was alright.

When he let himself think about it, the worry about his mom was almost overwhelming. But, since there was nothing that he could do about it at the moment, he pushed it to the back of his mind and tried to focus on what was happening here and now.

CHAPTER 13

Scott wandered around looking for Emma and finally found her in the gym. He heard her before he saw her and peeked around the corner to see who she was talking to. He was surprised to find her all by herself, running on the treadmill and having quite a lively conversation.

"Seriously, Emma, how bad do you want this? You can do it, it's just another two minutes, you lazy thing. Lift those legs, move that ass, come on, how bad do you want it? It's not that hard, just shut up and keep running a little bit longer."

The words were getting a little further spaced apart as she continued to run. The neck and chest of her tee shirt were soaked and clinging tightly to her, sweat was dripping into her eyes and she had to keep wiping her face with the towel she carried in one hand.

"Thank God," she murmured, once the treadmill shut off and she stepped down from it. She wiped her face dry and bit back a scream when she pulled the towel away and saw Scott leaning against the far wall.

"What are you doing here? Damn, I almost had a heart attack." Emma put her hand dramatically over her chest as she stared at him.

He couldn't help smiling at her. "Do you always have to urge yourself on like that?"

"Not always, but some days I really don't feel like doing it, so I have to have words with myself."

"I see." He still couldn't get the smirk off his face and it was starting to irritate Emma.

"Well, you jog, don't you ever have to motivate yourself?"

"Not so much." He burst out laughing, couldn't help himself. By then Emma was close enough to playfully take a swing at him. He grabbed her arm and pulled her up tightly against his body.

"Actually, I found it quite stimulating."

"I can tell," she said, wriggling up against him, there was no way to avoid feeling the extent of his stimulation.

He lowered his lips to hers and pulled her in even tighter against him.

"No, I can't," she said, breaking away.

"Why, what's the matter?"

"I'm a sweat hog." She pulled the soaked tee shirt away from her body and raised her eyebrows at him.

"I don't care." He grabbed her hand, pulled her close and successfully maneuvered her down onto the mats covering the floor without injuring either of them, then he rolled her over on top of him.

"But, I smell."

"Trust me, after what I just smelled you have the scent of a rose in bloom."

She frowned down at him. "What...ooh."

He had reached up and pulled her head down towards his own, capturing her lips. Emma moaned and stretched out along the length of him, rubbing her body against his.

They froze when they heard someone delicately clearing their throat. Emma sat up and realized that she was sitting square on Scott's private parts and wasn't sure if she should stay there and hide the evidence of his arousal or stand up and let him fend for himself.

"Oh, my," Katherine Carmichael giggled, "I'm so sorry to disturb you."

Her cheeks were flushed, but she didn't take her eyes off them, making Emma feel a bit protective, so she stayed right where she was.

"Apologies," Scott said, from his prone position on the floor, "I guess we forgot where we were."

"It's all right," Katherine said with another giggle. "I love to see you kids making the most of your youth. Don't mind me, I can come back another time. Just keep doing what you're doing."

"Thanks, but we're done here. It's all yours."

Scott held onto Emma's arm, keeping her in position on top of him.

"Thanks, anyway, I was looking for an excuse to not exercise and you just gave it to me. Take your time, I'll see y'all later."

She smiled broadly at them and left the room.

"That's odd," Emma said, after she was gone from sight.

"What?" Scott asked, delicately removing Emma from his lap and standing up.

"She was wearing a cardigan with a turtleneck top under it, and some kind of boots with a creepy fur trim around them, kind of looked like a dead animal wrapped around her upper calves."

"So what? We already know she isn't exactly a snappy dresser, what's so odd about it today?"

"What was she doing in here dressed like that? She certainly wasn't going to be exercising."

Scott paused and looked curiously at the door Katherine had just exited. "Good point, that woman really is a little freaky, I'm not sure what to make of her to tell you the truth."

"Me either," Emma added, as they made their own way out of the room.

*   *   *

Gabriel came over to their table to refill their water glasses later that day when they all got back together for dinner.

"So, guys, and gals," he added, blushing slightly as he looked over at Emma, "what are we are we up to tonight?"

Scott smothered a smile and shook his head. "Not a thing. Tim and I will take turns watching over the place again, but, hopefully, it'll be as quiet as it was last night."

"Anything else on the stuff?"

"What stuff?" Skylar asked curiously.

Scott frowned at Gabriel, hoping he would notice and shut his mouth.

"Nothing important," Tim said, reaching over and engulfing her hand in his.

She narrowed her eyes at him. "I thought we talked about that?"

"About what?"

"The secrecy, the lies."

He withdrew his hand and looked resigned before he even started to speak, having been through this so many times before, he already knew exactly how it would end. "You have to trust that sometimes there are things that you are better off not knowing."

"And, there are some times when I know that I'm not needed or wanted. You can stuff your secrets where the sun don't shine, Tim."

She stomped out of the room, leaving her uneaten meal sitting on the table and the four of them staring after her. Tim was just relieved that, at least this time, he didn't get doused with a drink to add emphasis to her exit.

Scott's eyes narrowed suddenly as he spied crewcut just off to the side of the doorway.

"Emma, is that the guy?"

"Yes, but, Scott, let's just talk to him."

"That big, burly guy over in the corner?" Gabriel asked.

Scott nodded, not taking his eyes off the fellow.

Gabriel lowered his voice. "Is he the bootlegger?"

"No," Tim said, "but we think he has something to do with what's going on. Do you know him?"

"Not really, we haven't had a conversation or anything, and seriously, dude, he wears sweater vests. I didn't even think they still made them, for cripe's sake."

Emma laughed and ended up choking on the wine she had just been taking a sip of.

"He's right," she said, once she could speak again, "and he does look a little odd in it, doesn't he?"

"It's all I've seen him in," Gabriel said. "It's like he has an evil grandmother that keeps knitting them for him and he can't escape her."

Emma giggled and even the corner of Scott's lip lifted in a slight smile.

"I'm going to go sit with him for a few minutes," Tim said. "See if he'll tell me what's up."

Scott watched the two of them closely from across the room, but they seemed civil enough to one another. They talked for a couple of minutes and then Tim came back to the table.

Tim spoke to them quietly, aware of how close they were to the other diners in the area.

"He suggested that we meet up in the bar in an hour or so, and we can try to talk things over."

"Fine, let's hear him out," Scott said. "But we give away no more information than we get, agreed?"

"Agreed."

"After we're done with him, do you want the first watch, or shall I take it?"

"I'll do it, after all, I got nothing better to do."

"She'll get it over it, Tim," Emma assured him. "A little thing like that won't keep her away from you, she was just making a point."

"I hope so," Tim said wistfully. "I had fun with her."

*   *   *

The three of them walked into the bar a little later and found their new friend situated at a table in the back, away from the other patrons.

They took a seat and there were a few moments of awkward silence as the men just stared at each other. The tension between them continued to build until Emma couldn't stand it anymore.

"Scott, Tim, meet Kevin McConnell, Kevin, meet Scott and Tim Devereaux, now will you all please just promise me that you'll play nice together."

McConnell stared at her curiously, Tim ignored her, and the corner of Scott's lip raised, just a little, as he looked at Emma out of the corner of his eye.

"So, what are you doing here? And why did you feel the need to kidnap Emma? That was not a smart move, my friend."

"Not your friend, not your call on what I do." His voice was gravelly and rough, his eyes never left Scott's.

Emma could feel Scott tensing up beside her. "Oh, it most certainly is. Don't ever touch her again or you'll answer to me. She asked me to let it go, this time, so I will, but don't think that I'll go easy on you if anything else happens to her."

McConnell bridled, and Emma was afraid this little meeting might be a big mistake, after all.

"Guys," Tim interjected, feeling the same as Emma, "let's put aside the bad feelings and figure out how we can help each other. McConnell, what are you doing here? Is it the bootlegged alcohol?"

McConnell looked at him in surprise, then narrowed his eyes suspiciously. "I knew you two were involved somehow."

Scott opened his mouth to speak, but Tim shook his head at him. Scott was about ready to fly off the handle and they needed to be able to have a civil conversation with this guy.

"Listen, we don't have anything to do with it. We just found out about it today. We can tell you what little we know, if you'll do the same."

McConnell seemed to be weighing a big decision as his eyes flitted back and forth from Scott to Tim and back.

"Fine," he finally replied, "you first."

"We actually know very little; the manager is involved but he, supposedly, doesn't even know the name of his contact here at the Lodge. Scott heard them talking last night, but never saw the guy. We found the booze down in the wine cellar. Whatever their plans were to get it out of here must have gotten screwed up by the storm. Your turn."

"We knew the alcohol was being moved through this Lodge, we weren't sure of the inside guy, but assumed it was the manager, he's a heavy gambler, and a bad one. We think he's working for Benny Scalfaro."

All three looked at him blankly.

"The Scalfaro crime family, in Brooklyn, you've never heard of them?"

They shook their heads in unison and he looked even more disgusted by their lack of awareness.

"It's a large crime family, we thought they were mainly into drugs, but it looks like they've branched off into bootlegging alcohol. Benny's a smart business man, he knows they can make a ton of money with the alcohol."

"But, alcohol is legal, how do they make money?" Emma asked.

"Tax evasion, that's what they ended up getting Al Capone for, you knew that, right?"

"Of course," Tim replied.

Scott nodded his assent. It was news to him, but there was no way that he was going to share that information with McConnell.

"So, what exactly are you doing here then? And why are you by yourself."

"Quid pro quo, your turn again. Why are you here?"

Scott hesitated, wanting to pop the guy a good one in his bent nose, but he restrained himself.

"Personal reasons, unfortunately, we just happened to pick this place to meet up with an old friend." Emma's hand snaked out and grabbed his tightly, and Scott felt himself calming down, a little bit, anyway.

"Not good enough."

Scott looked him straight in the eye. "Tough shit, that's what you get."

McConnell's mouth tensed in frustration. "What about this imaginary animal?"

"It's not imaginary, it's real enough to have killed five people here already." Tim said, debating on whether or not to provide any more information on the creature.

"What is it?"

"We aren't sure, maybe a bear, definitely something that big and that dangerous."

"Bears don't generally open up doors or windows to get inside buildings."

"No, they don't," Scott agreed, without adding anything further. "So, why are you here alone and what is the purpose of your being here?"

"I'm on vacation."

"Come again?"

"I'm not on a sanctioned assignment." McConnell looked uncomfortable, almost embarrassed, as he explained. "I had gathered some intel on this situation and told my superior. He didn't think we had sufficient cause to expend any resources on it. I disagreed and happened to have some time coming to me, so I decided to go skiing."

"That's precious," Scott said. "He doesn't know you're here, right?"

"Right," McConnell said, the embarrassment faded, and a wry smile lit up his face.

"You might be okay, after all," Scott said with a respectful nod in his direction. "But, if you really want us to take you seriously, you need to lose the sweater vest, it just doesn't work for you."

"What's wrong with it," he asked, peering down his crooked nose at the gaudy design on the sweater.

Scott just shook his head in his disgust. "So, what's your plan? Do you somehow intend to catch the contact person with his hand in the cookie jar, so to speak? Or are you going to arrest the manager?"

"I need to find out who the contact person is. All I want to do is put the pieces together, so that I can get the appropriate warrants once I get back to the office. That way we can get all the bad guys in one fell swoop.

I'm frustrated though, I can't understand why I haven't seen anyone here that I recognize. I've studied the Scalfaro family. I thought I knew all the men that are at the top of their food chain so, maybe it isn't Scalfaro, after all, that's what I have to make sure of first."

"We're going to take turns patrolling the Lodge tonight. You can have the first watch if you want, maybe your buddy will go back to visit Fluffernutter, I doubt it though."

"Who?"

"Noffsinger," Tim said, glaring at Scott. "You're doing that on purpose, dude, you know his name, use it."

McConnell just stared at the two of them curiously, then asked, "So, why do you doubt that our guy will meet up with him again?"

"They seemed to cover everything they needed to last night and nothing has changed today. I can't imagine he wants to take a chance at exposing himself."

"True, but why the night patrol?"

Scott and Tim looked at each other, not sure how much they should share.

"We think the creature could try to get back in. You carrying?"

McConnell lifted his outrageous sweater vest and they could see the pistol tucked in his pants.

"That will just piss it off," Scott stated matter-of-factly. "We have some rifles back in our rooms, you want one of them?"

"Sure, thanks. What exactly is this thing, I know you know more than you're telling me. I can't help if I don't know what I'm up against."

"Bigfoot," Tim stated bluntly. He was surprised at himself for sharing the information, but McConnell was right, if he didn't know what he was up against, he couldn't help. Besides, they would be endangering his life unnecessarily by not sharing what they knew about the creature.

"I know that sounds ridiculous, but we've seen it and that's what it has to be. It's huge, moves superfast and smells worse than anything you can imagine. Fortunately, just the stink alone will keep it from sneaking up on you."

McConnell looked back and forth between the three of them, waiting for one of them to break out laughing, at his expense, of course. But, not one of them did, their faces were set in a most serious manner and he had a sinking feeling that they were telling him the truth. At least, what they believed to be the truth.

"Let's say I buy what you're selling, what the hell is it doing here?"

"We think it tracked us. We killed one of them about a week ago."

"Sorry, but that's pushing the limits of reality a little too far for me."

Scott shrugged his shoulders. "You asked. You might as well wait an hour or two to start checking things out, until most everyone has gone to their rooms. I'll bring you out one of the rifles later, we don't want anyone getting nervous about it."

"That's fine."

"And you'd better be listening close, too, in case it gets in on an upper floor, which it obviously can. You should be able to hear it if does, just grab me or Tim and we'll head up there with you. You've got both our room numbers, right?"

"Yes, I've got them, and I'll be fine. No need for you to worry."

"Don't try and be a hero, I really mean that. If you hear anything, come and get one of us. You do not want to underestimate this creature. That would be a fatal mistake."

Scott and Emma headed back to their room and Tim went in search of Skylar, hoping he might be able to fix the mess that he had created earlier that evening.

McConnell sat silently where he was for a little longer, thinking about what they'd told him and wondering if they were all crazy or if this thing, this creature, could possibly be real.

CHAPTER 14

"What do you want?" Skylar asked, as she opened her door. There was a noticeable tension in the air when he stepped inside. Her long, thick hair seemed to have taken on a life of its own and her dark blue eyes snapped at him in anger.

Instead of answering her, he took one long stride forward, until there was no room left between them. She was tall, with legs that went on forever, but he still had to lean down as he took her face in his hands and slowly lowered his lips to hers.

At first, she resisted, pushing against his chest. But, only for a few seconds, then she melted against him and returned his kiss reluctantly. Tim wrapped his arms around her and tried to negotiate her towards the bed without releasing her lips, but she was having none of that. She pirouetted out of his arms and put the bed between them, hoping that she would be able to think clearly if she wasn't so close to that hard, strong body of his.

"Nothing has changed, you are still not being honest with me and I cannot accept that."

Tim shrugged, and his soft, brown eyes stared intently into hers. "There are things in my life that I will not share with anyone, including you. I like you, a lot. You're a very special person and one of the prettiest women I've ever met."

"Keep going," she said, her lips expanding into a Madonna-like smile.

"I like spending time with you, I really do, but, and this is the God's honest truth, I'm not ready for a relationship, I'm not planning on having you meet my mother or move in with me. I pretty much take one day at a time and, right now, I want to spend my time with you. That doesn't entitle you to know everything that goes on in my life. There are some things that I just can't share, I'm sorry if that offends you, but it's part of the package."

"Ironically, that offends me less than the fact that what you are really saying is that we have great sex, so you'd like to keep doing that, but you don't want to have to put out any emotional effort whatsoever, oh, and that you'll be heading on down the highway as soon as the road is clear."

Her dark blue eyes were really snapping now, and Tim realized that he probably hadn't worded that quite the way he should have.

"I just don't want you to have any expectations, that's all."

"Don't worry about that, you've made it perfectly clear that I'm nothing more than a temporary dalliance."

"Dalliance? No, you are much more than that. Come and sit with me, let me try to explain a little better, I really messed that up."

"No, just leave." As angry as she was, Skylar could still feel his arms around her, his lips bearing down on hers, and she was afraid that she would give in if he came anywhere near her. But she had been played by too many men in her life already and refused to let it to happen again.

Tim hesitated, and she looked him straight in the eye, the anger was fading now, and the hurt was taking over. "Please."

"I'm sorry." He had handled this completely wrong and felt like a shithead. "If you want to talk, you know where I am."

*　　　*　　　*

"Done already?" Emma giggled.

"Are you kidding? You're going to kill me if I'm not careful."

He loved the tousled look of her as she lay back against the pillow. She was still breathing a little heavy and there was a pretty blush to her cheeks.

"You are so beautiful," he murmured, tracing her jawline and then her mouth. He watched as her emerald eyes softened, and her lips parted slightly.

Slowly lowering his head, he captured them with his own and was savoring the moment, right up until Callie barked sharply and they both jumped. Somehow his lip got bitten, either by Emma or by himself, he really wasn't sure.

"What the hell, girl?" he asked irritably.

Callie was standing next to the bed, her tail wagging incessantly, happy that she had finally gotten their attention.

"I think she needs to go out," Emma said, blinking her beautiful eyes at him innocently.

Staring down at Emma's naked body, Scott sighed heavily and stood up to locate his own clothes. "Fine."

A few minutes later, he and the dog were headed down the hallway to a side door.

"Oh, my heavens," Katherine Carmichael stated breathlessly, as they narrowly avoided colliding at a turn in the hall way. She had her hand clutched to her ample bosom and looked like she might be having a mild heart attack.

"Are you okay?" Scott asked.

"Yes, dear, I'm fine. Just a little startled is all. Certainly, didn't expect to see you or this scary looking dog coming around the corner."

"I apologize, I didn't mean to upset you, and the dog is harmless, she wouldn't hurt anyone."

Katherine's eyes hardened a little as she stared at Callie.

"Didn't your friend say that the dog had gotten lost outside?"

"Yes, but she managed to find her way back, and we're both very grateful about that."

"Well, aren't you fortunate," she said quietly, still staring hard at the dog. Then her demeanor changed completely, and she started to giggle nervously and bat her eyes at Scott. "You wouldn't let her bite me, would you?"

"Of course not, I'm sorry again, but, I'd better get going, the dog needs to go outside."

"Don't let me hold you up." She turned and watched as Scott and Callie continued down the long hallway.

"Oh, hell," Scott muttered when he reached the door. He forgot to bring the key with him and the doors were locked from the outside, meaning he wouldn't be able to get back in the building.

He really didn't want to head back to the room and possibly run into Mrs. Carmichael again, she gave him the creeps for some reason.

Callie was beginning to whine and Scott knew he had to make a decision and do something quickly. He spied a coffee table down the hall with a fake plant on it, tossed the plant and dragged the table over to the doorway where he used one of the legs to block it and keep the door from being able to shut completely.

Feeling pretty darn clever, Scott headed outside with Callie, trying to find a reasonable place for her to do what she needed to do.

The wind was whipping and Callie didn't want to be out in the storm any more than Scott did, so she quickly went about her business and they headed back towards the building.

They hadn't been gone long at all but, as they got closer, Scott could see that someone had pulled the table out of the doorway, and it was shut and locked tight.

He peered in through the narrow piece of glass along the side of the door and could see the end table over against the far wall, there was no way that had slipped accidentally, someone had removed it. Someone did it on purpose, hoping to strand him out in the storm, someone wanted him out of the picture, for good.

*   *   *

It was still snowing and, although the wind seemed to have died down a bit, it was brutally cold as Scott pounded on the door. But there was no one around and it remained shut tight. Fortunately, he'd slipped his coat on, but had no gloves and was just wearing a scuffed-up pair of work boots.

"What do you think, Callie?" She tilted her beautiful black face at him and then looked towards the front of the building. "Yeah, me too, we have a much better chance of being seen at the glass door out front, except if your Mom comes looking for us, it won't be over there.

Let's hustle around the building and, with any luck, we'll be out front and someone will let us in before she even realizes the stupid predicament that we've gotten ourselves into."

He decided to take the long way around, the sidewalk and part of the parking lot had been shoveled earlier in the day and was easier to walk through than the huge drifts along the side of the building. But, the snow was still quite deep and, after trudging through it for several minutes, Scott's jeans were soaked and his hands were frozen. His whole body began to shiver before they were even half way to the front of the building.

All of his worries about the cold fled from his mind when he noticed that the wind was carrying something more than just snow pellets, he was able to pick up a scent, faint but nasty, and as they continued around the building, the smell got stronger.

The hair on Callie's back was up, but Scott wasn't sure if it was because she smelled the same something or if the wind was doing it. He wasn't taking any chances and pulled his gun out from the waistband of his pants. Releasing the safety, he tried to hold it steady in his trembling hands while he looked around in the dark shadows that surrounded them.

Scott stumbled through the snow and tried to pick up the pace, he did not want to be caught out here alone with the creature, not when his hands were almost numb from the cold and he only had a pistol to defend himself.

He breathed a sigh of relief when he finally spotted the carport and hurried underneath it to the glass doors. Scott had banged on them several times with no results when he first heard a loud growl, somewhere way out in the woods. Or at least he thought it was pretty far away, but he couldn't be sure with the wind whipping like it was.

Scott debated with himself about whether or not it was the creature or just the wind playing tricks on him. If it was the creature, and he suspected that it probably was, he could only hope that it was far enough away that it did not pose an immediate threat. But, Callie was growing more uneasy and was staring hard out into the darkness.

Scott glanced out in the same direction but could see nothing, but his own apprehension was increasing exponentially, and he knew that he had to get them both inside without any further delay.

Callie began to whine and rub anxiously against his leg, as Scott continued to pound desperately against the glass door, knowing that time was running out and that the creature could be upon them any moment now.

He banged on the glass with such force that it actually shook, but when that also went unanswered, Scott accepted the fact that there was no one around that was going to be able to let them in.

"This will probably scare you, girl, but I need you to stay with me okay, no bolting. It'll be loud, but I promise it won't hurt you."

He wrapped her leash tight around his hand and aimed his pistol at the glass in one side of the door, he hated to do it, knew that he was creating another opening for the creature to get in, but he was out of options. He raised the gun and prepared to fire, but slowly lowered his hand when he saw McConnell running towards the lobby, waving his arms back and forth.

"What the hell are you doing out there?" he asked, after pulling the door open and letting Scott and Callie into the building.

"I blocked open a side door, someone decided they didn't want me around and shut it tight so we couldn't get back in." Scott explained as he stared out into the blackness, unable to see the creature that blended so easily into the night. But, he knew it was there and that it was watching them this very moment.

"What?" he asked, turning his attention towards McConnell and trying to force thoughts of the creature out of his head, so that he could deal with the more direct threat somewhere inside this Lodge.

"I asked if it was this door?"

"No, over around the side."

"Did you see who shut it?"

"No," Scott replied slowly, suddenly feeling a little suspicious about his inquisitive savior, but then, if McConnell locked Scott out, why would he turn around and come to the rescue like he did? Maybe as a way to gain his trust? Scott couldn't be sure one way or the other.

The man didn't seem to be acting suspicious or deceitful, so Scott decided he had better give McConnell the benefit of the doubt, for now anyway. But, he planned on keeping a close eye on him just the same.

"Have you seen anyone walking around?"

"No, but I just left my room a little while ago. Was it our bootlegger?"

"Most likely, but, damn, how did he get by me like that?"

"I'll keep my eyes peeled for anything, or anyone, out of the ordinary. You better go warm up."

"I will, thanks." Scott headed down the hall but stopped and turned back to McConnell. "Hey, maybe it was the wind playing tricks on me, but I thought I heard it out there, not too far away either. Keep your eyes and ears peeled and let Tim or I know if you see or hear anything unusual. I'll be back to relieve you in a couple of hours."

"No problem, I'll make sure to watch all the exits. It won't catch us by surprise on my watch."

Scott just hoped McConnell could back up his bravado if, and when, circumstances called for it.

*   *   *

"Where have you been?" Emma asked, rushing over to Scott as soon as he came through the door. "My goodness, your face is frozen, come here, get that coat off and let me run you a hot tub. I almost went out looking for you, what happened? Why did you stay out so long?"

Emma ran into the bathroom to start filling the tub with warm water. Scott followed her and began to remove his soaking wet clothing.

"I forgot the damn key to begin with, and then after Callie got done, I found that someone removed the end table that I'd placed in the door to block it. The door was shut tight and we couldn't get back in that way."

"I should have gone with you, I'm sorry."

"Not your fault," Scott pulled her close against his naked body and kissed her, realizing that he'd found a way to warm up his body without even having to touch the water.

"You didn't see anyone out in the halls?"

"Not a soul," he replied, lowering his head to take possession of her lips, but then stopped with a frown. "No, wait, I did see Mrs. Carmichael, scared the crap out of her when we ran into each other going around the corner. She's a creepy thing, I don't really like her."

Now it was Emma's turn to frown and look confused. "What was she doing over here, her room is on the other side of the building?"

"Don't know, don't care," Scott said with a shrug, as he tried to get back to business. He pulled Emma tighter against his body and this time managed to kiss her thoroughly before she backed away and pointed to the tub.

"Get in, please."

Scott thought about dragging her in with him, but she sensed the direction of his thoughts and stepped even further away. "Behave yourself and maybe I'll wash your back."

"That's not even close to an even trade."

"But, it's all you're going to get."

Scott sighed heavily and put on his best pouty face as he stepped gingerly into the hot tub. But, he did have to admit soaking in that water melted away all the remaining iciness that was flowing through his veins, and he was beginning to feel almost human again.

Emma kept her promise and washed his back and, as she moved around to his chest, Scott leaned against the tub and let his heavy eyelids close for a few minutes as his whole body relaxed for the first time in quite a few days.

She managed to get him up and dried off and then tucked him into the bed with a heavy comforter over him. He made her promise to wake him up in two hours, so he could take over for McConnell, then immediately fell into a deep sleep.

The time passed quickly and, even though Emma wanted nothing more than to allow him to sleep just a little longer, she did as she was asked. A few minutes later, after quick kiss goodbye, a thoroughly refreshed Scott headed out of their room, with Emma trying to understand how anyone could function so well on so little sleep.

*   *   *

It was only a few hours later that the screaming began. Callie barked sharply, waking Emma, and that's when she first heard all of the commotion. Her heart started thudding heavily in her chest as she tried to clear the sleepy confusion out of her head.

She had crashed on top of the bed right after Scott left and was, thankfully, still fully dressed. Throwing on a pair of sneakers, she grabbed Callie's leash and her gun and ran to the door.

"Shhh, Callie." She put her ear up against it but couldn't hear anything. The screams were echoing down the hall, but they were distant, not near her room.

Emma opened it a bit, peered out, saw nothing and pulled it open the rest of the way. They slowly made their way down the hall towards the lobby, which was also the direction that the screams were coming from.

Her heart was now skittering nervously and the pistol was shaking violently in her hand. Callie was rubbing up close against her leg as they slowly moved down the hallway. That help eased Emma's nerves a bit, but not much.

She heard someone, or something, running towards her, just as she was approaching the corner. She raised her pistol and aimed it, trying to ignore the nervous tremors and hold it steady as the sounds got closer.

"Wow, it's just me, put it down." Scott said, coming to an abrupt stop as he rounded the corner, both of his hands in the air, one with a much bigger pistol in it than hers.

"What's going on, I hear screaming."

"Lower the gun, Emma."

"Oh, I'm sorry," she said, lowering her arm and waiting for her mind to catch up with her eyes and realize there was no threat in front of her. But, the screams were still echoing down the hallway and her mind and body were primed for some sort of an assault.

"Are you alright? What's going on? I can't stand that screaming."

"I'm fine, but it got in, somehow. We think through one of the upper floors. We heard it moving around but haven't gone up there yet."

"Is someone else hurt?"

"No, we were just trying to round everyone up, get them all together, and some of the women got a little hysterical. As far as we know, everyone is okay. I still have to gather the rest of the people down this hall, why don't you head to the banquet room with the others. I'll be there in a few minutes."

Scott saw her hesitating. "I'll be okay, there's just a few more rooms and I have to make sure everyone is safe. Please?"

"Alright, don't be long." Emma's voice caught in her throat, she was scared, very scared, and couldn't bear the thought of his being out of her sight, even for a few minutes.

*   *   *

Scott and Tim met outside the banquet room and confirmed that they'd rounded up everyone and they were all safe and sound inside, for now at least.

"I haven't seen McConnell since all the commotion started though, how about you?"

"No," Tim replied, "he headed off in one direction and I never saw him again. You don't think that he would have gone upstairs by himself, would he?"

"Damn, I hope not. Let's take one more look inside and make sure, but if he isn't there, we're going to have to look for him while we're upstairs checking on whether or not McStinky is still here."

"Best case scenario, maybe he already took care of the creature for us. I haven't heard any sounds from upstairs in awhile."

"Me either, including gunshots and McConnell had one of our Winchester rifles. If he had used it, we definitely would have heard the shots. If he didn't have an opportunity to use it and isn't down here somewhere, I don't think it looks good for his chances."

"I'm not feeling real positive about that, myself," Tim replied. "Let's just hope McConnell's around somewhere and is okay, and that we finally kill this sucker once and for all."

"I'm with you on that, brother," Scott said, lifting his rifle in acknowledgement.

It didn't take long for them to check the room and confirm McConnell was not there. Emma joined them while they stood by the main door, looking out over the crowd.

"You didn't see McConnell in there, did you?" Scott asked.

"No, I don't think he's anywhere in here."

"That's what we thought, we aren't sure where he is."

"If you have an extra gun, I'd be happy to help," George Carmichael, the lottery winner, interrupted as he walked over to their little group standing in the doorway.

"Do you know how to shoot?" Tim asked, looking at the bespectacled man a little skeptically.

"Born and bred in Texas, I been shooting since I was knee high to a grasshopper."

His soft, almost effeminate voice did not match the bravado of his words, but Scott and Tim needed all the help they could get.

"This thing is like nothing you've ever hunted before."

"I kind of figured that, but I can help."

"Okay, we're going to make a run to my room and bring back some of the extra rifles we have, we'll be sure you get one of them."

George gave them a half-smile and turned to go back and sit with his wife. Neither of them were guffawing or giggling now. As Emma watched them, she couldn't help but notice how calm and focused they were, and she had faith that they really could help with this situation.

Other people were not reacting quite so gallantly, some of the women, and even the men, were panicking, and nothing had actually happened to them, not yet, at least. One of the men began to hyper-ventilate and some of the staff had to risk going back to the kitchen to find a paper bag for him to breathe into. Emma was just grateful that there were restrooms within the safety of the banquet hall, otherwise half these people would have been pissing their pants.

Scott and Tim made it back with an armload of guns and, very selectively, handed them out to some of the men. They weren't being sexist, none of the women, other than Emma, and surprisingly enough, Katherine Carmichael, wanted anything to do with the guns.

They placed the men at intervals around the perimeter of the banquet room and prayed they didn't shoot anyone inside of it, particularly Gabriel, who wasn't exactly coordinated.

"Wait, wait, wait," Emma said, running over to Scott as he was preparing to leave the room. "What are you doing?"

"We have to go upstairs and see if it's still in the building. Don't worry, we won't get close to it, I think we can recognize its stench pretty easily by now and from a distance. I think once daylight hit, it took off because no one has heard it since then."

"Let me come with you."

"No, I mean it, Emma. Stay here, we won't be long. If you see McConnell, tell him to stay put in here until we get back."

"Damn it, Scott. You have to stop risking your life with this thing. You're scaring me to death."

"Did I ever tell you how much I love you?" His words, plus the mega-watt smile that he bestowed on her, were almost enough for her to forgive him for what he was doing, almost, but not quite.

With his free hand, he grabbed her around the waist, pulled her in close and gave her a very long, very passionate kiss.

It wasn't until Tim began clearing his throat, quite loudly, that Scott finally released her. And, at that point, Emma would have forgiven him for anything.

"I'll be back soon." He headed out with Tim and left George and Gabriel behind to guard the door once they'd closed it behind them.

CHAPTER 15

Tim and Scott crept up the stairs as stealthily as they could. They slowly made their way through the second floor and found was no evidence of McConnell or the creature, although there was a slight rancid scent in the air. They couldn't tell if the creature had been there and it was faint because it had been gone for so long, or if might be wafting down from the third floor.

They adjusted the grip on their rifles as they headed for the staircase to the third floor.

"It's getting stronger," Tim whispered, as they approached the top of the staircase. Scott nodded his agreement and went to the right side of the hallway. Tim stayed to the left and they checked each door along the way, making sure it was securely closed and locked.

They both stopped dead in their tracks when they happened upon a room where the door was not completely closed, there was something blocking it, a piece of clothing or something.

Scott stood to the side of the door and slowly pushed it open with the barrel of his gun. Tim positioned himself across the hall, facing the doorway with his rifle lifted and ready to fire.

Scott shoved it the rest of the way open and stepped aside, waiting for the monstrous creature to rush out, but nothing happened. The door banged against the wall and bounced back, stopping again when it hit the dark item of clothing that was blocking it. Scott cautiously reached down and picked it up.

"This isn't good," Scott said, as he unrolled the wadded item and showed Tim the gawdy design on the sweater vest that had been used to block the door open.

"Only one person I know wears those stupid things. And there's no stink," Tim commented quietly, "but I see blood."

"Damn it," Scott said, as they slowly made their way further into the room.

"What?"

"McConnell didn't make it, looks like it got him across the chest, same way that other one hit you. There's blood all over the carpet, he must have been cut pretty deep."

Tim walked over and knelt down beside the body. "Wait a minute, Scott, look at this."

"What do you see?"

Tim ripped open the blood-stained shirt from McConnell's body, his chest was cut deep where the creature had slashed him, but there was also a small hole, a bullet hole, directly over his heart.

"Holy shit," Scott exclaimed, "do you think he got whacked by the creature, came in here to hide and got shot by our bootlegger? Or found the bootlegger and got shot, then Stinky gave him a swipe while he was laying here, either dying or already dead?"

"Either way, it's one more death that asshole is responsible for. Man, McConnell could have really helped us out, too. What do we do with him?"

"Nothing for now, we can't bring him downstairs and tell everyone that we have a human killer in the Lodge, as well as a monster, oh, and by the way there is no way for you to escape because of the storm. I just don't see that going over too well with people here."

"You're probably right," Tim agreed.

"We'd better finish checking this floor, for our killer and for Stinky. Damn, I feel bad about McConnell. I didn't trust him a hundred percent and the stunt he pulled with Emma was not smart, but he was one of the good guys and this is just wrong."

"I know. We'll get the asshole that did this, and the creature. But, we have to be really careful every step of the way, we can't just focus on the creature any longer. There's more danger than just it waiting for us now.

"Agreed, we need to be on high alert and ready for anything, don't even think about leaving your room without a gun. The danger is all around us and we need to look out for Emma, also. She'll be an easy target for him, so we can't let her out of our sight."

"Understood, come on, let's finish this up and get back downstairs."

*   *   *

Emma wandered around the room for what seemed like hours, waiting for their return. She was exhausted and scared and avoided talking to anyone. Callie paced along beside her, without a leash.

Emma couldn't help but hear some of the obnoxious comments being made as she and Callie continued their meandering. Having no leash on the dog was obviously not going to be overlooked, because apparently even in these extreme circumstances, the Lodge rules must be followed.

For all their muttering and bravado after Emma and Callie passed them by, none had the backbone to say anything to Emma's face or risk agitating the large black dog walking close by her side.

"Funny how not everyone has to abide by the rules, isn't Samantha? Apparently, if they carry guns, they get to make their own wherever they go," Travis Benham said with a snigger, after Emma and Callie walked past them.

"It's reprehensible," his tight- faced wife agreed, holding their Shih Tzu securely in her arms. "You can bet I'll be sending off a detailed complaint to Yelp about this Lodge, and by the time I'm done with them, no one will ever stay here again."

Emma had had enough at that point, she was worried sick about Scott and Tim, and about everything else that was going on, and refused to put up with any more nonsense from these small-minded people.

She stopped abruptly, turning back towards the two of them. The angry set of her face was almost as frightening as the low growl coming from deep in Callie's chest.

"There is a freaking monster loose somewhere in this building that has been tearing people apart. Two of my friends are upstairs risking their lives right now, to save yours. Are you jackasses telling me that your biggest concern is Callie being in a common area without a leash? For God's sake, what is wrong with you? Where are your priorities?"

The stunned look on their faces almost made Emma want to break out laughing but, instead, she shook her head in disgust and walked away.

Just then Scott and Tim returned, and Emma, with a loud sigh of relief, hurried over to greet them.

"Everyone," Scott called, "we checked each and every room, on every floor. It's gone, for now. Looks like it came in through a window on one of the upper floors, it never made it down to this one though."

"What do we do now? It's still storming outside, we can't drive away. What are we supposed to do?"

"Hey, Jerry, don't you have some snowmobiles or a Zamboni, or something we could use to get through the snow?"

"Oh, for Christ's sake," came the unmistakably annoying voice of Travis Benham, who was still angry at being reprimanded by Emma. "A zamboni is used to clear the ice on a hockey rink, don't you know anything?"

He was close enough that Scott was standing directly in front of him within seconds. They were about the same height but, while Scott was broad and strong, Travis was a skinny little weasel. They were toe to toe and Scott stared him straight in the eye.

"You know," he said calmly, "this was supposed to be a nice, quiet little vacation. A time for me to get to know my girl again, you understand, right? Brandy and a warm fire, that kind of thing. Instead, I've been finding dead bodies, smelling a stench worse than anything I've ever smelled before, and dealing with dickheads like you. So, if you want me to save your bacon, you shut your mouth and stay out of my way. If you give me anymore lip, you'll be on your own, and you don't strike me like the kind of guy that can do anything for himself. So, back the fuck up, I'm done with you."

It was a long speech, all said in a calm and straight-forward manner. But, Travis could see Scott's eyes as he was speaking, and it frightened him in a way that he had never experienced before. He clamped his lips shut and turned away without another word.

"Jerry," Scott yelled over to the manager, "answer my question."

"Um, yes, we do have several snowmobiles out in the garage. I have the keys in my office."

"Of course, you do. Ladies and gentlemen, it is safe to go back to your rooms, if that's what you want to do. I think the kitchen is going to put together some kind of a brunch buffet for everyone, right?"

Jerry Noffsinger did not reply immediately. After wiping the sweat off his forehead and quickly trying to calculate the extra cost to the Lodge, he finally nodded his head.

"Of course, John, please see to that and have it set up in here, so we can all be together. Let's hustle and have it ready within the hour."

"Do you plan on taking the sleds out of here yourself?" John Hubbard asked.

"I haven't thought that far ahead, but I don't think so, we'l probably ask someone else to take it and go for help. Tim and I can be of more use here."

"I think so, too, thanks."

The three of them stayed together and waited until most of the room had cleared out. Scott noticed that Emma had quite a perplexed look on her face as she watched the last few people make their way out into the hallway.

"What's up?"

"It's probably nothing, just me trying to be supersleuth."

"What do you mean?"

"Again, it's probably nothing but, did you see what George the lottery winner was wearing?"

"You're kidding, right?"

She exhaled loudly. "Of course, you didn't notice. Well, he has on a nice cable knit sweater over a white dress shirt."

Scott was looking at her curiously, trying to be patient, but not quite understanding the relevance.

"He was also wearing a nice pair of dress slacks and an expensive pair of black loafers."

Both men were still looking at her, wanting to understand, but beginning to lose interest, and Emma was starting to think she might be way off base.

"I don't get it, Emma. They won the lottery and have lots of expensive things now. So, what's the deal?"

"Never mind, I was just thinking about how easy it would be to take off that sweater and the glasses, throw on a suit coat and, boom, you've got your well-dressed, nondescript man. I'm sorry, I still can't figure out why Scott saw Katherine by our room that night he got locked out, or why she showed up at the gym when we were there, and I guess it's made me a little suspicious of the two of them."

"Holy shit," Scott murmured. "Hiding in plain sight, that would really explain things, wouldn't it?"

"Damn straight, good catch, Emma, we never would have noticed that."

"But, you don't know for sure, right?" She was not one hundred percent confident in her deduction but beamed with pride at the compliment.

"Not yet, but now we know who we might be looking for, at least. Nice going, Scott, you gave him one of the good rifles and some ammo, didn't you?"

"Yeah, he didn't bring it back before he left either, did he?"

Tim shook his head.

"Well, if he's our guy, we know he's got a pistol already, anyway. Since we know for sure that he's packing, we need to be really careful, you too, Emma."

"Why, what do you expect to happen?"

"Anything and everything. You can't have any expectations, just preparations."

"Why did you say that you already know that he has a pistol? How do you know that? What haven't you told me?"

Scott hesitated, he didn't want to upset her any more than she already was, but he had promised to be honest and upfront with her so, he looked around to be sure no one was within hearing distance and quietly told her about finding McConnell."

"Oh, no," she said, tears springing into her eyes. She didn't know him well, but still couldn't help regretting that he was a good man whose life was just thrown away, all so that someone could have more money that they didn't earn or deserve. It was sinful and heartbreaking.

"Don't dwell on it, Emma, there's work to be done. Once we get the son of bitch, we can take the time to mourn another stupid, wasteful death, but not right now. Come on, let's get ready and check out those snowmobiles."

Emma, Gabriel, Scott and Tim bundled up and met at the side door before heading outside. Callie came along, but Emma held tight to her leash, she wasn't taking any chance of losing her again.

The snow had let up for a little while, but the angry clouds billowing above left no doubt in their minds that the storm was not over, it was just taking a temporary respite.

"I think we took too long to get out here," Scott said, as soon as they reached the pathway to the garage.

"What's up?" Tim asked, he was bringing up the rear of the group and couldn't see the footprints in the snow ahead of them. They actually weren't so much footprints, more of a furrow through the deep snow towards the garage. No one had used the snowblower or the shovels to clear any paths out this far.

"I think someone beat us to the punch," he said, nodding towards the passageway someone had made before they arrived. He slowly drew his gun and released the safety.

"Emma and Gabriel, you two stay back away from the garage until we make sure it's safe."

Tim and Scott slowly made their way to the side door. They stood to either side of it and Tim swung it open as Scott stepped inside with his pistol raised and ready.

They both quickly disappeared from Emma's sight and she almost lost her hold on Callie when she tried bolt at the sound of the gunshots. Emma's heart was jumping in her chest, the shots kept ringing out periodically and she had no idea what was happening inside the garage.

"What do we do, Gabriel?"

He just stood frozen in place, staring at the building.

"Gabriel," she yelled, finally getting his attention. "I have to do something, I can't just stand here. Can you hold onto Callie for me?"

He looked at her as if she were speaking a foreign language. "Gabriel, snap out of it."

She slapped him lightly across the face and he blinked hard.

"What, what should we do?"

"Can you hold onto Callie for me, please? Do not let her go. I have to see what's happening."

"Okay."

"Hold her tight, I mean it."

"I will, I promise, I'm alright now."

Emma waded through the snow, the sound of the gunshots were louder now and seemed to be spaced farther apart. She pulled her own little pistol out of her pocket and held it tight.

Just as she was approaching the doorway there was a volley of gunshots and George Carmichael came sprinting out the door. He and Emma spied each other at the same time, she started to raise her pistol, but he was too close. In the time it took her to get it in position, he was able to get close enough to smash her arm with his own gun. It went numb immediately and the pistol fell from her fingers.

Another step and he had one arm around her neck and his pistol in the other, the barrel resting against her temple. He turned so that they were both facing the door of the garage, Emma in front, shielding him from Scott and Tim who were slowly exiting the building.

"Don't come any closer," George said calmly.

"Let her go, she has nothing to do with any of this."

"I'll let her go when you toss those pistols down into the snow."

Both men knew that if they dropped their guns, George wouldn't hesitate to shoot them, and Emma. They were the only witnesses and, if they were dead he could go on with his little charade until the storm was over and cleaned up, and no one would be any the wiser.

"Now, George, you know you can't get away with this."
Scott was trying to buy time until they could find a way out of
this predicament, but it wasn't looking good. The man had
Emma almost completely blocking him, so they had no chance
at getting a shot off without the possibility of hitting her.

"Your bootlegging is common knowledge."

Scott was gratified at the look of surprise on George's face
and tried to bring home the reality of the situation. The deep
snow on either side of Scott and Tim prevented them from
rushing George, so their only option was to try and reason
with him.

"You really screwed up by killing McConnell though. Why
did you think you had to do that, anyway? He's a Federal
agent, they know all about you and now, you're going to fry for
that. Doesn't matter if you kill us or not, they already know
who you are."

George frowned momentarily and pushed the barrel of his
gun even tighter against Emma's temple, making her wince in
pain. Tim had to grab hold of Scott's arm to restrain him and
keep him from running straight into a bullet from George's
gun.

"They don't know who I am, and they never will. And he
wasn't any agent, or I would have known he was sent here.'

"Friends in high places, huh? Well, they really screwed you
this time."

"That guy was just a stupid man who got in my way. He
followed me upstairs and found the room I was using to hide
some of my things in while I'm here, since you two were being
so damned nosy. Seems he and your monster both arrived up
there at the same time and I had to make a sacrifice of your
friend, in order to save my own life from that thing."

"Listen, he knew, and we know all about the alcohol in the
wine cellar and where it's going, so you might as well give
yourself up now. You have no other option. Just do the smart
thing for once in your life."

"You should have minded your own business," George said, deciding that what they'd been telling him about McConnell was nothing more than a last-minute attempt to save their own miserable lives. Feeling confident and in control again, he knew what needed to be done, and would not hesitate to do it.

"Enough with the chit chat, just drop your guns and do it now, or I swear I'll kill her."

"What good would that do?" Tim asked. "Once she's out of the way, you're a dead man."

"Maybe I just wound her, badly, and leave her here bleeding in the snow for your big, hairy friend to find, after I finish off the two of you, of course," he said, continuing to slowly back up along the trail they'd made on their way to the garage.

He paused and aimed his gun down at Emma's leg, watching Scott and Tim for their reactions. "Wouldn't bother me a bit, or I could just wound her, drag her along with me as a shield until I get to the Lodge and lock the three of you outside. I'm pretty sure I could convince everyone left in there that you two are the bad guys. Then the three of you would be at that monster's mercy. I think I would enjoy watching how that played out."

Scott and Tim looked at each other, neither could see a way out of this and they knew they couldn't just drop their weapons. Scott was mentally preparing himself to take a shot at George and just had to pray that Emma didn't get hit in the crossfire. But, then he saw Callie silently running up the pathway behind George.

Gabriel had been hiding behind a snowbank, watching everything that was going on and had removed Callie's leash and sent her off. She ran effortlessly along the path they'd made, low to the ground and completely silent as she neared her prey.

When she was close enough, Callie leapt up onto George's back, knocking both him and Emma into the deep snow. Once she had him on the ground, Callie started to growl and snarl and snap at him in a mindless fury.

George struggled to turn over in the deep snow, burying Emma even further down underneath it, until she was unable to breathe. He freed his arm and aimed his pistol at Callie's head while she snapped viciously at him, but he never had a chance to fire.

Scott stood above him, the barrel of his gun smoking slightly, the bullet he had just fired struck George in center of his forehead and killed him instantly.

"Good girl, Callie, get back now." She was still attacking him in a frenzy and it took a moment to get her away from George's dead body. As soon as they were able to pull the dog away, Scott started digging through the snow to get to Emma.

He pulled her up and she gasped in huge breaths of cold air and then started coughing uncontrollably.

Scott pulled her up against him, breathing a huge sigh of relief that she was okay.

"You going to be alright?" he asked quietly.

She coughed once more and nodded her head. Gabriel had run up and joined them by then. He was more than a little frightened by Callie's attack and handed the leash to Emma.

Rubbing her ears and telling her what a great dog she was, Emma hooked the leash to Callie's collar and wrapped her arms around the dog. Burying her face in the warm fur, she started to cry uncontrollably.

The men stood back to give her a moment.

"Good job, Gabriel, you saved the day."

Gabriel gave them a hesitant smile, not quite able to speak just yet.

Scott extended his hand towards Emma, Callie was still being a bit protective and he didn't want to get his hand too close to her just yet, so he let Emma reach out the rest of the way to him.

"Come on, let's get you inside."

She let go of the dog and with a last pat on her head, stood up and grabbed Scott's hand.

"Gabriel, will you escort her inside for me, please?"

"Sure."

"Emma, we just need to check out the sleds and then we'll be in, okay?"

She still looked a little shell-shocked, but she'd stopped crying and was getting a little color back in her cheeks.

"Okay, I'm going to buy my hero a drink. Meet us in the bar, alright?"

Gabriel blushed as she took his arm and started trudging back towards the Lodge.

"Hey, guys," Tim called, "for now, let's keep what has happened out here between us, okay? No need to share with anyone else or let them hear you talking about it, alright?"

The two of them nodded their understanding as Scott and Tim watched them walk away.

"I'm not sorry that he's dead," Tim said quietly, "but, maybe the Feds would have found him more useful alive. It might have made McConnell's death worth something."

"You're probably right," Scott acknowledged. "But, I wasn't thinking about McConnell at the time. All I could see was the gun that he had pointed straight at Emma's head, and then at Callie's. I couldn't take any chances with him, he wouldn't have hesitated to kill any one of us."

CHAPTER 16

Scott and Tim went inside the garage and found three sleds. Unfortunately, George had gotten to one before they arrived, its hood was up and there were some significant parts missing, parts that they couldn't find in a cursory search of the garage. George must have thrown them into the snow out the back door.

Fortunately, the other two roared to life when they turned the keys. Oil and gas levels were checked, and now they just had to find the right people to take them to try and find help.

It was still pretty early in the day, so when Tim and Scott met up with them in the bar, it was empty other than the bartender. They sat at table in the back, out of his earshot, where they could speak freely.

"What exactly happened in the garage?" Emma asked, once they were all situated.

"If it wasn't for you, Emma, we probably would have been dead as soon as we walked in."

"What do you mean?"

"We saw George over by one of the sleds," Tim explained. "He started giving us his 'aw, shucks' routine and telling us he thought he could help get the sleds ready, but at the same time his hand was sliding into his pocket for his pistol. If you hadn't given us the heads up about him possibly being the bootlegger, we would have probably been sucked in by his act and we'd be dead right now."

Emma reached out and grabbed Scott's hand, feeling only slightly reassured when he squeezed it back and smiled tenderly at her. "But we aren't."

"What did you do with the, um," Gabriel couldn't quite get the word out of his mouth.

"Body?"

"Yeah."

"We dragged it around to the back of garage and left it for now. We need someone to go out and use those snowmobiles, so we couldn't leave him in the garage, there would be too many questions."

"Who is going to take them for help?" Emma asked, noticing that Scott and Tim gave each other an odd look. She'd have to find out from Scott what that was all about a little later.

"What about you, Gabriel? You must know this area?"

"I really don't," he responded regretfully. "This is my first season here and I haven't been able to check it out at all."

"So, who do think might be our best bet?"

"Rocco and Jimmy work in the kitchen. They're young and strong, and I think they both live in town. From listening to them talk, I think they've lived in this area their whole lives. They'd probably do it for you."

"Alright, let's go find them and get this show on the road. Hopefully, help will be here before nightfall."

*   *   *

Gabriel brought the two men, boys actually, into the bar to talk to Scott and Tim.

They looked to be in their early twenties and both seemed fit and energetic.

"So, what do you think, are you up for this?"

"Hell, yeah, this is dope, man," Rocco replied with complete and total confidence. "I've been sledding in this area my whole life. I know the quickest route to get us into town and to the police station. We can be there by late afternoon, if we get going soon."

Tim needed to be sure they both realized the danger that they could be in. "You do know that the creature is still out there and that it can move fast, real fast, even in this snow. This is not a fun run, it could be very, very dangerous."

Rocco exuded raw excitement as he replied, "I've been a Bigfooter since I was fifteen years old. This is the opportunity of a lifetime for me."

"What the devil is a Bigfooter?" Scott asked.

"It's a group that hunts Bigfoot. There are chapters all across the country, most of us hunt with cameras, but there are a few chapters, in the really remote areas, that hunt with guns. Once I share this story, I'm gonna be 'the man' for our chapter. We have no actual photos, none that you can for sure tell it's Bigfoot anyway, so I'm gonna get a great picture of this one."

"Don't take this lightly, Rocco. This creature is nothing to underestimate. Don't stop once you head out, I don't care if you see it and think it's too far away to get you, it isn't. You cannot stop to take its picture, it's faster than you could ever imagine and we're counting on you. You're our last hope to get help here as soon as possible. Do you understand?"

"Sure, man, I get it." But, neither Scott nor Tim were convinced that Rocco appreciated the full extent of the danger that he might be in.

"We're good," Jimmy added. "Nothing's gonna catch us once we get going. There's nothing for you to worry about."

They both looked so excited about the trip they were undertaking, and Scott and Tim just hoped this would end up being the adventure that the boys were anticipating, and not their last hurrah.

"Emma, Tim and I are going to go out the garage with the boys and make sure they get off okay. I'll be back in just a bit."

"Okay, but can I talk to you for a minute first, alone?"

"Sure," he said, standing up and moving out of the way for the others. "You guys go ahead, I'll catch up."

Once the others were out of hearing distance, Emma said, "Scott, what aren't you telling me?"

He smiled down at her and ran his finger along her jaw and around her lips. "I think you are starting to get to know me better than I realized. I'll have to watch out for that. We saw some other tracks out behind the garage when we took Carmichael out there. They were stink monster tracks, we think."

"And?"

"We're just going to check them out, see where they came from and where they went as far as getting in to the Lodge."

"You don't intend to follow them, do you?"

"No, we just want to get an idea of its comings and goings."

"You better get back here soon."

"I will, do not coming looking for me, understand?"

"Yes, I understand." She gave him a quick peck on the lips and watched nervously as he went away to join the others.

*　　*　　*

"Son of a bitch," Scott said, "that's how he did it."

Rocco and Jimmy had taken off on the sleds, feeling free and adventurous, gunning the engines as they made their own trails into the woods.

Tim and Scott followed McStinky's path back towards to Lodge. They found a huge bank of snow along the back side of it, the wind must have blown it up against the building there and, having nowhere else to go, it piled up into a small mountain. Bigfoot only had to climb up it a bit and get through the sliding glass door into one of the deluxe rooms on the third floor.

"But, didn't we check that door? It was locked, wasn't it? As smart as this creature is, I'm pretty sure it can't pick a lock."

"Let's go check it out."

Once inside, they dropped their coats and gloves off in Emma's room and let her know they were back before heading up to the third floor. They found the room in question fairly easily and the sliding glass doors opened with no problem, the lock had been broken off from the outside.

"But, I know we checked that the other day and it was locked."

"Maybe it just happened last night. When we looked around this morning, we only looked for unlocked doors, broken windows, things like that. If we even looked in this room, nothing would have been out of place."

"So, you're telling me that it closed the door behind it, so we wouldn't know how it got in?"

"I don't know, do you have a different explanation?"

"Not just yet, but I'll find one." They pushed the bureau over in front of the door and then piled as much other furniture as they could. It wouldn't keep the creature out, but it should cause enough commotion that they would know it had gotten back into the building before it could catch them by surprise.

"You ready for lunch? We still have a lot to figure out and I can't think on an empty stomach."

"We'll get you squared away soon, but we have one other thing that we need to do first."

"What's that?"

"Katherine Carmichael, she doesn't seem very gangsta, but he fooled us, so maybe she did too. Anyway, we need to find her and make sure she isn't going to cause any trouble."

They made their way down to the lobby and, fortunately, Mitzi was behind the desk. She was able to give them the room number for the Carmichael's, but there was no answer when they knocked. They used their passkey and went in with their pistols drawn, but it was empty.

Tim couldn't resist and opened the closet door where several expensive suit coats hung.

They had no better luck when they checked the common rooms for her and decided they could postpone looking for Katherine until another time. Neither of them felt threatened by her, so there didn't seem to be a dire need to find her right away.

*   *   *

After some much-needed food and coffee, the four of them tried to figure out what they needed to do next. Gabriel had somehow become a permanent part of their little group and, although he hadn't been formally invited, no one complained about it, particularly since he was the one that saved their lives earlier that day.

Scott once again realized he was probably opening a door that he shouldn't but couldn't help himself. Overall, he found Gabriel's responses pretty amusing, and a nice break from the reality of their current situation, so he had to ask.

"Hey, Gabriel, what does your tee shirt say? Most of it's blocked by that ratty sweatshirt you're wearing over it."

"Oh, this?" He proudly opened the sweatshirt and pulled the shirt underneath away from his skinny little torso, so they could read it.

"Surely they weren't all kung fu fighting?" Scott read out loud.

"It's a gag on a song, man."

"Yeah," Tim interrupted with a laugh, "we get it."

Scott just shook his head with a grin. "Alright, back to business. So, even if the cops come and save the day for all of us, what do we do about Mr. Yeti?"

"Well, technically, the Yeti is found in Bhutan or Tibet, it's also called the abominable snowman, and is white. Our friend is not white and, as far as I know, we are not currently in Tibet, however, it does feel slightly like the Twilight Zone."

"Are you done now, smart ass?" Scott asked. "So, what shall we call him? Bigfoot, or maybe Mr. Stinko, what would you suggest, Professor?"

"Believe it or not, there are stories of all kinds of Bigfoot type creatures across the country, and the world, for that matter. Each region has developed its own name for it. I guess we could make up our own too, if we want."

"I'm stunned that there have been that many sightings of it. I just thought it was something people in the northwest United States made up."

"Actually, Emma, these creatures have, allegedly, been spotted all over the world for centuries. As for the Mr. Stinko name, some of the southern states have a skunk ape, stink ape or even a swampsquatch, because, apparently the swamp monsters smell much worse than their northern relatives."

"Don't even go there, Tim. Nothing could possibly smell worse than this bad boy."

At that point, Gabriel decided to join in. "I haven't smelled it when it was close by, but just the residual smell that it leaves makes me want to gag. It's worse than limburger cheese, sitting out in a henhouse on a hot summer day."

They all just stared at him, until finally Scott said, "Very descriptive, Gabriel, makes me want to throw up a little in my mouth just thinking about it."

"Yeah, what he said," Tim agreed.

"So, do we just hang for now?" Gabriel asked.

"I think that's a good idea, we should all be getting a little rest, just in case the cavalry doesn't make it before dark tonight."

"Good idea," Tim said. "I think I'll go check on Ms. Carrico first."

Scott smiled. "The masseuse lady?"

"Yeah, you got a problem with that?"

"No sir, just don't forget, get some rest."

"Right back at ya," Tim said, as Scott stood and grabbed Emma's hand. "Besides, Skylar still isn't even talking to me, so I don't think that's going to be an issue."

"What about me, what am I supposed to do?" Gabriel asked.

Scott ignored him and led Emma back towards her room. Tim just raised an eyebrow and walked away.

*   *   *

The bells over the office door jingled softly and Skylar looked up to see who was coming in. Her hand froze in midair when she saw that it was Tim's body blocking the doorway, and the pen fell out of her lifeless hand.

Tim smiled hesitantly, noting the look on her face and not feeling very encouraged by it.

"Can I help you?"

"Are you busy right now? Do you have a client?"

"No."

"Can I buy you a drink and just talk to you for a few minutes?"

"It's a little too early for me. It's not even noon, is it?"

"How about a cup of coffee then, or if you want to get really crazy, we can make it tea."

She almost allowed herself to smile, but regrouped and pinched her lips together, refusing to allow him to charm his way into her good graces.

"If you have something to say, just say it here and now."

"I'm sorry," he said quietly, rubbing his fingers against his forehead, as if trying to bring his thoughts together.

Skylar waited, but nothing more seemed to be forthcoming. "For what?"

"For being so callow, for not giving any thought to what I was saying before it spewed out of my mouth like a piece of rotten fruit."

"Thanks for the visual," she replied dryly, but he could see that she was a little less tense and hoped that he might be able to get her to re-evaluate their situation, after all.

He walked over to the desk and looked down into her luminous blue eyes, losing himself in them as he grabbed her hand and led her around the desk and over to the settee.

"Listen, I'm not real good at explaining myself, to anyone. And I never try to justify myself, to anyone. I just wanted to be honest with you, not to discount whatever this is between us. I like you, but I live a different kind of life and I just didn't want to hurt you once this situation is done."

"But, saying things like that are very hurtful to me, how do you not get that?" Tears gathered in her eyes as she stared up at him. "I can't just be a plaything for you."

"I know that, and I'm not saying that there is no possibility of a future together. I'm saying that, although it might be great if it happened, it isn't likely."

Skylar was wearing a pale green stone on her gold chain. It was shaped like an obelisk and she was twirling it round and round on the chain as she stared into Tim's eyes. She had chosen today's gemstone with great care because she was struggling a bit to keep her mind clear and needed to strengthen her positive energy.

The adventurine stone's shades of green were supposed to provide a stabilizing influence on the heart chakra, as well as relieve stress from chaotic emotions. The chain allowed it to hang low enough on the center of her chest to ward off feelings of depression and loneliness, it was a heart healer.

Skylar needed it today because, although she hadn't known Tim very long, her feelings for him were strong, and he had managed to hurt her deeply when they spoke the last time.

She wished that she had been wearing it when she first encountered Tim, it might have saved her some heartache because it was also useful in counteracting emotional extremes and preventing its user from developing impulsive, unstable attachments.

"*Maybe,*" Skylar realized, "*with my track record, I should be wearing this stone every day. Just in case.*"

She had to give Tim credit for his patience, he hadn't said another word while she silently mulled over his explanation, but the expression on his face showed how important it was to him that she understand. When Skylar finally replied, her voice was husky with emotion.

"It's funny, but I think that it might be me that's looking at this all wrong, and I just, this very moment, realized it. Maybe I should be appreciating your honesty, rather than being upset by it."

"What do you mean?"

She continued to twirl the pale green stone as she looked deep into his eyes. "I told you before that I've been with my share of undesirables and, maybe, the biggest difference between you and them is that, although they had the same feelings as you do, they didn't tell me until I'd already trusted them with my heart and thought we had a relationship. They just walked out and left me to pick up the pieces and try and figure out what had happened between us.

I guess that you are laying your cards on the table at the outset and, maybe, I should appreciate your honesty because you are letting me know exactly what I'm getting myself into.

"But, you did say maybe, so where does that leave us? Can you understand and appreciate where I'm coming from or not?"

"You certainly don't tread lightly, do you? Can I appreciate your honesty? Yes, I can. Can I enjoy being with you and have no expectations for the future? I don't know. I like you. I enjoy our time together, but I don't know how I'll feel being intimate with you and knowing that its only temporary."

"I enjoy being with you, too. Much more than I think I've been able to explain to you. Can we just take it one step at a time and see where it leads us?"

Skylar hesitated, knowing ultimately that she was going to end up, if not with a broken heart, at least with a significant wound in it when he left, but she had to admit that all she wanted right now was to be with him. And when he did leave her, which was inevitable, she would have only herself to blame.

"What the hell," she said, with a shrug and a smile. Tim wrapped his arms around her and pulled her close, lowering his lips to capture hers and seal the deal.

As Tim slid his hands under Skylar's sweater and started to caress her soft, bare skin, the bells over the door tinkled and they both turned to find Christian standing in the doorway, staring daggers at them.

CHAPTER 17

Just as Tim and Skylar were beginning to reach an understanding about their relationship, Scott and Emma experienced another hiccup in theirs.

They'd had an energetic romp together and were laying back against the pillows, collecting their breath and waiting for their hearts to settle back down to normal.

"Did you ever picture me when you were having sex with Jeremy?"

Emma rolled over and stared at him in disbelief. "Why would you ask me about that, especially right after what we just shared?"

"I don't know," Scott replied, folding his hands behind his head as he stared up at the ceiling. "Sometimes, I can't help getting caught up in the past. You have no idea the pictures of you that swirled around my head, day after day. Maybe, if so much time hadn't gone by, they wouldn't have had a chance to eat away at my mind like they did but, they are there and try as I might, I can't always make them go away."

Emma sat up and wrapped the thin sheet around her body as she looked down at him in concern.

"Scott, I thought we went through this already."

"We did," he replied, not taking his eyes off the ceiling tiles. "I told you that sometimes my issues were going to rear their ugly head, well, they just did, I don't know why. The timing of it sucks but, right now, all I can think about is you and Jeremy together, and I cannot clear that picture out of my thoughts."

"Well, you're going to have to find a way to put all that behind you if we are going to be able to make this work. I believe I am supposed to remind you how much we care about each other right now, and how lucky we are to be together."

"Tell me again, why you waited so long. Maybe, if I understand that better, I can let some of this go."

Scott still wouldn't look her in the eye and that worried Emma a great deal. Just when she thought they were in a good place together, one of them kept throwing a wrench into the mix and messing it up all over again.

"Once Jeremy and I were split up, I had to be sure of myself, what I wanted from my life. I needed to be sure that I wasn't going to change everything in my life to chase a dream."

"What do you mean?"

"We were together at a very emotionally fragile time for me, because of the house and because of Jeremy. You were my hero, Scott, you were bigger than life in my memories, and I just needed time to be sure of who I was before I tried to find you again, just in case you weren't really the man that I had built you up to be in my mind."

"That doesn't make any sense to me, why take all that extra time to think about who I might be, when you could have just contacted me and found out for yourself, a long time ago. And you could have saved me from months of torment."

"Scott, I am sorry for any pain that I caused you, and I'm sorry if my timetable seems unreasonable to you, but I needed to take care of me, before I could even think about taking care of you."

"See, that's just it Emma," some of Scott's anger was beginning to show in the tone of his voice, "I didn't need you to take care of me, I just needed you to be with me. That's all."

"That's where you're wrong, Scott. That's all that a true relationship is, it's about two people taking care of each other, helping each other get through the bad times and helping to make the good times exceptional. It's keeping them safe and happy and being there for them, always."

Scott finally turned his head to look over at Emma, her green eyes were open wide and he could see the doubt and concern on her face. He wished he could reassure her, but at that moment, he just couldn't.

"Ay, there's the rub," he quoted. "If keeping a person safe and happy, and always being there for them, is love, then how could you let me suffer so much for so long? I just need you to be honest with me, Emma, I can't completely buy what you are telling me. I'm sorry, I just can't."

"I don't know what else to say to you, Scott. Everyone has to find their own way of dealing with what is happening in their life at any particular moment. I had to do what I thought was right.

I certainly never intended to hurt you and drag out your pain. I wanted to be with you, but I wasn't ready yet. I was in a marriage for a long, long time. I had children to consider and, maybe I was afraid, maybe I was afraid to step back into another relationship right away and possibly get hurt as badly as I'd allowed Jeremy to hurt me."

Scott continued to stare into Emma's eyes, almost challenging her, and she couldn't tell if anything that she was saying was making a dent in the armor that he had built up around his heart. Sadly, she knew that armor was as thick as it was because of her and, somehow, she had to find her way back through it.

"Did you think that you couldn't trust me? That I might treat you the same way that he did?"

"I'm not sure," Emma said quietly, tears collecting in her eyes. "I was with him for twenty years, I thought we were perfectly happy and never in my wildest imagination did I think he could ever hurt me the way that he did. So, how can I ever be sure of anyone again?"

"I am not Jeremy. Never have been and never will be anything like him."

"I know that and all I can tell you is that I love you. I never stopped loving you and I never tried to intentionally hurt you. I just had to take care of, and be sure of, myself first, and that is the absolute truth."

Scott turned his gaze back to the ceiling, thinking over what she'd said. He couldn't understand why he was putting Emma through this right now, particularly with everything else that was going on around them. Maybe he was just plain scared. She was his first, and his only true love, and she held so much power over him that just the thought of it was frightening.

He had never felt fear like he had when he saw the muzzle of Carmichael's gun up against her temple. It was almost debilitating, and he never wanted to feel that helpless again.

But, the only way that he could save himself from that kind of fear would be if he left Emma. And, by doing that, he would never again experience the depth of the feelings that came with loving her totally and completely. Somehow, he was going to have to reconcile all of those emotions running amuck inside of him. But, before he took on that battle, he had to be sure of her feelings.

"Come here." He held out his hand to her and she laid down next to him, her head resting on his shoulder, her arm across his chest, twirling his chest hairs around in her nervousness.

"I understand the damage that Jeremy did to you, but can you let that go? Can you have faith in me and trust that I will never cheat on you or hurt you like he did? If I want out, I'm going to tell you that straight up because that's who I am. So, you need to be sure, can you trust me?"

Emma hesitated, mulling over his words. "I know who you are, the kind of man that you are, and I know that I have to let go of the past and focus on the here and now. You have issues that you are still working on, I accept that. But, I still have issues too, and I'm trying every day to deal with them and let them go. Is that good enough for you, are you still willing to try and make this work?" Emma asked.

It was not the response Scott was hoping for, but if he was asking her to give him the benefit of the doubt, then he owed her no less.

"Of course, I am," he replied, running his hand through her hair, enjoying the feel of her naked skin against his. Scott knew they belonged together and that he was going to have to find courage like he'd never needed before, to conquer the destructive thoughts he'd had while they were apart and to make sure that he didn't drive her away with his anger because of them. And even more importantly, to somehow keep his fear of losing her at bay.

"Are you? I'm still a work in progress and you're going to have to be patient with me while I continue to work things out. Things that might rear their ugly heads at the most inopportune times. Can you do that?"

"Yes, I can. I actually have had a lot more time get my head wrapped around this situation than you have. I forget that, although we weren't together yet, I knew where I was going and where I planned on ending up, and you didn't. I guess I should have realized that we weren't going to be able to just fall into a happily ever after. But, we will get there, I have no doubt about that. It's just going to take a little bit of work, on both our parts. You just have to keep talking to me when it comes up, don't keep it inside and let it fester."

"Have you ever known me to keep my thoughts to myself?" Scott asked with a slight grin.

"No, I guess not," she replied softly, still twirling his chest hairs.

He tilted her head up and lowered his lips onto hers, caressing them softly until she turned and gave herself to him completely, trusting that the depth of their love would help them get to where they needed to be in order to move forward with their lives.

*   *   *

"Is there something that I can do for you, Christian?" Skylar asked, her smoky voice slightly agitated.

"I guess not, I didn't realize your services now extend to paid sex."

Tim stood up and stepped towards Christian. To give him credit, Christian did not back down, but his hatred was almost palpable as he stared up into Tim's eyes.

"I think you'd better leave," Tim said.

"Go to hell, Skylar and I have a history. I need to talk to her about something that is important to the two of us, something you do not need to stick your nose into."

Tim's hand curled into a fist, he wanted to knock the arrogance off Christian's smug face. He held himself back from doing any violence because he heard the concern in Skylar's voice when she tried to intercede and settle them both down.

"It's alright, Tim. I'll take care of this. Christian, I'm not sure what you think we have to talk about. You know as well as I do that whatever we had is over and done. I think you should leave."

"I need to talk to you, alone."

"Not right now, I'm busy."

"Sklyar, I'm not leaving until you've let me explain some things to you."

"Christian, the time for explaining was before you hooked up with, was it one or two of those snowbunnies that left just before the storm hit?"

"They didn't mean anything, look, I can't talk to you with Lurch here staring me down. Come with me for a few minutes and I'll explain everything."

"No, I want you to leave."

Christian started to plead with her, but his mouth snapped shut when Tim grabbed his arm and turned him towards the door.

"She asked you to leave. I won't ask so nicely, now get out of here."

Christian yanked his arm from Tim's grasp and turned back to Skylar.

"Listen, you little tramp, no one treats me the way that you have."

Without even thinking, Tim just reacted and punched Christian forcefully in the jaw. Christian fell backwards into wall and slid down onto the floor. Rubbing his jaw and scowling at Tim, he slowly stood back up and started walking towards the door.

"This isn't done yet."

"Yeah, I think it is, get the hell out of here." Tim was walking right behind him when Christian turned quickly and gave him a powerful straight punch of his own, his large gaudy ring cutting Tim's cheekbone.

With an uppercut, Tim lifted Christian off his feet and the brawl was on.

They matched each other blow for blow, to the stomach the face. Skylar was in the background, begging them to stop, but neither of them heard her.

It was when Christian tried to kick Tim in his privates, that Tim's full fury was released, and he didn't hold back any longer, pummeling Christian until he fell onto the floor and buried his head in his hands like the coward that he was.

Tim started towards him again, but Skylar put her hand on his arm to hold him back. Tim reluctantly managed to restrain himself from inflicting any more damage, although it would have been very satisfying to knock him upside the head just a couple more times.

Christian hesitantly stood back up and made his way to the door, ignoring the two of them. Tim followed close behind and once Christian hit the hallway, Tim slammed the door in his face and made sure the lock was turned, so they wouldn't be interrupted any further.

Skylar was pacing now, turning the adventurine stone around and around in her fingers. Their romantic moment was obviously lost, but Tim took her back into his arms and just held her until she calmed down.

"What did you ever see in that asshole?"

"He can be very charming when he wants to be. Unfortunately, it doesn't last long. He doesn't forgive and forget either. I'm sorry that happened, are you okay? Let me get you some ice for your face."

"I'm fine and don't worry about him, he doesn't concern me, I'm just a little worried that he might bother you when I'm not around."

"He's really just a big baby, he doesn't scare me. He likes to make the rules and I didn't behave the way he wanted me too. But, he would never physically hurt me. I'm shocked that happened between the two of you, I've never seen him like that, or you either, for that matter."

"I'm sorry that it happened, but he didn't play nice and I kind of lost my cool."

"I saw that, you can be pretty scary, can't you?"

"I try not to be. Do you think there is any possibility of getting back to what we were doing before he so rudely interrupted us?"

"I'd love to," she replied. "However, I do have a client coming in five minutes and, although you may be able to accommodate that time frame, I'd prefer something that takes just a little longer than that. Can we meet up later?"

"I'm not sure exactly what's going on, but I'll check in with you once I do know, okay?"

With a quick kiss and wistful glance, he was gone.

*   *   *

It was much later that afternoon when Emma awoke with a start. Callie was whining softly, and Scott was snoring loudly.

Emma let him sleep and quietly got dressed. Then, she and Callie left the room and headed out to the lobby, feeling extremely grateful that Mitzi happened to be behind the desk just then. She still didn't feel one hundred percent comfortable going outside alone, even with the passkey to get back in.

"Hi, Mitzi, Callie and I are going to step outside for a few minutes, are you going to be here, just in case we have a problem with the door."

"Of course, I'll keep an eye out for you." She walked around the counter and petted Callie gently. "How's our beautiful girl today?"

Callie's tail wagged excitedly, and Mitzi couldn't help petting her for just a few moments more, loving the feel of Callie's soft fur in her hands. She found it very soothing after all the stress they'd been living with these last few days.

"Thanks, Mitzi, we'll be right back."

The sky was still spitting a little snow here and there, but the wind had lessened quite a bit and it seemed like the storm might finally be winding down.

Emma got a crick in her neck trying to look around full circle the entire time they were outside, positive that the stink monster was out there somewhere, just waiting for them. She knew that she was being silly, Callie would let her know if it was there, but it didn't matter, Emma still couldn't shake her uneasiness.

With unsteady hands, she was able to let herself back into the building once Callie was done.

"What now, girl?" Emma was a little bored and, since she didn't want to wake Scott from his much-needed slumber, she decided to wander around the Lodge, keeping to the first floor, of course.

Most of the guests were in their own rooms, or together in the main lounge, playing card games and trying to take their minds off what was happening, both inside and outside the Lodge. Emma really didn't feel like being around people just then, so she and Callie walked the hallways.

They explored a corridor along the back of the building that Emma hadn't been down before. She was admiring the pictures on the walls and was amazed at the feats those professional skiers were able to accomplish on the slopes, and the heights they were able to reach when they jumped

The photographers were just as talented, in their own way, and were somehow able to catch the skiers at just the right moment to showcase their amazing skills.

Callie started whining suddenly and Emma thought she might be getting bored, but then she caught a whiff of something rancid and her chest seized up in fear. They had dug her little pistol up out of the snow after Carmichael knocked it out of her hand earlier, but she didn't have it with her right now. Not that it would have made any difference, it certainly wouldn't be able to actually hurt the creature, but Emma felt completely helpless without it.

The smell suddenly engulfed her completely and at the same moment, Emma saw the hair on Callie's neck raise and the dog began a low growl.

Emma took a breath, trying not to panic, or to gag at the smell. The dog was staring back down the way they had just come, so Emma continued forward, until she realized that she was at a dead end. They were going to have to either take the stairs up to the next floor or head back the way they came, and there was no way she was going to do that.

The smell became even stronger and tentacles of fear crawled up Emma's spine. She knew that she needed to make a decision quickly and get out of there, but she felt frozen and unable to move.

Callie started barking frantically, freeing Emma from her paralyzing fear and prompting her to turn and run up the stairs, pulling Callie's leash along behind her. The dog held back for a moment, but then understood and raced up the stairs, almost tripping Emma as she passed her by.

Emma let loose a horrific scream, born of terror and panic, when something grabbed her foot. She tried to shake it loose, but whatever it was held tight. How could it be the creature? Nothing could have moved that fast, it wasn't even in the same hallway they had been in. Her mind was reeling as she tried to figure out what to do, but she was too petrified to turn and see what had ahold of her. Afraid that she would literally die of fright if she saw that it was that thing.

But it wouldn't release its grip on her leg and was starting to pull her backwards, down the steps.

Emma threw the leash up the stairs, so at least Callie would be able to escape. Trying not to cry, she finally turned to face her nemesis. The stench was now so strong that Emma could barely breathe, and the size of the creature was staggering, almost crumpling what little courage she still possessed.

It filled the stairwell and, although it stood several steps below her, its head was even with her face. It was large and hairy, it's eyes glowed red and it was making some kind of mewling noise in the back of its throat that made Emma's skin crawl, and then it yanked on her leg again.

Emma screamed as loud and as long as she could, but when it yanked her leg out from under her, she fell backward, and her spine smashed into the hard stairs, momentarily knocking the breath from her body.

It stared down at Emma intently and its nostrils flared as if it were checking out her scent. Emma gasped, trying to get her breathe back as she stared up into those hateful, little red eyes. When it did return, she groaned loudly and then started to scream again.

The creature had unusually long arms, it reached down and grabbed Emma with its huge hand and threw her over its shoulder, knocking the breath out of her once again.

As soon as she was able to draw a deep breath again, Emma started to scream and squirm and struggle to break free from the creature's grasp. Her head was upside down and was periodically banging into its furry shoulder blade as it continued to move along the hallway.

She couldn't help getting some of its hair in her mouth and was retching at the smell and the taste of it as she desperately tried to spit it out. The creature held her tight, even though she continually hammered at it with her fists and tried to scream, hoping to catch someone's attention, but so far no one was coming to her rescue.

Emma knew she was verging hysteria, the blood was all rushing to her head and the smell was so overwhelming that she was afraid that she might pass out. But, through it all, she realized that this thing, this creature, could have just flicked her with one finger and knocked her flying, but instead, it was patiently tolerating her, even when she continued to beat at it.

It hadn't tried to hurt her at all, for some reason, and was almost trying to be gentle, which was a crazy thought, but there was no other explanation for what was happening.

Quicker than Emma could have believed possible, they were at the other end of the hallway. At that point, the creature did finally reach the limits of its patience, or maybe it heard people approaching, regardless, it tightened its grip on her painfully and turned down another hallway, the one that led to a side door.

"Emma," she heard Scott yell from far away.

"Scott, help me, I," but she got nothing else out. The creature bopped her gently in the head, knocking Emma unconscious immediately and then picked up speed as it approached the door.

Callie was at its heels now, barking and nipping. It slowed a little and stared down at the dog, but Callie didn't relent. Scott was running up behind them, his rifle raised, but he was afraid to shoot because he might hit Emma.

He watched in stunned disbelief as the creature banged open the door, went through it and then held it open for Callie to come outside and join it. With one last hate-filled look at Scott, it was gone, and the door slammed shut behind them.

"What the hell is going on?" he screamed, as he ran towards the door. But, by the time he got outside the creature had covered so much ground there was no way he could catch it, even the Shepherd was barely able to keep up with it.

CHAPTER 18

"Damn it, damn it, damn it," Scott yelled, looking around for something to throw or to break.

"Scott, Scott, hey, calm down, what's going on?" Tim asked, looking disheveled and like he got out of bed hurriedly.

"That freaking thing just took Emma."

"It took her, it didn't kill her?"

"No, and I swear that I saw it hold the damn door open, so the dog could go with it, too."

"What the hell?"

"I don't know, Tim, but get bundled up, we've got to go after her. The snow has let up, but it's frigid out there and all she has on is a sweater. We don't have any time to waste."

"I'll meet you back here in ten minutes."

"Hey, man what's going on?" Gabriel asked, as he approached Scott nervously, not loving the angry set of his jaw.

"It took Emma and we're going after it. You stay here," he said, much to Gabriel's relief. "Hopefully, the police will show up soon and get you guys some place safe. You keep everyone together while we're gone, okay?"

"Yeah, sure. Can I do anything for you?"

"It'll take us forever to plow through that snow on foot. We're going to need snowshoes, I assume they must have some extra ones here, right?"

"Yeah, I think so, in the sports shop, but that's over in the next building."

Scott could see his hesitation and understood it completely.

"Gabriel, I just watched the creature take off down that trail to the left, it's nowhere near the building you have to go to. You'll be safe, just hurry back to the Lodge when you're done, alright?"

Gabriel swallowed hard and Scott could have sworn his scraggly little beard was shaking in fear, but he looked Scott in the eye and nodded, then ran off in the direction of the other building.

*   *   *

When Emma woke up, her body was shivering violently from the cold and her jaw and entire head ached. Callie licked her face, then turned to watch the entranceway of the cave.

She looked around in confusion. The cave that they were in was large, some sunlight made its way in through the opening, but it was murky and damp inside. She could see several openings along the back of the cave and assumed they were some sort of tunnels.

Emma's entire body tensed up when the creature ducked down and entered the cave. It stared curiously at Emma, who laid completely still, and then looked intently at Callie.

The two of them made soft sounds in their throats, almost as if they were communicating, and they never took their eyes off each other. Callie made sure to stay between it and Emma at all times, and only growled once, softly, when it began to move closer to Emma.

When Callie growled, the creature pulled back its lips in response, exposing obscenely long canine teeth that could have ripped Emma and Callie to shreds. At the same time, it made sounds that seemed more impatient than angry. It snarled once, and then turned and headed back outside of the cave.

Although grateful that she'd at least been wearing jeans and a heavy wool sweater, even those weren't able to keep her warm and Emma was chilled to the bone and couldn't stop shivering. All she wanted to do was crawl into a ball and go back to sleep, but Callie wouldn't let her. Callie grabbed Emma's sweater in her mouth and tried drag her off to one side of the cave. Emma didn't understand what she was trying to do and brushed her away.

Callie took two steps in the direction that she had tried to drag Emma, and turned to see if Emma was following, but she wasn't. Callie went back to her, grabbed the sweater again and tried to pull Emma over in that direction.

"What are you doing, girl? Stop it."

Callie let out a sharp, little bark and then dropped on her belly in front of Emma when she saw the creature's shadow fall across the entrance again.

They both froze in place until it moved away, then Callie tried again, taking a few steps in that direction and turning to look at Emma.

"Okay, show me what you want me to see," she whispered, through chattering teeth.

Callie's tail wagged briefly, and she headed over to a shadowed corner, standing in front of one of the openings that led to a tunnel down through the rock. It was dark and smelled bad and Emma had no desire to make her way down it blindly.

Callie took a few steps into the darkness and turned back to Emma, waiting for her.

"Oh, Callie, I can't go down there."

Callie then did something that she had never done before in her life, she walked over to where Emma was standing with her arms crossed around herself and reached out and bit her leg. Her bite didn't break the skin, but she definitely got Emma's attention.

"Callie," Emma yelled, and then shut her mouth tightly when she heard the creature approaching the entrance to the cave once again, neither of them moved a muscle until they heard it wander away again.

"What is it doing?" she wondered. *"What is it waiting for?"*

It was almost acting like it was on patrol and suddenly Emma understood completely, the reality of it hitting her like a sledgehammer between the eyes. *"Oh my God, it's using me as bait. Somehow, it knows that Scott and Tim will come looking for me, will easily follow our trail and walk right up to this cave, where it will be waiting for them in the darkness."*

Deep down, she couldn't believe that this rancid, disgusting creature could have that much intelligence, but there was no other explanation for what was happening.

Emma was freezing, her entire body was shivering, her hands and feet were beginning to go numb already, but she realized there was no choice, she had to escape this cave and find Scott and Tim before they got too close, before it had a chance to get them.

Callie was back at the entrance to the tunnel, whining quietly, and Emma relented and went to her. Callie's tail swayed back and forth spastically, and she started forward, turning back to be sure that Emma was following her.

"Alright, baby, you've never lied to me before, so I'll trust you now. Get me out here, girl, as fast as you can."

Emma placed her hand on the dog's back and followed her into the tunnel. Emma couldn't see anything, and her heart was pounding violently in her chest, she just had to place complete blind trust, literally, in the dog, and hope there was another exit.

It was difficult for Emma to estimate how long they had been wandering along the tunnel, the darkness and the cold made everything seem to take so much longer. She still held onto the hair on Callie's back and used her other hand to feel her way along the wall.

The tunnel continued to get more and more narrow and, after bumping her head on the top of it several times, she had to walk stooped over.

After what seemed like forever, Emma was finally able to see light shining through an opening. It was on the side wall, just about at eye level. Emma thought she might be able to shimmy out through it, but then looked down at Callie.

She picked up the heavy dog and tried to get her up to the opening, but she wasn't strong enough and the dog wiggled and squirmed and fell out of Emma's arms.

"Callie, I can't go without you," Emma said, her eyes filling with tears.

The dog whined anxiously and kept looking back towards the cave. Emma knew what she wanted.

"I love you, Callie, girl," she said, wrapping her arms around the dog's neck and hugging her tight. "You stay safe and I'll be back to get you as soon as I can. I promise."

She looked back once, and Callie was wagging her tail excitedly as she watched Emma start crawling through the small opening.

Emma managed to squeeze through it and fell forward onto the ground which, fortunately, wasn't that far because of all the snow. But, although she didn't think it was possible, she was even colder now. The soft powdery snow had gone down the back of her sweater when she landed and felt like it was instantly freezing her skin wherever it touched.

Emma stood up a little wobbly and looked around. She was in the middle of the forest. There must have been a path from where they'd come, but it would be in front of the cave, where the creature was stationed, so she couldn't go that way.

Emma headed further into the woods, hoping she wouldn't get too lost before she was able to backtrack onto the path. She had to locate Scott and Tim before they got to the cave.

Staying in the thicket of trees where the snow wasn't quite so deep helped a little, but it was slow going and her leather Uggs were soaked through in no time. Emma just kept placing one foot in front of the other, not knowing how much further she would physically be able to go but refusing to stop until her body gave out on her completely.

*   *   *

Fortunately, for Scott and Tim, the creature made quite a trail due to its size, and Callie had packed it down even more as she followed, so the walk with the snowshoes was a little easier than they had anticipated.

"What the hell is this about?" Tim asked. "Don't get me wrong, I am really happy that it didn't hurt Emma, but why didn't it? What is it up to?"

"Feels like a trap, doesn't it?" Scott asked. "But, that's crazy, it's an animal, it couldn't possibly be smart enough to use Emma as bait to get us out here, could it?"

"Hell, if I know, but that's what it looks like. And it worked, didn't it?"

"Yeah, it did. Keep a sharp eye out, both in front and behind us, we can't let it catch us by surprise."

"Right." Both men remained vigilant, looking for tracks that might indicate the creature doubled back on them but, so far, they just kept heading straight.

"So, are you going to tell me what happened to your face?"

"What do you mean?"

"Well, the black eye, the cut on your cheek, kind of looks like somebody got in a fight. You could at least let me know if you won, and who it was in case they try to get even with you by coming after me."

"No chance of that, it was Christian Hebel, he's a sneaky, dirty-fighting little snake."

"That sounds serious."

"The bastard cold-cocked me. Otherwise, he never would have gotten in such a good shot."

"Did you kick his ass?"

"Why, yes, I did, and I just might do it again if the need arises."

"Good, he is a douche."

They continued on for a few minutes and the only sound was their loud breathing as they tried to cover ground as quickly as possible.

"Oh, damn it," Scott said, a few minutes later, coming to an abrupt stop.

"What?"

"The sleds." Scott pointed over into the woods where the two snowmobiles were almost buried in red snow. "I don't think our boys made it."

They trudged over and, ignoring the bloody snow, they found the keys still in the ignition and turned the machines off. The batteries would be dead by this time, most likely, but they couldn't risk trying to turn over the engines right now, they had no idea how close they might be to the creature and didn't want to warn it that they were coming.

There was no sign of the boys, other than the bloody snow, but neither of them held out much hope that they were still alive.

Scott picked up a camera out of the bloody snow next to one of the sleds and slid it into his pocket. The moisture had damaged it, so he couldn't tell if Rocco had finally gotten his proof that Bigfoot existed or not. He shook his head sadly at the waste of yet more lives because of this creature.

"Shake it off, Scott. There's nothing we can do for them right now. Let's get going, we can check the sleds out on the way back."

Tim hoped they would actually have an opportunity to make their way back, but wasn't feeling completely confident about that.

*   *   *

Emma was frozen, her teeth were chattering so hard that she thought she might have chipped a tooth. It took everything that she had to force each step as she continued on through the deep snow. Every bit of her clothing was soaked and clinging to her body and she couldn't feel her lips, or her fingers.

"Please, God," she prayed silently, "let me find my way back. I'm just getting started in my new life with Scott and I truly want to see how that turns out. And my children still need me. Please let me have more time with them. I want to see them graduate and share their lives with them as they grow up, get married and have families of their own."

"Please, God," she mumbled between frozen lips, "please give me a little more time. There is still so much I need to do."

She stumbled out of the patch of evergreen trees and almost started to cry when she found a packed down trail in the snow. She headed back along it, but even with her brain all fogged up from the cold, she realized that, in addition to the huge path made by the creature and Callie's paw prints, she was also seeing snowshoes tracks, and they were heading back to the cave.

Tears started down her cheeks and immediately froze to her skin. It was Scott and Tim, they were coming to rescue her, she was sure of it.

Hugging her arms around herself, trying to keep in what little warmth there was still left in her body, she turned around to follow their tracks. She would have called out to them but had no voice left.

Using the last of her reservoir of strength, she hurried along the trail, finally spotting them up ahead of her.

"Scott," it came out as a hoarse whisper. "Scott."

Her voice cracked, and it felt like she may have burst something in her throat. With numb fingers, she grabbed a handful of snow and made a snowball out of it and threw it in their direction. It didn't even come close. Emma made a few more and ran towards the men, the snowshoes had packed the trail down a little and she was able to move faster than she'd thought possible as she tried to cover some of the ground in between them.

When Emma thought she was close enough, she threw the other two snowballs that she had been carrying. They didn't hit Scott or Tim but came close enough to get their attention.

They both turned, rifles raised, until they saw that it was Emma. Shaking his disbelief, Scott started running towards her, just as she fell unconscious, face first into the snow.

*   *   *

"Holy shit, she's ice-cold." Scott took off his own coat and wrapped it around her.

"We have to get her back, fast." Tim said. "I'm going to run ahead and try the sleds, see if I can get at least one of them running again."

"Good, go." Scott had a little difficulty carrying Emma in the packed snow, but he kept moving along. Her lips were starting to show a pale blue tint and her breathing was shallow. He had never been more scared in his life and breathed a huge sigh of relief when he heard one of the snowmobile engines roar to life.

Tim came back for them, but they couldn't all ride on one sled. Scott got on it and placed Emma in front of him.

"Don't waste any time, Tim, it'll be dark soon. Don't be out here alone in the dark."

Tim nodded his understanding and watched them fly down the trail, Scott maneuvering it as well, and as fast, as he could back to the Lodge, while at the same time trying to keep Emma securely on it.

Tim tried the other sled a couple of times but couldn't risk staying out in the open like that anymore, not when he had no idea where the creature might be. He trotted back along the path to the Lodge, looking over his shoulder frequently.

By the time he got there, Scott already had Emma in her room and her wet clothes were off and thrown into a pile in the middle of the floor.

"Tim, grab me some more blankets, and run down to the bar and get me a bottle of brandy."

After throwing Scott a couple of extra blankets, he ran down the hallway, turned the corner and almost knocked Skylar over.

"What's the matter," she asked, seeing the panic on his face.

"It's Emma, she was out in the frigid weather with no coat, she's frozen. I'm going to grab some brandy for her."

"No, no alcohol, go to the kitchen and have them brew some hot chamomile tea, hurry."

Skylar ran to Emma's room to see what she could do to help, and Scott looked at her in relief when she walked through the door.

"Will you run a hot bath for her and help me get her into it? I think that might help."

"No," Skylar said firmly. "The hot water could affect her skin, or it could give her an irregular heartbeat, we can't take that chance. Maybe later, when she has recovered a little from the hypothermia."

"Are you sure?" he asked, an unmistakable edge to his voice. He wasn't taking any chances where Emma was concerned.

"Please, trust me, go into the bathroom and get all the towels. I have a clothes dryer in my spa, put them in there and let them tumble until they get nice and warm and get them back here pronto."

"I'll keep an eye on her until you get back," she assured him, seeing him hesitate. "Do you know CPR?"

"No."

"Then get out of here and do as I asked, if she has trouble breathing, I can help her, you can't. Now, go."

With one last look at Emma's ashen face, he ran out of the room with an armful of towels.

Tim was back a few minutes later and Skylar was able to force a little bit of the warm fluid into Emma's mouth. She was starting to revive but was shaking uncontrollably.

When Scott arrived with the warm towels, Skylar lowered the blankets and started to apply them to her neck and chest. Wanting to help, Scott grabbed one and started to rub her arm with it, but Skylar reached out and put her hand over his, stopping the movement.

"Please, don't do that," she said patiently. "We can only apply the towels to her neck and chest. If you rub her arms or legs with it, the cold blood will be forced back towards her heart and lungs, and it will lower her core body temperature and make things worse. Just step back and let me take care of her, okay?"

Scott scowled at her and, although she was a very serene person, even Skylar found the hostile look in his eyes to be a bit unnerving.

"Tim, can you take your brother to the bar for that brandy, at least until I get this situation under control?"

"Sure, come on, Scott, let her take of care of Emma. We need to get out of the way."

Scott only began to relax about halfway through the second snifter of brandy.

"Damn, that was close," Scott said. "We could have missed her and Emma would have died out there, all alone."

He gulped down the remaining liquid in his glass and waved the bartender over for another.

"But, we didn't, Scott, and we still have a major problem on our hands, and no other help is coming. Get a grip, we need to be sober and figure out our next move. Nightfall is coming fast, and that thing will be coming for us."

The bartender set down another brandy in front of Scott, he lifted the glass, swirled the amber liquid around it and downed it in one gulp.

"No worries, Tim, I don't think it would be possible for me to get drunk today, but you're right. We do need to figure out what we're going to do. Let's find the manager first."

They ran into Gabriel in the hallway and then found Noffsinger in his office, nursing his own bottle of spirits.

"You came back," he said, his words slurring slightly, as he waved his vodka bottle in front of them.

"Yes, we did." Tim and Scott looked at each other in disgust, realizing he would be no help at all in this state.

"Gabriel, head to the kitchen. Tell the staff to cook up enough for everyone for dinner, grab bottled water, soda, anything you can carry, and get it to the banquet room."

Scott thought for a moment and then turned to Tim. "You go tell everyone to collect there within the hour and get our weapons. I'll look around for some tools and wood. We are going to have to put some blockades in place."

"But, Scott," Gabriel asked hesitantly, "if we barricade ourselves in, how will we know when the police get here?"

Scott clapped him on the shoulder and shook his head sadly.

"They aren't coming, Gabriel. I'm sorry, but, your friends didn't make it out."

Tears sprang up in the boy's brown eyes and the blood drained from his face, leaving his rusty freckles standing out starkly against his ashen skin.

"Okay, I'll get to the kitchen." He slowly walked out the door, his shoulders slumped and his eyes downward, unable to look either of them in the eye because he was afraid that he might burst out sobbing like a baby.

"Noffsinger, get to the banquet hall, we'll all stay there tonight. We should be safe if we stay together."

"I'm good, right here." His eyes were bloodshot and his hand was shaking as he lifted the bottle to his lips.

"We aren't going to babysit you, if you don't show up within the hour, you're on your own. We won't be back to save your ass."

"I'm good, right here," he repeated, as he leaned back in his plush chair with a drunken smile on his face.

"Let's go," Tim said.

"I'm going to check on Emma first, I'll catch up with you later."

Scott was pleased to find Emma doing much better when he got to her room.

He ran his finger along her cheek and pushed an errant strand of hair off her face. "You look much better. Nice to see some color back in your cheeks."

She smiled up at him, but there was such a depth of sadness in her eyes that all he wanted was to be able to hold her and make it go away.

"You aren't okay though, are you?"

"I feel much better but, no, I'm really not. I think I've lost Callie. She saved me Scott, she saved me and stayed there with that monster, so I could get away."

Her voice broke and she started crying in earnest. Scott sat down and held her close, letting her pour out her sorrow in his arms, because that was all he could do to try and help alleviate some of her pain.

"Emma, if she is still alive, we'll get her back. I need you to be strong now, okay? Skylar, wait," he called out, as she was discreetly trying to make her way out of the room.

"First, thank you for helping us get Emma back. Second, we all have to get to the banquet hall before dark. We'll stay the night there together and everyone should be safe. So, please, collect whatever you need and head over there, okay?"

"I will, thanks."

"Emma, are you okay to get up and dressed on your own?"

She smiled weakly. "I think I can manage that, go do whatever it is you need to do. I'll head over in a few minutes."

"Don't make me come looking for you."

She took his face in her hands and pulled him close, her lips were still cold against his, but she felt the life starting to circulate in her body again.

"I'll be there, I promise."

CHAPTER 19

The guests of the Lodge were safely deposited in the banquet hall well before dark. Everyone, except Noffsinger, who never did manage to make his way there.

"Should I go get him?" Gabriel asked.

"You're a good kid," Tim said. "But, no, you'd have to drag him here and he'd only make trouble in the state he's in."

The banquet hall was in the center of one end of the Lodge, so there were no windows to worry about, but there were several doorways leading into it.

Scott and Tim had seen some large planks of wood out in the shed housing the generator and they ran out there together to grab some of them. They found a box of nails and a hammer and managed to get them all back to the banquet hall without any unwelcome incidents. They nailed them across all of the doorways except one.

They knew that the little barricades wouldn't hold back the creature for long, but they were hoping that it would at least give them time to get into position and shoot it. Both of them kept their rifles slung over their shoulders, and they also had their pistols wedged snugly into the waistband of their jeans, just in case a little additional firepower was needed.

"I still haven't seen Katherine Carmichael, have you?" Tim inquired quietly as they continued to work.

"No, but she couldn't have gone far. She could be hiding out in one of the Yurts, or even down in the basement, for that matter. I'm not going to worry about her right now, we have too many other people to look after. Once we get this creature good and dead, then we can spend some time trying to locate her and we'll finish up that situation."

"By the way," he added with a smirk, "are you enjoying our vacation, Tim? First time we ever took one, isn't it?"

"I think it is, and hey, who could ask for more, how did you phrase it, hot tubs, hot toddies and hot chicks, something like that, right? And you weren't wrong, we've had that and so much more."

But, the smile faded from Tim's face as he looked out over the crowd and wondered if they were all going to make it through the night alive. Finishing up the last doorway, they threw the extra supplies into a pile along the wall and headed over to the one open doorway.

Emma was exhausted and still couldn't keep warm, even though she was fully dressed and was wrapped up tightly in a heavy blanket. They had pulled some chairs over around the doorway and she and Skylar sat with Tim and Scott as they kept watch over the closed door.

Scott kept one arm around Emma, sharing his own warmth with her as she rested her head against his shoulder, her eyelids drooping tiredly. He made sure to keep his other hand free, and within easy reach of his pistol that was resting on the table in front of them. There were also several rifles leaning up against the table, close enough that, within seconds, Scott and Tim could have them raised and aimed at anything that tried to come through the door.

"What's all that fuss about?" Scott asked a few minutes later, hearing some type of argument going on over in the corner.

"I'll check it out," Tim said, "I'm going to grab a couple of waters while I'm up, do you guys want anything to eat?"

"Thanks, but I'm good and Emma's almost asleep."

"I'll come with you," Skylar offered and followed along behind him as he made his way over to the men arguing in the corner.

"What's the problem?" he asked.

Suddenly three or four people all started talking at once. Tim held up his hand. "Wait, one at a time. Gabriel, what's going on?"

"It's him," Gabriel said, nodding his head towards Travis Benham. "He's being a jerk and yelling at John 'cause he doesn't like the food, the free food, that we put out for everyone."

"How many times do I have to tell you?" Travis asked, in his high, nasally voice, "My wife and I are vegans, we cannot eat this garbage. I insist that you go make us an appropriate meal."

His wife was once again peering over his shoulder, her face screwed up tight and their little dog was wrapped up in a blanket in her arms.

"What the hell's the matter with you?" Tim asked, just about out of patience with all of these people, particularly the Benhams.

"What's the matter with us, that's rich," Travis said. "We paid good money to come here, and to say it hasn't been the best vacation ever, is a massive understatement. At the very least, we expect to be presented with a meal that we can actually eat."

"Shut the hell up," Tim said quietly, brushing Skylar's hand off his arm when she reached out to him, trying to calm him down. Tim had no intention of getting physical, but he needed to tell this buffoon off once and for all.

"Do you understand what is happening here? Do you realize that people have died and that more may lose their lives if this thing gets in tonight? Do you get that? This is not a game, this is life and death."

"I'm not an idiot, I know what's going on."

"Then explain to me why you would ask John and these other employees to leave the security of this room, to go back to the kitchen and risk being torn limb from limb, just so you can have some freaking tofu? Why don't you just suck on a bottle of water for now and try and put this whole situation in perspective. If I hear you causing trouble again, I'll throw you out of here, and your little dog, too."

"Now, listen…"

"Travis, I think we'd better do what he says." Samantha gave Tim a scorching look, grabbed Travis' arm and led him away to another part of the room.

"Thanks, Tim," Gabriel said, wanting to high five him, but thinking that might not be well-received. Tim didn't scare him as much as Scott did when he was angry, but it was close.

"No problem, let me know if there is any other trouble."

He grabbed ahold of Skylar's hand after snagging a few bottles of water with the other and they made their way back across the room.

"I'm sorry about brushing you off like I did. I didn't mean anything by it, I was distracted by the dickhead."

"I understand, after what happened with Christian, I was a little worried about what you might do."

"That was completely different. Where is my good buddy, anyway?"

"I saw him slink off to a far corner when he came in, I think he might be trying to avoid you for some reason."

"Wonder why?" Tim asked, his lip curling up in a smile.

*   *   *

The mood was somber in the room and no one was very talkative. Nevertheless, very few seemed to be able to relax enough to get any sleep during the night.

Most of the people had enough sense to bring their blankets and pillows and, after filling their bellies, were finding as comfortable a place on the floor as possible. No one anticipated being able to sleep much, but they were all giving it their best shot.

Scott, Tim and the two women kept watch all night long. Emma spent most of it snuggled up against Scott, sound asleep. She was still so exhausted from her ordeal earlier that day that she could have slept on a bed of nails if she had to. Skylar wasn't feeling quite so comfortable around the men and was only able to catch a few winks here and there.

There were strange noises coming from the group of people laid out all around the room, grunts and snores and moaning, and Skylar was getting restless and just wanted to be away from all of them, but she was too frightened to actually leave, so she decided she would find something relaxing to do so that she could take her mind off all of the ugliness and fear.

Scott watched curiously when she walked around behind Tim and gently began massaging his neck and shoulders. Tim's face immediately relaxed into a look of exquisite pleasure and Scott was actually feeling a little jealous. Every muscle in his body was tight, he'd been on watch for hours, never knowing when the creature might burst in, and he hoped once this was all over he might be able to convince Skylar to work on him, too.

Scott moved his body a little to stretch out his own muscles and Emma woke up. "What time is it?"

"I'm not sure, it's just about dawn, I think."

"What's that all about?" she asked, pointing at Tim and Skylar.

"He's getting the royal treatment. Can I expect something similar at some point?"

"But, of course, my love. Just don't expect me to be anywhere near as good as she is."

"Wow, that feels great," Tim said quietly, his eyes remaining closed as he enjoyed every minute of the neck and backrub he was getting.

"You know, Tim, I can watch the door for awhile, if you want to go have a little quiet time with your friend."

Tim opened one eye and looked at Scott balefully. "Why do you have to ruin everything? Just shut up, we're all fine right here. I'm just going to relax and let Skylar loosen me up a little, so I'm ready for the stink monster when he shows."

"I wasn't being an asshole, I meant it, go off for a little while and relax, I can cover."

"And what if it does show? We both need to be here, you know that."

"Do you really think it will?" Skylar asked, taking her hands off of Tim's shoulders and grabbing for the necklace that she was wearing. It was on the same gold chain, but today's stone was a much deeper color of green and Skylar was cradling the gemstone gently in her hands.

Scott nodded and started to expand on his answer, but Emma jumped in, seeing how nervous and upset Skylar was, she wanted to try and take her mind off the creature for a few minutes.

"That is a beautiful necklace, what kind of stone is it?"

A serene smile lit Sydney's face. "Green Jasper, it's been used for centuries as a protection stone."

She looked down at the olive-green chalcedony and twirled it around in her fingers. "I thought it would be appropriate for tonight, it provides protection from evil spirits, harmful fantasies and all types of evil and venomous creatures."

"Have any more of them? I think we could all use one."

The serenity dropped from Skylar's face when she looked at Scott. She wasn't sure if he was being serious because he believed that the creature really was coming, or if he was just mocking her.

Whichever scenario it was, Skylar was now even more upset than she had been, and Emma elbowed Scott in the ribs, making him grunt in pain.

"What?"

"Sometimes, I wonder about you."

"We all do," Tim agreed, reaching over to grab Skylar's hand with his own as she sat down heavily beside him, looking glum and uneasy.

"The creature will be here, but you have nothing to worry about, we'll keep you safe."

"How do you know that?"

"How do I know what?"

"That you can keep me safe?"

"Because that's what we do, we'll keep all of you safe and we'll kill this damn thing."

Tim felt as if her luminous blue eyes were looking into his very soul, she was a special person, an innocent in so many ways, and he knew that he would do whatever it took to ensure her safety, above all the others.

There was a loud crash and then they heard a muffled scream through the heavy door, and it seemed to be coming from the direction of the Manager's office.

Scott and Tim looked at each and Scott shook his head.

"No, Tim, we warned him, and we couldn't possibly reach him in time, anyway. He's probably dead already."

Skylar looked like she was going to pass out and Tim lightly tapped her cheek. "Are you okay?"

"I don't know, what do we do now?"

"Nothing, just wait," Scott said, releasing the safety on his pistol as he stared towards the doorway.

"Gabriel, get back here," he yelled suddenly, as the boy sprinted past him and grabbed the handle.

"It's Mr. Noffsinger, didn't you hear him?"

"Gabriel, stop." Scott tried to grab him before he got through the doorway, but just missed him. "Damn it."

Scott pushed the door open, followed Gabriel out into the hall and saw him turn the corner towards the manager's office. He hurried that way with his pistol raised, but moved a little slower than Gabriel, as he checked each alcove and doorway along the hallway. He had rushed out of the room in such a hurry that he neglected to grab his rifle and was pretty much naked without it. The smell of the creature was wafting throughout the first floor and it was difficult to tell what direction it was coming from.

Hearing Gabriel's ear-splitting scream, he sprinted the rest of the distance to the office. Gabriel was standing just inside the door, he looked to be unharmed, but Scott couldn't tell for sure because there was so much blood everywhere. It was splattered all across the carpet and the walls.

He made his way gingerly into the room, trying not to step in any of the blood or gore. As he made his way over to Noffsinger's desk, he spied what was left of the manager lying on floor behind it.

Scott quickly walked back over to Gabriel, grabbed his arm and started to drag him out of the room. Stepping into the hallway, Scott froze in place when he saw that their way forward was blocked by the creature. He hesitated, looking around for another escape route, but was almost knocked to his knees when the creature let out an ungodly roar that made Scott's head scream.

"This way, quickly," he yelled at Gabriel, pulling him along the hall in the opposite direction. Scott was constantly turning to look behind them and holding up Gabriel, who was tripping over his own feet as he sobbed in terror.

The creature started towards them and Scott sped up. He would use the pistol on it if it cornered them, but he wasn't confident that the weapon would do much more than make it angry.

It roared again one last time, just as Scott heard rifle shots ringing out. He assumed it was Tim coming after the beast and could only hope that the last roar was because it had been fatally hit.

Taking advantage of the creature's distraction, he grabbed Gabriel again and they took the staircase to the second floor, where they waited for a few minutes. Scott couldn't hear any heavy footsteps, nor was the smell getting any more intense. He thought they might be safe for now, but just then heard another volley of gunshots, this time from further away.

"Damn, that sounds like its coming from the banquet hall." He ran his fingers roughly through his hair, checked to be sure his pistol was fully loaded and turned to Gabriel.

"You stay up here," Scott told him in no uncertain terms, needing him safely out the way, so that he could go help fortify the banquet hall. Gabriel nodded and curled up in a corner as he watched Scott run back down the stairs.

The creature had torn apart the blockade at one of the doors and got into the room where it was unprotected. People were screaming and running helter-skelter all over, most were running out of the room through the one open doorway, and Scott had to elbow his way through the oncoming traffic to get in.

Tim was closing in on it with his rifle. Emma, literally shaking in her boots, was behind him, carrying additional weapons in case he needed them, and Skylar was nowhere to be seen.

The creature gave another horrific roar, louder and more painful than if a thunderclap went off right next to their heads.

Tim had to stop and wait for the echoing to dissipate and then refocused on the creature. He raised his rifle and aimed at its heart, he was just about to squeeze the trigger when it's abnormally long arm swung wide and knocked a small table in Tim's direction. He had to duck to avoid it knocking him on his ass and, by the time he got back into position, he no longer had a clear shot.

Out of nowhere the little Morkie-poo ran at the mammoth-sized creature, continuously yapping and even being so bold as to try and nip at its feet.

It hesitated a few seconds as it considered the little dog, which it could have crushed just by stepping on it.

"Simba, no," Wiggy screamed from the other side of the room. Totally disregarding her own safety, she ran straight at the two animals, intending to save her little dog, no matter what the cost to herself.

When Tim realized what she was doing, he sprinted over to get between her and the creature. She was almost able to get past him and he had to dive and tackle her to the ground to keep her from being swatted by the creature's obscenely long and deadly arm.

From the floor, Tim, wrenched his pistol out of the waistline of his jeans and aimed it carefully at the creature, Wiggy was moving violently and he wasn't able to get off a head shot, but he was pretty sure that he hit it somewhere on the chest or the shoulder.

The creature still hadn't done any harm to Simba, but it stared hatefully at Tim and seemed to be debating what to do. It chose to run back out towards the front door and was picking off any stragglers it found in the hall, taking a swipe at them, its long nails lacerating whatever they touched, blood blossoming on people's shirts or pants or wherever they were struck.

And the entire time, Simba continued to chase after it, nipping at its heels all the way, somehow under the impression that he was scaring the great creature and was the sole reason that it was running away.

"Hey, you freaking, stink mutant." Scott had to yell for it to hear him over the din of people screaming and trying to escape its wrath.

It swirled towards the sound of Scott's voice and was opening its mouth to let loose another eardrum-shattering roar when Scott let go with his Winchester .308.

The blast was deafening inside the building, but the sound of the creature's howl of pain was excruciatingly louder to anyone still in the vicinity.

It continued its ungodly roar as it ran towards the front doors and smashed through them, shattering the glass and letting in a rush of cold air.

Tim joined up with Scott and the two of them ran to the doorway, staring out into the early light of the dawn at the vanishing creature.

Scott heard a pitiful little whine coming from under one of the overfilled chairs in the lobby and went over to check it out.

Only brave little Simba's nose was sticking out from under it and Scott was barely able to get ahold and pull him out. The dog was shaking from head to toe, not because of the beast, he obviously wasn't afraid to attack it, but the loud gunshot filled him with enough terror that he immediately left his prey in order to find somewhere to hide, which had probably saved his life.

"Simba, thank God you're okay." Wiggy came running over and grabbed him out Scott's arms and, after glaring at Tim for interfering when she tried to rescue her dog, she walked away, holding Simba tightly and murmuring endearments to him, ignoring the crying and moaning of her fellow guests as she passed them by.

Skylar, Emma, Mitzi and a couple of other people were going from one person to the next to find out how badly they were hurt. They had towels and tablecloths and were helping people clean up and wrap their wounds. None seemed like they would be fatal, but many of the lacerations were deep enough that they would need stitches, but that would have to wait until they were able to get out of here and reach a medical facility.

Tim looked at the injured people scattered around the room and felt angry, very angry. "We need to finish this, Scott."

"I know, it has to stop now. Let's get ready and head out."

CHAPTER 20

"Listen, those caves go all over into the mountainside. I was only able to find a way out because of Callie, you'll never be able to find the creature in there. You can't go inside the caves." Emma's eyes glistened with tears. "Please, Scott, its suicide, it'll be waiting for you. I can't let you do it."

The three of them were in the main lounge, Tim and Scott were putting on their winter gear, getting ready to begin the hunt.

"Emma, we don't have a choice." Scott took her into his arms and held her close. "Look, the storm is over, people are starting to dig out their vehicles, someone will make it out to get more help. We have to follow it now, while its hurt and there is a blood trail to follow."

"But, Scott..."

"I might be able to help." Christian Hebel interrupted, walking over with a handful of walkie-talkies. "Take these, I have my drone and I can send it in ahead of you to find that thing. Once I do, I can tell you on the walkie where you need to go. I can get you in and out safely."

Tim and Scott looked at each other, trying to quickly determine the pros and cons of Christian's idea. He was still sporting a shiner, thanks to Tim, and it was obvious from his tone and the look on his face that there was no love lost between the two of them.

"I think that could work," Tim said cautiously, "but why do you want to help us? We aren't exactly pals."

"Oh, I know that we're not, don't get me wrong." Christian flashed his brilliant white smile at Tim, but his eyes were deadly serious. "And we will finish our business, but I want to get out here alive first. If that means helping you kill whatever this thing is, then that's what I'm going to do."

"Of course," Scott said, "your drones film as they fly, right? And footage like that would make you a ton of money, wouldn't it? No more Podunk little ski resorts for you."

Christian shrugged his shoulders. "Does it matter? You get the benefit of my drones, too, right? I keep you safe, I make some money. It's a win-win for all of us."

"Yes, that's true, but you damn well better keep them there until we find what we need. Rest assured that if you plan on stranding us with the creature and high-tailing it with the film, you'll be the first thing on our list after we waste it. I hope you understand that. Can we count on you to stay with us until we get back out of those caves?"

Christian didn't hesitate. "Of course, you can, like I said, I want out of here alive. I need you two to make that happen."

"Alright, as long as we're clear," Scott said, unable to hide the doubt in his voice. "So, how do we do this?"

"How long will it take you to get there?"

"Maybe ten, fifteen minutes on the sleds."

"I'll wait till I think you're almost there and send off the drone to meet up with you."

"Do we just keep in touch with the walkies, so you know where we are?"

"I should be able to see your tracks and have the drone follow along them."

"If we get to the cave first, what do you want us to do?"

"If it's safe, wait outside the cave until my drone gets there. If the creature is in the cave, I'll send it in while you two wait. I can tell you which tunnel to head down once I spot it through the drone."

"We don't even know for sure if that's where the creature went."

"I'd bet on it," Emma said. "I believe that's where it's been hiding, it's out of the weather and it's dark, and no one can catch it by surprise in there."

"So, we'll have to have pistols and rifles. If we come upon it in one of those tunnels, the range will be too close for the rifles and we'll need the pistols. I think if we try to hit it in the face or head, that will wound it badly enough that we can finish it off with the rifles. I saw a little trailer we can pull behind on the sled. We only have the one sled, so we can use that to carry the rifles. You ready, Tim?"

Tim still couldn't help feeling suspicious about Christian and hoped they weren't making a deadly mistake by trusting him.

"I guess that I'm as ready as I'll ever be."

"Just remember, you only have forty-five minutes before the drone will automatically return on its own, don't putz around, make the best use of your time so you don't get left in one of those tunnels."

The two of them just stared hard at him, still questioning whether or not they could trust him, but knowing that without him, they would just be walking in completely blind anyway.

"I'm going with you."

"No, Emma, you aren't. Only two of us will fit on the sled, we'll take that and catch up to it in no time."

"I'll follow on foot, then."

"No, you won't. Stay here with Christian and help direct us to it."

He lowered his voice and pulled her up close against him. "Keep an eye on Christian, make sure you have a walkie of your own to communicate with us and I'll feel a little more comfortable knowing you've got our back. You have to stay here, that's how you can be the most helpful, okay?"

"Sometimes, I hate you."

"I know." He gave her a quick kiss on the lips and went to collect his gear.

Emma nervously pulled on her earlobe a few minutes later as she watched the two of them jump on the sled and head off down the creature's most recent trail.

Scott and Tim tracked it easily and, fortunately or not, it did return to the cave that it had held Emma in. The drone arrived just a few minutes after they did and hovered in the air above them. They turned on the walkie-talkie and told Christian to send it in.

They waited a couple of minutes and then entered the main cave with their rifles raised. They stopped just inside the entranceway, it was murky, and they could barely see into the deeper recesses of it. The creature's tracks led right up to the opening, but they would have seen it if it was in this part of the cave, so it must have headed down into one of the smaller tunnels.

There were three of them that went off in different directions, the drone had gone down the one to the left, according to Christian. It returned a few short minutes later.

"Dead end," came the report over the walkie.

They waited impatiently for it to go down the second trail, but this time, it didn't return for what seemed like ages. While they waited, Tim wandered around the cave, the light did not penetrate very far and he needed his flashlight for the dark corners.

The cave stunk like the creature, but his nose wrinkled in disgust as it got much worse over in a far corner and was mixed with some other horrible stench, something that smelled like death. He covered his nose with a gloved hand and directed his flashlight in that direction, then stepped back in stunned silence.

"Scott," he said quietly, "look over here, I can't freaking believe what I'm seeing."

Scott turned and moved closer, aiming his own light in that direction.

"Holy shit, is that the one we killed?"

"It's gotta be." It was much smaller than the one they were currently hunting, and this one was now stiff as a board, its dark fur coated with hardened blood, and there was a bullet hole right in the middle of its forehead.

"But, why would it bring it here?"

"I don't know. Could this be it's child? It's mate? Could this thing actually be suffering from grief and keeping the dead one with it until it gets its revenge?"

"I can't even process that, Scott. How can this be?"

"I don't know, I really don't. Hey, that thing's been gone too long." He pulled out his walkie. "Christian, can you tell if it's still flying, or did the creature swat it down?"

"It's still checking out the tunnel, seems to go on a long way."

Emma was on the walkie now. "There is no blood along this trail, wouldn't we see some if this is the way it went?"

"Probably, if the drone doesn't come to the end of it, or see something, in the next couple of minutes, have him bring it back and we'll go in with it down the third tunnel. That would be the only other place it could be."

"Emma, you won't believe what we found."

"What?"

"The one we killed at the cabin. This one brought it along with it somehow. It's keeping the dead one here, for some reason, maybe until it finishes its business with us. I guess that answers the question of whether or not this was a coincidence, or if it really was hunting Tim and I for revenge. Mind-boggling, isn't it?"

"Yes, it is, I'm even more scared now, Scott. Please be careful."

"We will, the drone's back, so we have to head down the last tunnel."

"You're going to have to hurry," Christian said, "my little baby is going to run out of juice soon."

He sent it down the third path and Scott and Tim followed along, albeit a little slower, even with their flashlights.

"It's definitely the right path," Scott said, his light bobbing along, showing the spots of blood on the ground in front of them. "Tim, you keep the flashlight ready, I'll worry about the gun."

The two men continued on slowly, both feeling incredibly tense as they moved forward into the darkness. The stench of the creature filled the tunnel and was all around them. If it was hiding in the darkness, its smell would not give them any advance warning this time.

"Holy shit, guys, we have a problem," Christian said, his voice cracking as he started to panic.

"What?" They both stopped, waiting for the response.

"There's a big opening at the other end, it's not in there anymore. Get back here, hurry."

In the background people suddenly started screaming and the unmistakable roar of the creature could be heard clearly over the airwaves as it began its attack, just before their connection was lost.

*　　*　　*

Both men were hurrying back out of the tunnel the way they had come in when Scott grabbed Tim's arm. "Wait a minute."

"What? We have to go, they need us. Come on."

"I know, but I heard something. There it is again."

There was a soft whine coming from an alcove off to the right. Scott took his flashlight and shined it around the cavernous area.

Very slowly, from a dark corner, Callie scooched out on her belly, whining gently the entire time.

"Hey, baby girl," Scott said quietly. "What's wrong?"

"Scott, we don't have time for this, we'll come back for her later."

Scott ignored him. "Looks like a problem with your leg. You going to let me pick you up or are you going to bite me?"

"For God's sake, Scott, seriously?"

Scott reached out towards her slowly, the dog moaned a little when he picked her up, but she let him carry her and they made their way clumsily to the snowmobile. Scott laid her down in the trailer they were pulling along behind them as gently as he could before jumping on the sled behind Tim.

"Okay, let's go. And Tim, we don't stop this time until that bastard is dead. I don't care what it takes."

"Agreed."

*　　*　　*

As soon as the screaming started, Emma jumped up and ran out of Christian's room. She had her little pistol with her but knew that wouldn't be much help against the creature. She knew that Tim had a couple of extra rifles in his room and headed that way. The screams and commotion were coming from the front of the building, so she kept to the back hallways.

227

"Damn," she said, when she got to his room and realized that she didn't have the passkey to open it. "What now?"

Without a weapon significant enough to protect herself, Emma decided that the only smart thing to do would be to find a safe place to hide until Scott and Tim got back.

Emma shuddered when she heard the creature give an earsplitting roar, followed immediately by screams of pain and horror that she knew would haunt her dreams for a long time to come.

The chlorine smell from the pool apparently kept the creature from getting a specific scent and she didn't want it honing in on her, so she figured her best bet was to hide in there. Just as she arrived and was about to slip through the door, a shot rang out and hit the wall right beside her head.

Emma stopped short and turned to find Katherine Carmichael heading towards her, with a pistol aimed straight at Emma's heart. In all the commotion that had ensued since the fracas with George Carmichael, Emma had forgotten all about her.

Katherine looked like a different woman now, the vapid look on her face was completely gone, replaced by a venomous determination that was aimed directly at Emma as she closed in on her.

Emma had very little time to figure out what do before Katherine would be upon her. The pool room was no longer a viable option, not with a gun involved, so she turned and ran down the hallway, hoping those first shots came so close for no other reason than that Katherine got lucky.

"Where is my husband, you little tramp?" she screamed after Emma.

More shots rang out, but they weren't even close this time. Katherine was having trouble trying to aim the gun while she was hurrying down the hallway, so Emma realized that she just had to keep moving as quickly as she could.

She sprinted along the hallway, thanking God for giving her the motivation to get out jogging so often, when obviously Katherine did not.

It was a long hallway and Emma was pulling further and further away, so Katherine stopped to take the time to get off a steady shot at her. In doing so, she almost succeeded in bringing Emma down, but the bullet whizzed past Emma's ear, missing her by mere inches.

As Emma turned the corner, she had a new decision to make, the only way out was up the stairs or around the corner and back into the creature's realm. Emma could still hear the screams echoing down there so she headed upstairs, hoping Katherine wouldn't follow.

Taking the stairs two at a time, she kept looking over her shoulder, but Katherine wasn't behind her and there was no sound coming from the stairwell.

Emma hurried down the empty hallways and finally stopped to catch her breath. When she did, she realized that there was a whiff of something really unpleasant in the air and her heart started pounding frantically.

She looked behind her, but the hallway was still clear, so she sprinted along further and turned another corner, halting abruptly when she saw Katherine standing at the top of one of the other staircases, just a few feet in front of her, her pistol pointed directly at Emma's chest once again.

"Emma, my friend, you didn't answer my question." Katherine was still huffing and puffing a little, she had to hurry from the other staircase to this one, and then up the steps and was having difficulty catching her breath. But, her plan had worked and Emma was now at her mercy.

Katherine waved the gun as she stepped towards her, making Emma back away from the staircase. Circling around, she now had Emma with her back to the steps and no way to escape down the hall.

"Where is my husband? I am not asking you again."

"He's dead," Emma replied, her nose beginning to fill with the stench of the creature.

Katherine smacked her in the cheek with the butt of the gun, and Emma cried out at the sudden excruciating pain.

"That's nothing, sweetheart, if what you just said is true. I can't believe you namby-pambies could ever get the jump on my George, but if you got lucky and you killed him, you're going die a slow death, and so are your menfolk. Now, where is he?"

"Katherine, he's a criminal, did you know that?"

"Of course, I did, do you think I'm stupid? But, of course you do. I saw how you looked at me, you arrogant little tramp. With your pretty blonde hair and green eyes, you think you're all that, don't you? But you're stupid and so are your men. It was so easy to play all of you that it's not even funny. So, don't give me any crap about George being dead. Where is he being held? Tell me now or I shoot you."

"Katherine," Emma didn't know what to say, she was pretty sure that Katherine was going to shoot her no matter what response she gave. And the monster stench seemed to be getting stronger, although it could have just been wafting up the stairs.

A gunshot rang out and Emma felt a burning pain in her upper arm, she grabbed hold of it and watched as the blood from the wound seeped out under her fingers.

"Damn you," she said, glaring at Katherine.

"Where are you holding my husband? Next time, it'll be one of your legs, then maybe that pretty little face. Answer me."

Emma hesitated again and then her eyes got as large as saucers. "Katherine, we need to go now, it's not safe here."

"Answer my question, or you won't be going anywhere ever again."

"George is tied up out in the garage, I'll take you out there and show you where. Please, we have to hurry."

"Oh, I'm pretty sure I can find him on my own now," Katherine said with an evil grin, as she leveled the gun. Emma was staring down its barrel when the huge creature came around the corner, took a couple of very long strides and smacked the back of Katherine's head with its razor-sharp claws.

She had a surprised look on her face, just as her head fell to the side, almost completely severed from her body, which crumpled silently to the floor.

It raised it's dark, furry face to the heavens and let out a roar that made Emma almost fall to the floor herself, but she scrambled backwards and hurried down the steps, with the creature right behind her.

*   *   *

It was chaos when Scott and Tim arrived back at the Lodge, bodies littered the parking lot, the people that were trying to dig out their cars had been caught by surprise when it came back, and they had nowhere to run.

Jumping off the sled before it even came to a complete stop, Tim and Scott, grabbed their rifles and more ammo and headed into the Lodge.

Callie laid on the trailer for a few moments but, with a ittle howl of agony, she managed to get down and drag herself towards the Lodge.

Scott nodded to the right and Tim headed that way while Scott went off towards the left. More bodies were strewn around the lobby, and he paused only to reassure himself that Emma was not among them.

They could still hear screaming but couldn't tell exactly where it was coming from. The stench was all around them so that didn't help pinpoint where the creature was either.

Tim made his way over to the banquet hall, it was empty now, except for the bodies littering the floor, but there was blood and gore everywhere. He stepped lightly around the bodies, relieved to find that some were still alive, after all. They were moaning softly and calling out for help, but, he couldn't stop now, not until the creature was put down for good.

He was just about to leave the room when he thought he heard his name being called. Tim turned and scanned the room once more. Sitting over against the far wall, partially hidden by a large, overstuffed chair, he finally saw Skylar, her large blue eyes staring at him in relief.

He ran over to her, wiping the blood off her cheek and, grabbing a tablecloth off the nearest table, he wrapped it tightly around her torso. The creature must have swiped her as she was running away and she had some deep cuts on her back that were going to need medical attention, but they weren't life-threatening and Tim breathed a deep sigh of relief.

"Can you get up?"

She nodded and winced as he helped her to her feet.

"Stay with me," he said, walking slowly towards the door, with Skylar right behind him.

*   *   *

Scott made his way cautiously down the other hall, using the barrel of the rifle to swing open doors so he could make sure it wasn't hiding in any of the rooms. It was taking too long, and he was getting anxious.

He heard someone let out a horrific scream and his heart almost leaped out of his chest when he realized that it was Emma. Scott hurried in that direction and found her backing down the staircase, the creature was just two steps above her.

"Turn and run, as fast as you can, Emma."

She heard his voice and turned towards him, her beautiful green eyes were wide as saucers and she was panting through an open mouth in fear and panic.

"I said run," Scott yelled, just as the creature made a swipe at her, catching the back of her sweater and causing her to fall down the rest of the four or five stairs.

She winced in pain and hobbled past Scott, giving him a clear shot of the creature on the stairs.

Scott aimed and shot multiple times, hitting it each time, but the creature kept coming.

Emma grabbed Scott's arm and pulled him out of the way as the creature ran past them, towards the front of the building, bleeding profusely, screaming out its rage and pain.

They followed after it, Scott trying to reload while on the move.

They stopped short when they saw the creature standing in the parking lot looking down at Callie. The animals' eyes were locked, and they seemed to be communicating in some way.

There was a deafening boom as Scott shot the creature in the back, knocking it to its knees. From there, it rolled onto its side and gently reached out towards Callie, who did not appear frightened at all.

With a sympathetic whine, Callie laid down beside the great beast and rested her head on it, comforting the creature while it struggled to take its last breath, its life fading quickly from its body.

When it did, Callie raised her head and howled mournfully. Goosebumps rose on their skin and Scott wrapped his arm around Emma.

Tim, Skylar and several others came up and stood next to them, silently cheering the fact that the monster was finally dead, but unable to comprehend the bond that had developed between the two animals, a bond strong enough that the dog had actually tried to comfort the savage creature as it died and was now mourning its passing.

"Maybe they aren't that different, after all," Emma said, as if she'd read their minds.

Scott pulled her up even tighter against his side and, dragging his eyes from the aberrant creature lying on the ground in front of them, he looked over her head towards his brother.

Only the two of them could really appreciate the lengths that this creature had gone to, just to get retribution for the death of its loved one.

And Scott knew that, given similar circumstances, both of them would be willing to go to those same lengths to get revenge on anyone, or anything, that caused harm to Emma or any of their family.

Their eyes met in mutual understanding and Scott uttered the words they were both thinking. "Maybe it wasn't all that different from us, either. Let's hope we never have to find out."

THE END

I wanted to thank all of you for spending your time and your money on Devil's Retribution. It means so much to me and I hope it was worth your while and that you enjoyed reading this novel as much as I enjoyed writing it.

This is the second installment of the Devereaux Chronicles and the third, Devil's Gathering, is now available. I've included the first section of that book for you to take a look at.

I hope you'll join me for that adventure, as well as all of their future exploits.

Please feel free to visit me at debbieboek.com to contact me or for more information about me and my books. I would love to hear any comments you have about the characters, the book, the storyline, anything that you would like to share.

You may want to also check out my blogs at debbieboek.blog where I talk about the writers who have inspired me, about books, and about the monsters and urban legends that keep our imaginations fertile.

If you did enjoy the book, I would appreciate it if you could write a brief review. Reviews aren't just good for the author, they also help other people find good books to read. So, please let the world know about whatever books you're reading, not just this one, by writing a brief review.

Thanks again and I'm looking forward to our next adventure.

Debbie

DEVIL'S GATHERING

CHAPTER 1

The creature stood on the knoll, its red eyes staring down into the valley, locked on its prey. The voice was still chanting, echoing in its head, and a low, deep growl of frustration emanated from its chest. The wiry, black fur along its spine stood on end and its lips were pulled back in a grimace, exposing long, sharp teeth.

Unaware of the creature watching them from above, Caleb and Leona wandered slowly back towards their house, enjoying the brilliant shades of red and orange shimmering over the valley as the sun set behind the rocky bluffs. The temperature was dropping as the sun went down and Leona pulled her shawl tighter around her shoulders.

Caleb reached out to grab his wife's hand, but found that she had stopped suddenly and was staring almost trancelike up into the hills near the old abandoned mine.

"What is it?" Concern made his deep voice even more coarse than usual.

When she continued to stare mutely up into the hills, Caleb turned in the same direction, trying to find what had caught her attention so profoundly. But, try as he might, Caleb was unable to detect anything out the ordinary.

He reached over and took both her hands in his own, trying to rub some life into them, but they remained inert and motionless.

"Leona, honey, what is it? You're acting like you're off your nut, what do you see up there?"

She didn't respond, the sun was continuing to lower in the sky and Leona strained her eyes to catch sight of it again, but to no avail, it was now lost among the shadows that were forming.

Caleb moved directly in front of her, his large frame blocking her view, forcing her to focus her attention on him. Looking up into her husband's intense gray eyes, the haze finally cleared from Leona's mind, she bit back a sob, wrapped her arms around him and rested her head against his broad chest.

"You're scaring me, Leona."

"It was the dog," she whispered, starting to shiver violently.

He pulled her in tighter against his body, and asked, "The Black Dog?"

She didn't answer, but he could feel her head nodding in the affirmative as her tears burned through his shirt.

He stepped back and held her at arms' length so that he could look into her beautiful pale blue eyes as he spoke.

"Leona, there is no Black Ghost Dog, that's nothing more than an Urban Legend. If it was real, I would know it."

Leona searched his face, already knowing what she would find there. She and Caleb had been down this road before and he wouldn't accept that the dog was real ten years ago, so she knew it would be even harder for him to acknowledge it now.

She would not back down from the hard, steely gaze of his gray eyes. Leona had no doubt in her mind that the Black Ghost dog did exist and what it was capable of. It had killed her father and now it was coming for her.

Caleb knew what a logical person Leona was, not at all prone to foolishness, so it was disturbing to see how deeply this was affecting her.

There was a quiver around her eyes and her mouth was open slightly as she inhaled quick little breaths, trying to relieve some of her apprehension.

"Honey, you probably saw a stray or a coyote up there. It was no damn omen of death, so get that nonsense straight out of your head, right now."

Leona's face began to relax and a sad smile sat on her lips. For a few moments she had been overwhelmed by the knowledge of what she saw, and by the terror that had flooded her body as a result of it.

Her life had taken many unexpected twists and turns and because of that she learned to roll with the punches. Her pulse was now slowing down and her heartbeat was returning to a normal rhythm, allowing her to think clearly again.

"It's here and you know it, Caleb. I realize that you won't even discuss what happened with my father, but what about Michael and Clint?"

"What about them? Michael got bit by a snake and Clint got kicked in the chest by a horse. Both freaky, unusual incidents, but not supernatural in any way, shape or form."

"But they both saw the dog a day or two before they died."

"Says who?"

"They told me about it right after it happened."

"Why didn't you bother to share that information with me until now?"

"Because I knew what your reaction would be. At the time, I thought the same thing as you do, a coyote or a stray, nothing to worry about. Until I saw it myself. It was a huge, black dog, not a coyote, and it was staring straight at me. I could feel it's eyes boring into my very soul."

"Being a little melodramatic now, aren't you?"

Her smile had long since faded and now her eyes snapped in anger at his response. "No, Caleb, I am not being overly dramatic. I saw the thing and now I'm scared, very, very scared, so the last thing that I need is you belittling me right now."

She bit back a sob and Caleb closed his eyes and rubbed the bridge of his nose.

Slowly reopening them, he fixed his gaze on his wife and said, "Sometimes, woman, I cannot even begin to understand where you come up with the things you say and do. There's no damn Black Ghost Dog and it most definitely is not an omen indicating that you are going to die."

"I never said that it was."

"But that's what you think, right?" he asked, his gravelly voice even deeper than usual.

"When will the Devereaux brothers be here?"

Caleb had to think for a minute, she'd changed the direction of their conversation so abruptly that he almost didn't catch the question.

"I heard from Tim, he'll be here in the morning. Scott won't be here until sometime after that. He's bringing some new little piece of calico with him."

Leona frowned at Caleb. "You can be so disrespectful sometimes. I hope you don't intend to be that crass in front of her."

"Maybe I will, maybe I won't. I don't need you treating me like some old coot that doesn't know how to behave," he replied, feeling his own anger bubble to the surface.

"Then stop acting like one." Leona's fear was fading and the encounter with the Black Dog began to feel like it had been a figment of her imagination, but her annoyance with her husband was very real and growing exponentially. She turned and started striding back towards their house, the long gray braid that hung down her back swinging like a pendulum behind her.

"Why did you want to know when they'd be here?" Caleb asked, his long legs allowing him to catch up with her in just a few steps.

"Because, of all your friends, they are the two that I trust the most and I need to talk to them about this."

"About what?"

"The Black Ghost Dog killed my father, it killed Clint and Michael, and now it wants me. I am not going to let that happen without a fight and maybe they can help me stop it, since you obviously aren't going to."

"Leona,"

She stopped walking and turned towards him, her pale blue eyes filled with anger, hurt and frustration. "Don't say a word, Caleb. I cannot listen to any more of your condescending comments right now. You go meet up with your friends over at the saloon and don't worry about me, I'll take care of this myself."

Caleb watched her go, his lips pursed in frustration, battling within himself. He knew that he should go with her, be there for her and give her his support. But he couldn't bring himself to do that, wouldn't reinforce her silly notion that there was a mysterious black ghost dog haunting Windy Shot.

With one last look towards his wife, he turned, squared his shoulders and headed for the saloon so that he could visit with his friends, who had a little more realistic view of life.

www.ingramcontent.com/pod-product-compliance
Lightning Source LLC
Chambersburg PA
CBHW070601120726
47909CB00007B/2401